TYLER'S CAPE

TYLER'S CAPE

DARREN GREER

A CORMORANT BOOK

THE CANADA COUNCIL | LE CONSEIL DES ARTS
FOR THE ARTS | DU CANADA
SINCE 1957 | DEPUIS 1957

ONTARIO ARTS COUNCIL
CONSEIL DES ARTS DE L'ONTARIO

The publisher gratefully acknowledges the support of the
Canada Council for the Arts and the Ontario Arts Council
for its publishing program. We acknowledge the financial support
of the Government of Canada through the Book Publishing
Industry Development Program (BPIDP) for our publishing activities.

Printed and bound in Canada

National Library of Canada Cataloguing in Publication

Greer, Darren
Tyler's Cape / Darren Greer. — 2nd ed.

ISBN 1-896951-45-7

1. Title.

PS8563.R43T95 2002   C813'.6   C2002-905086-3
PR9199.3.G7598T95 2002

Cover Design: Angel Guerra and Tannice Goddard
Text Design: Tannice Goddard/Soul Oasis Networking
Cover image: Jon Wilkinson
Printer: Friesens

Cormorant Books Inc.
62 Rose Avenue, Toronto, Ontario, Canada M4X 1N9
www.cormorantbooks.com

For my grandmother
Madora Agnes Anthony-Keating
and
In memory of my grandfather
Leonard Michael Keating

To find the origin, trace back the manifestations.
When you recognize the children and find the
mother, you will be free of sorrow.
— LAO-TZU

Happy or unhappy, families are all a mystery.
— GLORIA STEINEM

PROLOGUE

My brothers and I were just boys when the whale beached itself off the shore below our house one Sunday afternoon. It had started raining shortly after lunch, a cold September rain that gave no warning it was coming and stopped just as quickly. My mother had gone out to test the skies and see if she could risk hanging her laundry out to dry. She came running back inside.

"Harold!" she called to my father, startling him so he nearly dropped the New Testament he'd been reading. We were gathered at his feet that day, as we were every Sunday, to listen to him read to us from his pocket Bible. When my mother burst back in the house we lost all interest in what Christ was doing, and my father jumped out of his rocking chair.

"What is it!" he cried. "Is everything alright?"

"Outside!" she said breathlessly. "Off the Cape. Come look!"

All of us went. My mother wasn't an excitable woman, and whatever she wanted to show us was without a doubt important. My brothers and I ran ahead of her out the front door, across the field, and to the edge of our property.

"Be careful," our father cried, struggling to catch up while we gathered at the edge of the cliff to peer cautiously down at the water and rocks below. My mother was coming up behind us all, shouting impatiently, "Not there, for heaven's sake. Out there!" We all followed her pointing finger to see a great grey body rising from the surf, perhaps three hundred yards off the shore.

"It's a whale," my father said, his voice struck with wonder. "Well, I'll be."

"It's beached," said my mother. "She ain't swimming."

My brothers and I were beside ourselves with sudden joy. "A whale!" we shouted, "A whale!" Even though we had lived our entire lives by the ocean, none of us had ever seen a whale before.

"Hush now," said my mother, though without any real threat in her voice. Even she, the most practical of women, was humbled by the sudden appearance of this miracle right below our house. "It's some size, isn't it?" she said, turning to my father.

"Yes," he answered her. "It sure is." We stood there and watched it in silence, and when it became apparent it was unable to swim as my mother had guessed, my brothers and I began to get worried.

"Maybe we should swim out and give it a push," suggested my oldest brother, Tom, who was only twelve and young enough to believe that with the help of his father and mother he could do anything.

"That won't work," said Billy, younger but slightly more

cynical than Tom. "It's too big. Why don't we go get Roland's boat and drag it back out to sea."

"Stop with that foolishness," said my mother harshly, turning on us. "There isn't anything anyone of us can do for that creature, so just settle down."

Though it was only my mother's intention to teach us the 'cold, hard facts of life,' as she often called them, we were so distressed by her words that she looked slightly ashamed despite herself. But she refused to take it back, only crossed her arms and looked out at the beached whale, perhaps still determined that nothing could be done. It was my father who challenged my mother, in that easy, unassuming way he had.

"I know one thing we can do," he said. To our expectant faces, suddenly turned up to him, he nodded, and quite unselfconsciously got down on his knees in front of us, clasped his hands together, and held them to the sky.

"Oh brother," my mother said, rolling her eyes. "Here he goes again."

Uncertainly, at my father's urging, we got down on our knees with him, my brother Billy having to pull me roughly down beside him when, bewildered by this sudden outbreak of religiosity, I made no move to kneel on my own. My mother stood apart from these proceedings as she always did, and just watched us with her arms folded disapprovingly across her chest. "Aren't you going to pray too?" I asked her. I was only five and too young to recognize the telltale signs of a skeptic when I saw them. My mother's reply was quick, and typically scathing. "I'll pray you don't catch your death of cold kneeling on that wet grass."

"Dear Lord," my father began, ignoring my mother's comment, though it was meant more for him than me or my brothers. "Please save this creature whom you made from its

3

death here on this beach. Send your invisible angels to rescue it."

I closed my eyes, opening them every few seconds to see if I could catch glimpses of God's angels lifting the whale out of the sea and back to deeper waters. But the whale only continued to struggle, sending up great walls of water with every sweep of its giant tail. When the rain started to fall again my mother said, "That's enough now. Come on in."

My father stayed on his knees, still mouthing his prayers, and paid my mother no heed.

"Billy, Tom, Luke. Come inside, I told you." But when we were with my father, my mother's commands, strictly obeyed at other times, had no weight. Especially when we were praying. God, our father had taught us, had more power than even the one who fed and clothed and made our beds for us. Eventually my mother gave up, and with a well aimed glare at my father started in out of the rain.

"Suit yourselves," she said as she went. "I hope you all catch pneumonia."

It was not my father's intention, I think, to keep us outside for very long. But often when he thought about God or was talking to him, he could forget where he was for extended periods of time. Only when he opened his eyes did he notice his three little boys kneeling beside him, without jackets even, shivering under the onslaught of cold, heavy rain. He seemed hesitant then, torn between his belief in prayer and his concern for us. With a sigh, and a last look outward at the whale, still beached despite his entreaties, he struggled to his feet and told us all to do the same.

"But what about the whale?" asked my brother Tom.

"We can pray inside as well as out," answered my father. "God doesn't stop at the door."

All afternoon we paced the house, praying for God to free the whale, and running outside to see if it had moved. My father, at one point, gathered us around his rocking chair, setting me, the smallest, on his knee, and read aloud the story of Jonah and the Great Fish. It was a short passage and when he was done Tom jumped up from his place at my father's feet and ran outside. Only minutes later he came running back into the house, excited and barely able to speak.

"It's moving!" he shouted. "Come see. It's moving!"

"A miracle," said my father.

"Yes," answered my mother drily, who had taken to her rocking chair to mend socks. "High tide. Happens twice a day."

My father, who was inured to my mother's sarcasm and had been for as long as I remembered him, only nodded while he put on his coat, urging us children to do the same. "Dora," he said on our way out the door, "are you coming?"

"No," my mother answered, refusing to look up from her knitting, as if even a glance in our direction might be too much encouragement. "I'll go see the miracle of high tide tomorrow."

We all ran outside to the edge of the Cape and stood in the rain to watch the whale swim back out to deeper waters — freed, as my mother had guessed, by the afternoon tide. Billy and Tom cheered as it went, and when it disappeared underneath the surface of the ocean, my father said to us with one of his rare smiles, "Isn't God's work beautiful?"

"What's God's work?" we asked him. Having grown up where we did, we could not think he was referring to the Cape and the ocean around it. Beauty is only recognizable if seen in perspective, and we had nothing to compare our landscape to. We had never been anywhere else.

"This," my father answered, holding out his arms, indicating everything around us. "This is God's work. Don't you understand that?"

We said we did, but my father knew better. He only sighed, looked out at the water, which contained the whale we could no longer see, and turned to go back inside again. My brothers and I stayed out and waited for the whale to resurface once more, though it never did. We stood there a half hour before our mother came and made us get out of the rain. This was one of the last times the three of us would be together with my father before he died, and my brothers and I share this memory as one of our strongest of him. Yet far from making us feel nostalgic for those times it is an unsettling memory, as if our father would always be somehow be above us, as if he would always know more and leave our questions forever unanswered. My second oldest brother, on the rare occasions when we three get together, puts it best. His words have all the flavour of ritual, obscure in origin and indefinite in meaning.

"None of us," my brother Billy always says, "has turned out to be the man our father was."

"Amen," my brother Tom and I always answer.

COMING HOME
❧

*O*ne Saturday afternoon in April my brother Tom called me at my apartment in Halifax to say our mother had broken her hip. She'd been carrying a basket of laundry down the stairs and the runner slipped under her foot. Luckily, he said, she was on the next-to-last step. If she'd been any higher she might have broken her neck.

"Those damned steps," Tom said to me. "I always said they should be widened and replaced."

Tom was a carpenter, and thus in his view practically any problem in the world could be rectified by the simple manipulation of wood. He was right about one thing, however. The stairs in our old house were treacherously steep and narrow. I fell down them once when I was fourteen and gave myself a pretty good bump on the head. My brother Billy fell down them too, but he was drunk, and so escaped unhurt, except for the lecture my mother gave him when she got up and found him passed out at the bottom of the stairs. I asked Tom if he had called our brother in Toronto and told him the news.

"I did," answered Tom. "But there's not a lot he can do."

Billy had been away so long that he sometimes slipped my mind for weeks on end. It was only when someone mentioned his name that I remembered I had another brother living somewhere in a strange city. But he was not going to be any help with my mother, who, according to her doctors, was going to be laid up at least two months.

"The thing is, Luke," Tom said. "Someone is going to have to stay with her."

"Bring her to your place," I answered. "You've got lots of room."

Tom didn't respond. He didn't need to. We both knew my mother would never move into Tom's house. She had many reasons, not the least of which being that the house had belonged to her dead father-in-law, whom she had hated.

"We could make her move there," I offered. "We could give her the choice between your place and a nursing home."

"I've looked into it," Tom said.

"And?" I was surprised Tom had even thought of it, knowing my mother. I had only been joking.

"They wouldn't take her," Tom said. "They don't take anybody against their will unless their mind is gone. And Mom's mind ain't gone."

"No," I said. "It isn't." I wondered if my brother could hear the note of regret in my voice.

The issue of my mother staying alone in Tyler's Cape wasn't a new one. Several times over the past year my brother and I had tried to get her to move in with him, where she'd have someone to look after her. It wasn't only that she was sixty-five and too old to be living alone, a fact which breaking her hip seemed to confirm, but that there wasn't anything in the Cape for her anymore. Her only neighbour, Etta Hunt, had died just two years before from a heart attack. While Etta's husband Roland had been around he'd driven my mother into town for groceries, but only last year Roland had put his house up for sale and moved to Carleton with his sister. He said he couldn't stand being in that big old house without his wife any longer. Tom, who lived forty miles from the Cape near the town of Trenton, had taken to driving down Saturday afternoons to take her into town for groceries and to help with the chores. But Tom owned a carpentry business and often worked on Saturday. Sometimes his wife went for him, until one afternoon she and my mother had a huge fight and she refused to do it anymore. Tom admitted he found it a burden, having to drive so far to look after our mother, but so far they had no acceptable solution, except one.

"You can work from anywhere," Tom told me over the phone. "You said that yourself. All you have to do is hook up your computer to her phone line. You can do that, can't you?"

"Do you honestly think Mom is going to let me tie up her phone with my modem, Tom?"

"What's a modem?" Tom asked innocently.

I smiled to myself at my end of the line. My brother Tom. The world was passing him by. It really was. "Never mind," I said. "The thing is, you can't expect me to stay down there forever. I do have a life here, you know."

"I know," Tom said, but he didn't sound convinced. I knew what my brother thought of my life in the city, although he was too kind to say so. In some ways I'm sure he thought Billy, with all his problems, was better off. "You don't have to stay

9

forever," he added. "Just until she heals up."

"And what are we supposed to do then? You're the one that's always saying she can't live there alone anymore."

"We'll cross that bridge when we come to it," Tom said. "Maybe while you're there you could work on her about moving in with me and Suzanne."

"Sure. And maybe I could convince her to run the marathon while I'm at it."

Tom laughed. He could afford to. He knew before he called that I would say yes.

⁓

Tyler's Cape is one hundred and nine miles from Halifax. For most of it you can take the 103 highway and turn off at the fourteenth exit into the town of Oldsport. The rest of the trip is a half hour drive back along the coast, on a narrow road that twists and turns so much it can make you ill if you're not used to it. The morning of April 7, 1992 I made the two-hour drive to Tyler's Cape, hating every mile of it. I had packed the back seat and trunk of my little Toyota with my clothes, my computer, and other instruments of diversion I'd need to survive the days of boredom that stretched out before me. I felt disturbed with the ease with which I had disassembled my life. When I told my boss at the advertising agency I'd worked at for eleven years he hardly even blinked. He wouldn't have cared if I moved to Spain, as long as I could send him my work by modem and fax.

I found myself glancing at the ocean as I drove the last few miles to my mother's. I did not miss it exactly. Halifax is, after all, a harbour town. But from my part of the city I could only catch glimpses of the ocean between buildings of concrete and glass, and it was comforting somehow to see a clear, unobstructed view again. In art school in my early twenties the ocean was pretty much all I painted. One of my teachers insisted once that I try my hand at something else.

"You've got to let yourself go," he said to me. "Your sense of structure is too confining."

Eager to please, I'd cast a bust of my brother Tom in bronze. When I showed it to the teacher with an explanation of who it was, he shook his head.

"Luke," he said, "you'll never make a living painting oceans and sculpting relatives."

I agreed, and took his advice. I let myself go, or rather, I let art school go. I gave the bronze bust to Tom, where it still sits on a low table beside his sofa, and applied to the graphic design school across town.

My mother, over the years, hadn't shown the slightest bit of interest in what I'd chosen to do. It was only when I talked to her over the phone, a few days before I drove down to stay with her, that she thought to ask about my work.

"Don't worry," I told her. "I'm bringing my computer."

There was a long pause on the other end of the line. "What do you plan on doing with it?"

"Work," I said. "What else?"

"What kind of work do you do with a computer?"

"I told you, Mom. I'm a graphic designer."

"I thought that was drawing pictures," she said.

"It is," I answered. "Sort of."

"Don't you draw with a pencil?"

I sighed. "Not any more."

"Then what do you draw with?" I often wondered if my mother deliberately confused what I told her. It was as if an act of understanding constituted some kind of surrender with her. And even over the phone, from a hundred miles away, in her hospital bed with a broken hip, my mother refused to surrender.

"Don't worry," I said, giving in to her. "I'll get my work done."

"Well, just don't get fired on my account," she said to me. "I can manage on my own if it comes to that."

I didn't bother to say that we both knew this wasn't true. With my mother, you have to state the truth obliquely. "It'll be alright," I assured her.

"Well," she said. "It'll only be for a few months anyway."

When I turned my car on the road leading up to my mother's house, I had to slow down considerably. The road still hadn't been paved, after all these years. And now, I supposed, with Roland gone and my mother never having learned to drive, it never would be. I only hoped she would agree to go to Tom's. I didn't relish the thought of spending the next two months arguing with her, then still having to force her out of the house at the end of it.

Tom's blue Chevy truck was parked between the barn and the house. He had brought our mother home from the hospital earlier that day. I pulled my little Toyota off to the side of the driveway, onto the grass, so he could back his truck out when the time came. He sauntered out before I'd even shut the engine off, zipping up his nylon jacket against the wind.

"You made it," he called as soon as I opened the car door. I got out and looked across the hood at him. "You wanna give me a hand with some of this stuff?"

He shook his head. "You better wait. Mom's on the war path."

I felt my spirit sink at his words. "What for now?"

"I don't know. Something to do with doctors at the hospital."

"She's not even in the hospital any more."

"I know." Tom attempted a smile. "But you know Mom."

I knew her alright. It started to rain, beating a delicate rhythm on the roof of my car. Suddenly, I felt thoroughly depressed.

"You coming in?" Tom asked.

"Do I have a choice?"

"I guess not."

I shut my car door and followed Tom into the house. Whenever I met Tom, I always followed him into a house, his or my mother's. It seemed he was just not comfortable inside, and would use any excuse to get out. He was like that when we were kids too. No matter how cold, he would want to stay out longer than the rest of us and play just one more game. It was funny. His chosen profession was building houses for other people to live in, but I always got the impression that houses for Tom were just a place to sit until you could drum up another excuse to go outside again.

My mother, as Tom had said, was upset. She was hobbling around the kitchen when we came in, muttering curses aloud, and for a moment I imagined I was a child again and we had committed some small crime for which she would beat us. But the fantasy didn't last long. She was supporting herself with a metal walker. It made her look a thousand times older. The walker wasn't permanent. The doctors had told her she could set it aside when her hip fully healed.

"Set it aside!" she'd cried derisively from her hospital bed. "I'll throw the goddamned thing into the trash heap." We all knew, however, that she wouldn't throw it away. One broken hip at her age, the doctor had told us, could mean more broken hips and bones, to the point where old bones get tired of being broken. But my mother didn't *sound* as if she was anywhere near this stage.

"It's about time you got here," she said to me when I stepped into the kitchen. "We thought you weren't coming."

"Wet roads," I told her. "I drove slow."

"Never mind," she said. "Those goddamned doctors. Did Tom tell you what they want me to do?"

"No." I found a place to sit. She complained that the doctors had wanted her to spend a few more days in the hospital. Tom stood by and listened politely. As soon as he could, he left. My mother barely noticed.

"Forty-three years I've spent in this house," she told me. "Forty-three years, and I'll be damned if a bunch of white coats are gonna tell me where I can and cannot sleep for a night."

"They're only trying to help, Mom."

"Help, my foot!" She sat down, calmed herself slightly. But the whole process still bothered me. It was what I'd grown up with — the senseless raving, the inability to get along with the world. I imagined I had two months of it ahead of me. I wished I hadn't agreed to this at all, that I'd hired a nurse for two months. But a nurse never would have put up with my mother, and my mother wouldn't have allowed one in her home. She sat in her rocker with the walker nearby, staring at it with a palpable hatred. After a half an hour of sitting like this, in total silence, I got up to retrieve my things from the car. My mother said nothing as I brought them in and took them up to my room. When I paraded by with the computer monitor she gave it a cursory glance and turned away again. I spent the afternoon setting up the computer in the living room, though I didn't hook in the modem. When I did I wouldn't tell her, and she wouldn't notice. That way I wouldn't have any trouble about use of the phone line. I wasn't worried about my mother missing calls. With Etta and Roland gone my mother received no calls. She didn't speak to her brother, my Uncle Joe, and he had no phone besides. But it was like her to complain about it, just for the sake of complaining. Once I was done I asked my mother what I could do to help out.

"Nothing," she said. Even with the walker she couldn't move about very well. Tom said she spent the morning in front of the television, and planned sleeping on the couch (she couldn't yet manage the stairs.) All the housework she could do was to cook meals and wash dishes. Even this caused her much pain. Our lunch was quickly prepared and underdone, she was in such a hurry to complete it and sit down. I thought I'd do what I could for her without taking away her dignity. Still, I was soon bored. I knew there must be something I could do to keep my mind occupied.

"How about the barn?" I asked her. "Maybe it needs a cleaning out?"

"What for? I don't use it for anything."

"Well, if I cleaned it out, maybe you could use it."

"With a broken hip?" she asked sarcastically. "What am I going to carry out to it?"

That was my mother all over. She only had a disability when it became convenient. But after a little more arguing, she gave in. She finally saw the benefits of having me do odd jobs outside. It would keep me out of her hair. If she needed me she could shout. Her accident had not reduced her lung power in the slightest.

My father had built the barn when he built the house. Neither design was original. The house was a small two-storey salt box and the barn was shaped like every barn I know. Over the years it had become a catch-all. Besides being a place for laying up wood for the winter, anything that wasn't immediately needed had been stored there. It had become a veritable junk room. I decided to take it on, clear out unwanted junk and save anything valuable. I began the next morning, in a pair of Tom's old overalls I'd found in the basement. Piece by piece I disassembled the pile. The junk — rusty bicycles, rotting milk cartons, moth-eaten pieces of cloth and oil-stained tarpaulin — I carried around to the back of the barn, where my mother couldn't see it and complain. I'd be able to load the smaller pieces easily into the trunk of my Toyota and haul it off to the junk yard in town. I set anything valuable aside, and not twenty minutes into the job I found the Sunbeam.

At first I saw only a rusted handlebar sticking out from the pile. I knew it wasn't a bicycle, because of the accelerator and metal hand brake attached to it. But I didn't remember the bike until I had uncovered most of it. It was in bad shape. I wondered if it would ever run again. Its leather seat was destroyed, slashed from the glacial motion of the pile of junk that had been resting on it for years. It was dented and bleeding rust. Its tires were flat, and too rusted to rotate. The chain was hopelessly seized. In order to move it I figured I'd have to clear out all the garbage and ask Tom to help me. I left it for the day but before long an idea occurred to me. I called Tom at his home that evening and asked him what I'd have to do to fix up an old motorcycle that had been sitting in one place, unused, for over twenty years.

"You mean that old thing of Billy's?" he asked me over the phone. "I thought Mom threw that out years ago."

"Apparently not," I said. "It's here."

"Well? What are you going to do with it?"

"Fix it up," I told him.

"Luke, you don't know anything about motorcycles."

"That's why I'm calling you."

Tom excused himself for a moment. I heard him say something to his wife about washing the dishes. They say that some men marry their mothers. This was not true of Tom. He did the dishes, the laundry, even cooked. My mother said she suspected Tom did all the housework. She considered it shameful that a working man couldn't depend on his wife for even the simple matter of cleaning up the home.

"Okay," Tom said, back on the line. "What do you want to know?"

"I don't know. How do I get started, I guess?"

He thought for a moment. "First thing you do, with a motorcycle that hasn't been started in twenty years, is make sure the oil pan is drained."

"And if it isn't drained?"

"Buy a new oil pan. This is going to cost a lot of money, you know."

"I know. I've got it to spend."

"Alright. It's your dough."

"After the oil pan?"

"Let me see," he said. "Just about everything will have to be replaced. The gaskets. Maybe the pistons if they're seized. The chain. Possibly the carburetor. You might not need new rims, but the tires will have to be changed. Hey!" he said suddenly. "Do you want me to come down there and take a look at it tomorrow? I've got some time. Maybe we could do it together."

"Sorry. I want to do it myself. What was it you said after gaskets?"

Tom sighed. "Why don't you start with one thing at a time? The oil pan first."

I hesitated only briefly before asking him where I might find the oil pan.

He hesitated back. It seemed my question wasn't as stupid as I thought. "On one of those old Sunbeams, I'm not sure."

Billy had bought the Sunbeam second-hand in 1967. By then it had ten years on it at least. Tom went on to say that getting parts for it wasn't going to be easy.

"Can't I customize it?" I asked him. "You know, put modern parts where the old ones can't be bought?"

"Maybe," Tom said. "You could always cut down the gaskets to the right size. I'm not sure about the engine though. You might end up building pretty much the whole thing."

"Then I'll build a whole new engine."

"Luke," Tom said, in wry amusement, "do you even know what a gasket is?"

I didn't, and Tom knew it. "So how are you gonna do this?" he asked.

"I'll find a way," I told him, and hung up. When I turned around, my mother was leaning on her walker in the doorway, looking at me suspiciously.

"What do you want with Billy's old motorcycle?"

I shrugged. "I want to fix it up."

"Why, for heaven's sake?"

"Something to do while I'm here."

"How long do you plan on being here?"

"As long as it takes you to get well."

"Lord's sake!" she said. "I hope I heal quicker than that old hunk of junk Billy tried to kill himself with."

I smiled, and the two of us sat and watched television for the rest of the evening, barely speaking to each other. I had no idea why I wanted to fix up that 'hunk of junk.' The idea just occurred to me, and quickly became a sort of an obsession. I caught myself watching my mother as she watched the television from her chair. As usual, the lights were off. Miniature square images of the TV screen reflected deep in each lens of her glasses. I didn't hate my mother. But neither did I feel love for her. It occurred to me I was incapable of any feeling at all. The few relationships I had been in were like that. I felt for the person only when they were not there, the way I felt for Billy, Tom, my father. When the people I loved in my life were present I turned inside myself, refused to allow any of my feelings to escape. Only over distances could I let myself feel for anyone, like a flower unfurling in the darkness to mourn the loss of the sun.

CAULS AND ANGELS

I was born with a caul, and although I've never had a genuine vision of the future, from the time I was old enough to speak my older brothers both believed in and indulged my imagined ability to see forward into time. When I was four years old they sat me down on the floor of our little barn, one cold January afternoon, and placed their most cherished artifacts in my hands. They hoped I would catch glimpses of them both as men. My oldest brother Tom gave me his jack-knife, with its scratched mother-of-pearl handle and a blade worn to a sliver from repeated filings. Billy gave me one of the fur-lined gloves he had received for Christmas.

"Something with sweat in it," he told us assuredly. "It's got to be something personal."

The three of us sat in a circle on the rough boards of the barn floor, sweating inside our hand-me-down snowsuits, and waited for flashes of insight. When I could tell them nothing (I was too young even to make something up) they took these things back undaunted and told their own futures.

"I'm gonna be a famous newspaperman," said Billy, holding the glove to his forehead, his eyes squeezed shut with the force of his concentration. Ever since he had published a story in the elementary school newspaper, Billy wanted to be a writer. One day, he told us, he would go to Toronto and someone would give him a job at one of those big newspapers we had always heard about. Tom was doubtful anyone in Toronto would give anyone from Nova Scotia a job, and sometimes he said so, but not then. He had opened his jackknife and was studying one damaged blade.

"I can't see that far," he said slowly. "All I know is that one day I'm going to shoot the biggest eighteen point buck that's ever been shot in this county."

Billy nodded solemnly at Tom's prediction. Neither of them was old enough to hunt, though Tom sometimes accompanied my father when the season was open. Yet Tom always dreamed of having a large rack of deer antlers to hang in our bedroom. And so, because these were Tom and Billy's strongest dreams, they always saw these things in their futures, and sometimes became disgusted with me because I couldn't see them too.

"Jeez Luke," Billy said to me once, "sometimes I think we were the ones born with the sight."

According to our neighbour, Etta Hunt, the caul I'd been born with was inseparable from the sight. She had known many with it, she claimed, in the old country. The 'old country' was Scotland. Etta was a Scottish immigrant who had moved to Canada and kept the thickest Scottish accent in stubborn defiance of the act. An old woman from Etta's village, who had also been born with the mysterious membrane, had predicted Etta's move to London, her marriage to a Canadian soldier and her eventual migration to Canada. This same old woman assured Etta she would be desperately unhappy there and would forever miss her home country, though she would never return to it. From then on, although she loved her husband, Etta regretted trading the rolling hills of Scotland for the salt-smelling flats of the south shore. Nova Scotia was never a 'New Scotland' for her. Once, years later, her husband offered to take her home for a visit, but the words of the Scottish seer spoken over twenty years ago still rang fresh in Etta's ears.

"We'd never have got there," she told my mother sadly. "The plane would have crashed, or been hijacked. I was told I'd never see the old country again."

"At this rate," said my mother acidly, "you never will."

My mother didn't believe in the sight, or in prophets. "Who wants to see the future?" she asked. "Most of us have enough to deal with right here in the present." She didn't believe in cauls either, and gave the one I was born with to Etta to keep. Often my brothers and I would make the pilgrimage across the field to her house on the smaller cape and ask to see it. We'd cut across our lawn, pick our way through the ravine, and wade patiently through the long grasses that neither Etta's husband nor my father ever bothered to cut, not knowing which one of them in fact belonged to that land. Our hair mussed, our faces more often than not dirty, we'd knock reverently upon Etta's porch door. If she was home, we would remove our shoes and boots and follow her through the kitchen into the parlour, where the caul was kept in a large glass pickle jar on the window ledge. Looking at it, a pink membrane curled and dried inside its airless prison, I could never understand how it had come from me.

"Go ahead," Etta always told us. "Touch it. Maybe you'll see something." My two brothers would crowd in and lightly trace their fingers over the outside surface of the jar. They often urged me to do the same, though I never would.

"Luke still hasn't had a vision," Billy said once. "I don't think he has the sight at all."

"Don't worry," said Etta, placing one hand on my shoulder. "He's got it. All who are born with the caul do. He's just got to grow into it."

Etta had been a witness to my birth. She had appointed herself midwife, claiming experience in the old country. My father always said that as far as he could see all she did was heat water on the stove. When it was over, he claimed, every bucket and basin in both households sat cooling around mother and child, so that no one could see us for the steam and the smoke from the tallow candles.

My mother had me on the parlour floor. By the time she realized I was coming she was so crippled with contractions she could no longer climb the stairs to her bed. There was no question of hospital. I came in October, during an electrical storm that felled telephone and power lines. The ambulance, employed in times of non-emergency as our grocer's bread truck, couldn't be called. We didn't own a car. It was 1957, and I bet altogether there weren't more than thirty cars in south-eastern Nova Scotia, none of which belonged to anyone we knew. The quickest route to town other than by car was by boat, a fifteen-minute row on a calm day. My father kept a dory, hauled up on the beach below our house. But the night of my birth wasn't calm, and a trip to town by boat wasn't possible. Even if it had been, he would never have chanced loading a pregnant woman into it. He was not a sure boatman at the best of times. He confessed to me once he was afraid of the ocean, and only kept the dory because we were Maritimers and lived by the water, and somehow he'd felt it was necessary.

So I was born in the house I grew up in. My father, according to Etta, could only look on helplessly, wringing his hands, his hair plastered to his forehead from the rain after fetching her from the second cape. He mixed mumbled scraps of prayer with frantic appeals to his wife. In his excitement he sometimes confused the two, casting his desperate glance heavenward when speaking to my mother, and looking directly at her when he addressed the Lord. My two brothers, then six and seven, stood back and looked on nervously. Roland, Etta's husband, didn't come, though he said he would if needed. He preferred, he told his wife, the miracle of radio to the miracle of birth. Etta was too preoccupied gathering the tools of midwifery — blankets, candles, a pair of tailor's scissors — to remember that the radio wouldn't work without electricity.

When I was a boy, every chance I could I pestered Etta to get the full version of the story. I would let her leave nothing out, not even those parts that might not be considered suitable for a boy to hear. She told me how she and my father had gently manoeuvred my mother from the chair to the floor, how she'd ordered Tom to fetch my mother's yellow mat for her to lie on.

"No!" my mother cried, even as my father and Etta laid her down on it. "It'll get bloodied!"

"A little blood won't hurt," answered Etta. "The hard floor's no place for a women about to have a child. It'll kill your backbone."

"That's why I wanted the sofa," my father complained.

"Be quiet, Harold," said Etta harshly, "and let me do my work."

My father, who lived in fearful consideration of my mother, and had always held a silent respect for our Scottish neighbour, stepped away. His work was finished, but God's wasn't. A flash of lightning whitened the room, followed by the obligatory rumble of thunder, and my father dropped to his knees beside his wife and her attendant and began praying aloud. Etta, kneeling before my mother, stopped long enough to throw him a glance, then turned away. She folded back the hem of my mother's skirt, unmindful of my two brothers watching fearful but fascinated from behind.

"You boys better pray too," Etta told them.

"But Etta," asked my brother Billy, "you've done this before, right?"

Etta only grunted in response, though she admitted later in the excitement she had never actually delivered anyone's baby before. Even in the old country, she said, she had never been given the honour. So my two brothers, unsure of whether Etta knew what she was doing, prayed. Not like my father, who prayed so much he only needed to adjust the words for the occasion, but in the manner of small children. Tom told me he prayed that our mother wouldn't get hurt too much and that I would be safe. Billy asked that the water wouldn't rise and wash our house away before he got a chance to see his baby brother, and added he hoped I wouldn't have two heads or four arms or anything like that, Amen. Etta offered my mother what words she could. She knew what would comfort her and what wouldn't.

"You won't have any trouble," she said once. "You've been through all this before."

"I know that," my mother snapped back. "What do you think I am, stupid?" It was these reactions, Etta said later, that she was looking for. Keeping my mother angry would keep her alert and participating in the birth, which would make it easier on all of us. Etta's plan must have worked, for the pain my mother had began to lessen, or somehow she gained mastery over it. She began to register events going on around her and, from her invalid position on the floor, made a desperate effort to regain control.

"Don't spill any!" she called to Billy, as the five year old struggled in with a cedar bucket brimming with steaming hot water. Billy was so startled by her shout that he did spill some, but because my mother was lying on the floor she couldn't see. He hastily wiped up the evidence with a towel. When Tom came rushing down the stairs with an armload of fresh sheets she cried out, "For heaven's sake, not those! They're my good ones!" And once, in the throes of what must have been a painful contraction, she cried "Joe! Go feed the cow!" Billy was halfway to the front door before he remembered his name was not Joe and that we didn't own a cow. My Uncle Joe only shrugged when he heard the story.

"We didn't have a cow either," he said. "Our father was a fisherman."

At Etta's urging my mother gave one final, desperate push and I slipped out into the sturdy arms of our neighbour. I didn't cry right away. There was at least a moment of silence, except for the storm and my father's frantic prayers.

"Billy said it first," Etta often told me. Or sometimes she changed her mind, and said it was Tom, or both of them together.

"It's got no face!" my brothers shouted, two small boys jumping up and down in the extremity of their terror and nervous exhaustion. "It's got no face!" Even my father stopped praying and looked over to see what God had done to him. My mother struggled to her elbows to see what kind of horror she had given birth to. I imagine at that moment even my mother prayed, though she would never admit it.

"Hush now," Etta ordered. "It's only a caul." My brothers, who had no idea what a caul was, and my father, who I'm not sure did either, watched in silent awe as Etta began to peel the membrane away from my tiny face. My mother sighed and lay back down again. Apparently she knew what a caul was. Etta, despite the disconcert in those around her, clucked happily to herself, and spoke while she worked. "This is a lucky one," she said. "There'll be no death by water for him."

Once Etta had peeled the thin membrane away, and placed it in a wet, wrinkled little pile on the floor beside my mother, she indulged my father by asking him to say a prayer out loud for me. He did, but not right away. For a few minutes, Etta said, my father could do nothing but stare at us as if he had found a new trinity to worship — Etta, me in her arms, and my mother collapsed on the yellow mat beneath us.

Once I asked Tom about the yellow mat. My mother had cherished it. It had been a wedding present from her brother, our Uncle Joe, and though she didn't much like the giver she loved the gift. She'd given it a position of honour in the centre of our parlour. It must have killed her to spoil that rug, but bloated and helpless, at the mercy of Etta and my father, she'd no choice. I believe part of her never forgave the two of them for forcing her down on it. For years afterward, long after I was in elementary school, she talked of it. But I don't think Etta ever understood my mother's fondness for a simple mat. My father knew, but he was locked into hysterical communion with his God, asking questions and listening for answers in the wind and the sheets of rain that assaulted our little house, and so was oblivious.

My mother scrubbed away at the stains for years, but by the time she got them out she had worn the nap down to nothing.

Where the rug had once blazed yellow in the centre of the room — slightly incongruous, I imagine, with the rest of our dark, cramped parlour — by the time I was old enough to notice it was a pale shadow of its former self, a weak autumn sun relegated to obscurity under a rocking chair in one corner.

Having heard the story of the mat from my brothers, and picked up what I could from my mother's grumbling, I used to crawl under the chair where it lay. I was young and small enough to fit there, but old enough to realize the mat's importance. I would sit on it, and try to imagine that night, or lie propped up on my elbows, tracing my imaginary history in its threads, searching for some clue to my existence in its composition. I even imagined I could see a rust-coloured stain, though my mother had long ago removed all traces of my bloody birth. I kept a *Brown's Atlas* borrowed from Billy's classroom beside my bed, and in my imagination the stain was shaped like Africa. This is the question I once asked Tom, about the actual stain, believing at first I'd had one of Etta's visions.

"Africa?" Tom said. "How would I know what the stain was shaped like, dummy."

"But you saw it, didn't you?" I said.

"For years," he answered. "But I don't remember if it was shaped like a fucking continent!"

Billy, lying in bed beside me, laughed aloud. Tom, from his own bed an arm's length away, whispered for him to be quiet. We lay silently in the darkness of our small, shared bedroom, listening for sounds of movement from our parents' bedroom directly down the hallway. When we heard nothing, Tom continued with the story of my birth, content my mother would not come to give us hell for still being awake. It was a story I had heard many times before, though usually I did not interrupt with questions about imagined blood stains.

"You should have seen it, Luke," he whispered. "You came out of there like a jackrabbit out of his hole." Tom, as usual, sounded awestruck. It endlessly fascinated my brothers that they had witnessed my birth, and they never tired of talking about it.

"I thought you were deformed," offered Billy. "I mean, you were all covered in blood and white shit. It was gross. But there wasn't anything wrong. Etta said all babies come out that way." He could not keep the disappointment out of his voice. Even then, Billy was gearing up to be a reporter. He just loved a good story, no matter what the cost.

"And then what did I do?" I said, although I didn't need to ask. They had told this story so many times, more often than not in the dark of our room after our parents were asleep, that I could have recounted it all without their help. But there was something comforting about lying between the two of them, having my history retold with such relish.

"You howled, Luke," Billy always told me. "Once you were born, you just howled to beat the band."

Tom and Billy hadn't known then that all babies cry when they are born. Tom thought I cried because of the storm, that the rain pounding on the roof of our little house had startled me to tears. Billy believed it was because I had just been through a terrible ordeal. He was near tears himself, and so could identify.

I would lie between my brothers, close my eyes, and see it. The wind and the rain, God's Voice, tearing at our little house with a vengeance. My mother giving one final screaming push, forcing me reluctantly out into the world. My father kneeling and praying beside her. Etta cleaning me off with a damp, warm towel, cutting the umbilical cord with a pair of tailor's scissors sterilized in one of the many buckets full of heated water, all the while murmuring the secular litany of the midwife. My two brothers, looking on with shocked faces. The story was told to me so many times by my brothers and Etta that sometimes I think I *do* remember it.

My father always referred to the night of my birth as 'The Miracle.' "It was wondrous, Luke," he often told me. "Truly marvellous." In my father's defence, he didn't always speak in superlatives. But he could use only these words to describe such an important, God-related event. He was careful, though, not to speak that way around my mother.

"If 'wondrous' means painful as hell I'd have to agree with him," she said once, when I'd innocently repeated his words. "If 'marvellous' means agony, then he's dead-on."

My father was considered something of an oddity in our town. Everyone we knew said prayers at meal times, or at bed times, but religion stayed in the church or home. My father carried his with him, in a pocket-sized New Testament with a white vinyl cover and gold leaf lettering worn away from years in the back pocket of his coveralls. It was a joke around town that he climbed poles for the Nova Scotia Light and Power Company to get closer to God.

He kept the Bible safely out of sight when he climbed to repair lines, but during his lunch break he would innocently draw it from his back pocket, plop himself down on the lowered tailgate of the utility truck or the nearest stump, and begin to read. Though he never preached, some of the other crew men — younger, single, and given to spending Saturday nights down at Carson's pool hall — grumbled to themselves and eyed him resentfully. Lost in his book, he was unaware of the discomfort he created. He'd complain to us over supper that the younger crew members didn't like him. After supper, he'd retire to his reading, and we could understand how his co-workers felt, for the Bible in his hands had a way of dampening our spirits and incensing my mother, who would exhaust her silent fury by washing the dishes or doing some other chore.

My father's wooden rocking chair sat in the kitchen next to the window, where he could look out and see the ocean. The other chair, my mother's, sat next to the wood stove. In the summer they were often empty. My mother was rarely idle. She might sit for a half hour in the evening, but even then she was constantly getting up to ply the wood stove with freshly split birch from the wood box. In the dead of August the wood stove still radiated heat, for my mother was always baking bread. My father couldn't stand it. Evenings and days off in the summer he could be found near the woodpile outside, in a pair of faded green work pants and a white T-shirt stretched from repeated washings, reading the Word of God. Even if the temperature in our kitchen had been comfortable, which in winter it often was, my father sometimes chose not to read inside. It wasn't that my mother forbade it, but each time he opened his Bible inside, it seemed the dust under his chair couldn't wait to be swept up, or there was a sudden and pressing need to gather the cushions on his rocker for washing. In the same way, she might decide to wash our sheets on a Saturday morning if she felt we were sleeping too long but it was too early to tell us so. More than once Billy and I awoke in our shared bed to see my mother standing above us, grimly and determinedly drawing the sheets right out from under our bodies. My mother wielded her household chores like a club. Everything gave way to an endless cycle of cleaning and sweeping and scrubbing. If my father happened to pull out the Bible on his day off, she would immediately arm herself with the straw broom from the pantry. Without a word, martyred in the eyes of his children, he'd close the book and take up residence on the wood block outside — his pulpit, as my mother often referred to it. At other times he might go for a walk in the field or along the shore. Occasionally we would follow, but he, caught up in a genteel world of angels and miracles, would rarely speak to us.

Sometimes my mother relented and allowed him to read to us from his Bible, especially at Christmas, when even she might listen from her rocking chair beside the stove. But more often than not, even then she'd abandon us and find some chore to do upstairs where the sound of his voice wouldn't carry. My brothers and I relished these times because, first, it was only then we got to share in his secret world, and, second, it was only then that my father lost his reticence about being in *this* world. He had a soft voice. Most times you had to strain to hear him. But when he read aloud passages from the Bible, the words fairly rumbled from his throat, as if bolstered by God himself. It wasn't only the New Testament we heard. In order to give us a complete picture of Christianity he'd bring out the family Bible and read to us about Isaac and Jacob, Job, Moses, and Jonah. But his enthusiasm for these stories was dampened by their impracticality. The flood, he said, was unconvincing. Jonah couldn't possibly have been swallowed by a whale and survived, and the parting of the Red Sea was, in his words, 'difficult.' It was problematic, for my father, that God ordered Noah to build a boat for one diluvial episode, and just forgot about boats with Moses, casually parting great bodies of water for him.

It occurs to me now, though it didn't then, that my father was quite heretical in his views for the time. But if his belief in the Old Testament was conditional, he made up for it when it came to the New. His favourite Gospel was Matthew. (I asked him once why he didn't name me Matthew. It made sense to me, even at that young age, that he should have named me after his favourite. "Luke used to be my favourite," he said. "I changed it.")

The story from Matthew we heard most often was that of the young man who wanted to follow Jesus but wouldn't give up all the things he owned in the world.

"Imagine!" my father would say. "Giving up the chance to be a disciple because of a few lousy camels!" I dreaded the second coming, because it was obvious what my father would do given the same opportunity.

"Imagine!" I could hear him say. "Giving up a chance to become a disciple because of a few lousy children!" But Jesus never came, and my father died unsummoned.

When the man from the power company, accompanied by a Mountie officer from Oldsport, came to our house that Tuesday afternoon and told us what had happened, all my mother could say was, "Stupid!" She kept repeating the word over and over, as if my father had actually gone out of his way to get himself killed in such a ridiculous manner. He'd been working on the power lines on the outskirts of town, replacing a faulty transformer that had left several houses without electricity. Somehow his safety belt had snapped and he fell directly into a string of live wires below. His death was viewed with religious awe in our town. It was said that when my father had finally stopped struggling, his head fell forward and his arms stayed outstretched, so that he resembled a man who had been crucified.

My own favourite story from Matthew was when the Angel of Heaven descended and rolled aside the stone from Christ's tomb. Matthew says of this angel, "His countenance was like lightning and his clothes were as white as snow." Whenever I pictured my father after his death, it was always this powerful angel I saw instead, as if my father had become him or hid behind his awesome wings. When I mentioned this to Tom he said, "There are no angels. If there were and I saw one, I'd shoot it."

This is the only time I remember Tom purposely setting out to hurt me. But the grief he felt for my father made him distant for the first few months after his death. He didn't cry at the funeral, or at the graveside, and if he cried softly to himself in our bedroom at night as Billy and I did, we didn't hear him. I'm inclined to think he didn't cry at all. My mother held up well at the funeral home and at the church. But when they lowered my father's casket into the grave, amidst a closed circle of mourners, she allowed one strangled moan to escape her. It surprised me because I had never heard her cry before. Billy stood next to me, weeping openly with Uncle Joe's hand on his shoulder. Tom stood next to my mother, glancing constantly back and forth between my father's casket and the minister, appearing almost unaffected by the whole event.

The minister stood alone and read passages of the Bible over the open grave. A large crowd had gathered. Nearly the whole town had turned out to see my father off, though he'd kept, as we were later to do, pretty much to himself. But in the Cape funerals were generally well attended. The minister had to shout for everyone to hear him.

"Let your heart not be troubled," he shouted. "Believe in God. Believe also in me. In my father's house are many dwelling places. I go to prepare a place for you." He paused. A short blast of wind ruffled his hair and pawed at the pages of the open Bible.

"And if I go and prepare a place for you," he continued, "I will come again, and receive you to myself, that where I am, there you may be also. And you know the way where I am going!"

We did, and we did not. "The only place I saw Dad going," Tom said bitterly, "was into a hole in the ground."

It was not only to us that Tom expressed the contempt he now found for religion. When the graveside service was over, and the crowd was walking slowly back towards town, the minister, perhaps out of some further attempt to assuage grief, layed a hand on Tom's shoulder and tried to pull him aside.

"Let go of me!" Tom shouted, and pulled away. Even the oldest of my father's co-workers, who wanted to tell him that as the man of the house, if there was anything he needed, he could come to him, had no success. In our kitchen after the funeral Tom listened to this man coldly, without expression. Only to my Uncle Joe did he make any response.

"Now you buck up there," Joe said, play-punching him lightly on the shoulder. "Things will get better, boy."

"I know," said Tom solemnly. "I'll make 'em better."

Many of those at the funeral followed us home that cold September day in 1963. All afternoon the kitchen was crowded with mourners paying their respects. Etta was chief among them, serving tea and coffee, and whatever sweets the guests had brought. It was common for neighbours to bring food to bereaved families, so that for the next week or so they could concentrate on mourning instead of cooking. My mother balked at the tradition, though she was too shocked by my father's recent death and burial to say anything. The food constituted charity, even when brought with the best intentions. The next day she gathered it up in cardboard cartons and we boys reluctantly delivered it to Etta's house, mourning the loss of such a feast — rose candy, chocolate cake, sweetbreads, tuna sandwiches, fried dough, brownies, even a jar of Lunenburg pudding. Over the next three weeks we made a few surreptitious visits across the Cape to help Etta and Roland eat it.

My mother was unused to having guests in the house. Indoors was strictly forbidden even to our friends. Three boys, in my mother's view, were more than enough care for. Other children often complained to their parents that even in the coldest temperatures my mother wouldn't allow them inside to warm their hands over the stove. As a result of this stricture, and with the natural curiosity of the young, Cape children were dying to see the inside of our house. They stood on their toes and attempted to steal glimpses of our kitchen through the window, until my mother caught them and chased them away. It irritated her, she said, "to have people nosing around, looking at what belongs to me and mine." On the day of my father's funeral she wanted to close up the house and pretend nobody was home, but Etta wouldn't let her.

"It's only right that people should come," said Etta. "And they will whether you want them to or not. So you'll just have to bear it the best you can."

Grudgingly my mother agreed, but when the first guests arrived she greeted them coldly, and even refused to let some of them in.

"There's no room!" she called out to a new wave of mourners who had jammed onto our front porch and announced themselves by a timid knock at the kitchen door. Etta stood with the door open and looked to my mother for guidance. My mother didn't even shift position in my father's rocking chair, where she'd been seated all afternoon, staring out the window.

"There's no room," she repeated. "You'll have to stand outside." Those already comfortably seated in our kitchen stared sheepishly into their paper cups. Etta quietly thanked those on the porch for coming and, as my mother had requested, asked them to wait outside. She closed the door on the disappointed but respectful mourners, and scowled at my mother.

"You could have let them in. It's cold out there."

"I told you," my mother answered. "There's no room."

Etta stood back abruptly from the stove, and looked long and pointedly into the immaculate, and empty, living-room parlour. Sighing and shaking her head, she lifted the teapot from the stove and started refilling paper cups. Those lucky enough to be seated inside our kitchen looked uncomfortable. The men squirmed like boys inside their suits, and the women kept folding and unfolding their hands and smoothing their skirts. In between whispered condolences and strained conversation, they threw my mother apprehensive glances, expecting her to turn on them and order them out of her house as she'd done time after time with their children.

After a while, Etta suggested that since my mother didn't allow smoking inside, the men might use the opportunity to light their cigarettes and pipes and give up their places to the women who stood outside. The banished guests hadn't gone away, but milled around the steps of the front porch, stealing looks through the kitchen window, apparently not giving up hope they would yet see the inside of our home. The men agreed, but slowly, some of them going only after being given curt nods from their wives. Each offered my mother their sympathies as they left. She accepted them silently, without thanks, and did not even turn away from the window long enough to acknowledge whoever was speaking. She sat silently in my father's chair long after the house had emptied. Etta was the last to leave. She hugged Tom, Billy, and me, and told my mother to call if there was anything she needed.

"Thanks," she muttered. "We'll be fine."

Etta nodded uncertainly, patted me on the head once more,

and left. The three of us packed away the extra chairs and loaded up the wood box. With nothing left to do we made our way upstairs, though it wasn't yet seven o'clock. We silently undressed and climbed into bed. After we had lain awake for an hour Tom said, "What in the hell are we supposed to do now?"

Neither Billy nor I had an answer. We heard my mother abandon her vigil in the rocking chair and slowly climb the stairs to her room. I'd always known what my father was thinking when he sat staring out at the ocean — the awesome glory of God. It's possible that my mother was thinking about God that evening as well, though I doubt she was singing his praises. From that day on religion was not practised in our home. The family Bible sat on a table in the parlour, but my brothers and I were forbidden to touch it. My father's New Testament had been buried with him. Along with his clothes, it had been fused to his skin with the violence of his electrocution. If my mother had sometimes indulged his reading of the Bible at Christmas, or tolerated his loud praises of the Lord, upon his death she never allowed the word God to pass her lips again, except as an expletive. When my mother buried my father, she buried God with him.

THE CAPE HERITAGE SOCIETY

$\mathcal{E}$tta Hunt was the only person in my mother's life who could speak up to her and get away with it. I was never sure why this was so. Perhaps it was because she was my mother's only friend, and my mother knew that if she didn't allow Etta some leeway, she would lose her. Even so, my mother would sometimes incense our neighbour by arguing with her. Their wills would clash. They could go days, even weeks, without speaking. In some ways, Etta could be as bullheaded as my mother. But she was always the more reasonable of the two. She was also more of a figure in town life, although more of an outsider, having no claim even to a Maritime heritage. She belonged to both the Ladies' Fire Auxiliary and the Cape Heritage Society. No one, least of all Etta, was sure how useful the Cape Heritage Society actually was. They held a lot of functions in town, mostly box socials and Sunday afternoon teas. Etta would occasionally take us to these, and we would eat sweets and drink grape juice out of plastic cups and play on the rusted swing set with the other children behind the town hall. My mother didn't like us to go, for the box socials had a five cent admission, and she could never afford to pay it, especially after my father died. But Etta insisted on paying it for us, over my mother's strident protests. Not only did my mother not like to take charity, it irked her to see even as little as fifteen cents go to the Society.

Ostensibly, any money raised by the Cape Heritage Society was intended to fix up the Collier house, a turn of the century mansion built by our town's founder one hundred years ago. But in all the years I lived in that town, the Collier house sat depreciating on the corner of Main and Sawyer Street. My mother, with her usual disdain, said they should lock all the members of the Society inside it, and just leave them to their tea and cakes and gossip.

"That way," she said, "an eyesore would hold an earful."

Etta was pretty much in agreement with my mother's assessment of the Society. She didn't have much use for wives of fishermen and lumberjacks pretending they were something they were not. But the Heritage Society gave her something to do while her husband was away those long months at sea. And the Ladies' Fire Auxiliary was entirely different, Etta decided. The Auxiliary was a *Cause*. The Cape Fire Department operated on an entirely volunteer basis, and they were always in need of money for new equipment. Also, on the rare occasion when there was a major house fire, the Auxiliary were called upon to help families who were burnt out and to feed the hungry firemen while they battled the blaze. This had happened only once in the entire time Etta belonged to the Ladies Fire Auxiliary, but once was enough for her to consider it worthwhile. Many times she tried to convince my mother to join.

"What would I want with those old battleaxes?" was my mother's usual response.

"Forget the battleaxes," retorted Etta. "It'll get you out of the house for a few hours a month."

"Out of the house? Why would I want to get out of the house? I have work to do, woman!"

"It couldn't hurt," said Etta, "to get involved with something, Dora. Everybody needs to be of service once in a while."

But my mother's idea of service was taking care of her family and her home. She had no concept of service to the community. "Fire's one thing," she said once. "Baking cakes and cookies is entirely another."

I was never sure what my mother meant by this. Etta admitted she was baffled by it as well, but I think she enjoyed antagonizing our mother, and in some strange way, I think our mother enjoyed it in return. At least, I'd never seen her get truly angry at our neighbour for trying to cajole her out of her inherent antisocial behaviour. If my father had tried it, or one of us boys, there would have been hell to pay. But Etta could get away with it, at least for a time.

There were instances, however, when Etta disapproved of my mother's cantankerousness, especially when she shouted at us in our neighbour's presence. Often Etta intervened on our behalf.

"Don't be so hard on them, Dora," she'd say. "They're just boys, you know."

This my mother took less lightly. "The day I tell you how to raise your children is the day you can tell me how to raise mine!" It bothered my mother not one whit that Etta and Roland had no children. She was only making a point. But Etta didn't take the slight lightly.

"Look woman," she said, heaving herself up out of her chair

and putting herself directly in my mother's way, so close that their noses almost touched. "I may have no children, and I may have never wanted any, but I damn well know you don't treat them like dogs!" With that our neighbour stormed out of the house and back across the Cape, her house dress fluttering around her bare legs in the autumn wind, her arms crossed tightly across her chest, muttering Scottish curses. My mother watched her go from the porch door, and when Etta disappeared inside her own house my mother turned, without a word, and went back to her chores. It was two months before they spoke again, and another two before Etta ventured back into our house or our mother into hers, and another week after that before they talked of anything but the weather, Roland's fishing, and my father's work at the Nova Scotia Power Company. This had been when my father was alive, and he suffered terribly because of it. My mother talked of Etta day and night, running her down as if they'd never been friends. My father, who never had a bad word to say about anyone, knew better than to defend Etta. That would only have caused an argument between him and his wife, and long ago he'd learned the art of co-existing with her. When she spoke to you at all, she was looking for neither agreement nor argument. She only wanted someone to hear. I don't think it mattered who it was, but it was always her husband or children. We all suffered, and during that time we boys weren't allowed to visit Etta, or see the caul, and that meant no cookies, or box socials, or even what I now consider much more important, the love that Etta gave us.

Etta knew we were never touched at home, unless it was by my father, and he was too preoccupied with thoughts of Jesus most of the time to remember we were there. So she tried to make up for it. She wasn't an especially demonstrative woman.

She didn't hug or kiss or even hold us, but sometimes she laid a hand on our shoulder, or patted our heads gently when we were with her. And she always fed us, sat us down at the kitchen table and served cookies and milk, or, at least for Tom, a cup of tea. Tom said later that he'd hated tea from his first taste, but drinking it with Etta had made him feel so grown up and important, he'd always drunk it to the dregs. It was Tom who told Etta he wished she was our mother. He just felt so comfortable with her one day, the three of us sitting around her kitchen table, talking about little happenings in the Cape. It just slipped out. We were all surprised at her response.

"Don't ever say that," she shot back. "Don't you ever say that again!"

"But Etta!" Tom stuttered. "I . . . I didn't mean . . ."

"I know what you meant," said Etta. "And I want you to promise that you'll never say such a thing to me again."

Tom promised, nodding his head, though we all saw that he was near tears. Tom made a point of not crying. Even when our mother gave us "lickings," a piece of kindling wood brought hard across the back of our legs, Tom bore it silently. Harsh words from Etta, however, who never in my recollection had spoken them to us before, were enough to bring him close. He lowered his head, and studied the pattern in the linoleum floor.

"You have a mother, Tom," Etta said softly. "And though she might not show it the way you want her to, she cares for you as much as I do. More, maybe."

"I just meant . . ." Tom began again, and this time lost the words. He wouldn't look at us, or even sit up to drink his tea. Etta waited only seconds before reaching over and placing one hand on Tom's shoulder. She had large hands for a woman, but they were soft and pink — perhaps, like my mother, from having them in buckets of warm water so often when cleaning

43

and scrubbing and washing clothes. One of Etta's hands placed casually on your shoulder could make you feel warm all the way from the inside out.

"It's alright, boy," Etta said to Tom kindly. "Now buck up, and drink that tea I've made you."

Tom did as he was told, and we left shortly after, for our mother would soon miss us and the two of them would have one of their famous arguments. Tom didn't understand why Etta had reacted so strongly, though he was careful after that not to wish for such things again around her. It was a long while before we realized that Etta knew certain things about my mother that we did not, and understood her in ways that went far beyond the simple powers of comprehension normally afforded to children.

We could always tell when my mother was ready to forgive our Scottish neighbour. It was when she got tired of one-sided conversations. We were only children, and did not have the proper appreciation for the news she picked up in town. It was then that she allowed us to visit Etta again. It always seemed like a casual move. She might say offhandedly, "Why don't you boys run over to Etta's house and get out from under my feet for an hour or two?" But she couldn't fool us. It was her way of making the first move without seeming to do so. Tom, Billy, and I would be ecstatic. It was like being let out of school. We'd calmly agree to my mother's suggestion, slip on our coats and boots, and then, once outside, let out joyous whoops and hollers and race each other across the Cape to the next house. Etta met our enthusiasm with studied casualness. She'd invite us in, as if it had been two days instead of two weeks or a month since we'd last seen her, and calmly give us our reward — endless cookies, milk, and tea. She'd ask us what had been going on lately in town. We never knew, so she'd tell us, making a point not to inquire after our mother. Once the visit was over she'd help us with our coats, lead us into the parlour to have a look at the caul, and then send us home.

Our mother feigned a lack of curiosity when we came back. We'd tell her what we had done, how Etta was doing, though she made it a point never to ask. We were part of the game, and played our parts instinctively. Then we waited.

Etta would never come over the same day. She wasn't as easy as all that. But usually by the next afternoon she'd magically appear at our front door, carrying a jar of pickles she'd just put up, or a tin of blueberries if they were in season. Sometimes we'd have to wait until the day after that, and that once when my mother insulted Etta deeply by mentioning the lack of children, we waited an entire week. For the first time we thought she might not come back at all. Even my mother seemed worried, although she didn't admit it. Several times we caught her staring across the Cape from our porch door. She told us she was only "testing the weather." But Etta finally came. She walked into our house like nothing had happened — blustering, windblown — and unceremoniously handed my mother a jar of homemade jam. My mother took the jar, and offered her tea and a seat with as much indifference as she could muster. This was a delicate time. They couldn't fawn over each other, yet at the same time they tried not to offend each other again. These visits were typically short and devoid of meaningful conversation. But it wasn't long before Etta was badgering my mother about the Auxiliary, and my mother would be responding with her usual sarcasm, and things would be the same between them as they had been before.

⁓

45

The Cape Heritage Society formed in 1954, three years before I was born, and though they never got a start on fixing up the "heritage site," as they called the old Collier House, they were a force to be reckoned with. Besides the box socials and teas, they started our town's first and only library — an unused stockroom at the back of Robichaud's grocery piled high with *Reader's Digest Condensed Books* and yellowed-out-of-date copies of *National Geographic*. Billy, our family's only reader, had struggled through everything in it by the time he was fifteen.

Another of the Society's incidental mandates, besides force-feeding what culture they could to the inhabitants of a small Nova Scotian fishing village, was to provide charity to those that might need it. Yet in a town with only two forms of employment — fishing and lumbering — all rates of income were roughly the same. When the fishing was bad, and the winter hard for fishermen and their families, everyone had a hard winter. Even our town's grocer would be forced to hand out credit and wait for better times to collect.

There was, however, one family poorer than most. They lived in a tarpaper shack on one of the back roads near Mackay's lumber mill. The father, Ernie Slowens, was accused of that one sin for which in a small town there is no forgiveness: criminal laziness. My Uncle Joe, living in his own tarpaper shack and drinking whatever money he earned from fishing, was more respected than this man, but only because Uncle Joe had no children and Ernie Slowens did. My mother always had something to say about Ernie Slowens and his ways.

"They should run that man right out of town," she said once. "I don't know why the hell his wife puts up with such foolishness, him starving her and her kids. She'd be better off on her own no matter which way you look at it, unless the woman's too stupid to think for herself."

Billy, Tom, and I went to school with several of the Slowens children. By Grade Eight most of them stopped coming. I can't remember names, or faces, and I have no idea how many of them lived in that one-room shack. Billy told me he'd been near it once, and that it was tiny. Etta, on a goodwill mission with the Cape Heritage Society one Boxing Day, described the place to my mother.

"It's terrible. One filthy room with a pot-bellied stove in the corner, and that nearly rusted through in places. They sleep on bedrolls, the girls on one side, the boys on the other, with nothing but a blanket to hide their bodies from each other. They don't even have an icebox. Imagine that, in this day and age! They keep their food, baloney and mustard I'm told, out in the snow to keep it from spoiling. It's a disgrace, I tell you, and we're just sitting here not doing anything about it."

"What do you want us to do?" my mother would always ask. "You look after your own. That's all a person can do."

"The least he could do is get rid of the old piano," mourned Etta. "Living with six kids and two adults in a house no bigger than this kitchen and having a piano taking up most of the room. I'm told one of the boys even sleeps under it at night."

Everyone in the Cape knew the story of Ernie and the piano. The instrument had belonged to the Collier family. Although no one knew for sure, it was assumed that Samuel Collier's daughter, Cordelia, had owned it. When the last Collier died, the piano, along with everything else, just sat in the house. The owners of the property didn't bother with it. No one else did either. In towns like ours you didn't take what didn't belong to you, even if no one else seemed to want it. Some of the town kids smashed windows and occasionally broke in to explore, but Tom, Billy, and I never did. My mother thought the Collier place dangerous. She told us if she ever found out we were inside she would beat us within an inch of our lives. Believing her, we obeyed. Besides, Billy thought the house was haunted, and Tom and I didn't wish to challenge him. Added to that was the fact that everything of value left there was already ruined by the time we were old enough to explore on our own. Or so we thought.

When Ernie Slowens found out about the piano, he gathered the few people around town who would help him, my Uncle Joe included, and relocated the ruined instrument from the Collier house to his shack on the other side of town. My Uncle Joe told Billy that they were drunk as lords when they did it.

"Took the three of us and hour and a half to get that piano up to Ernie's," he said. "And we dropped it three or four times." He said that each time they did, there was a loud, discordant but overwhelmingly musical crash and more than one light turned on in the middle of the night to see what all the fuss was about. My uncle said he felt really bad, even in his drunken state, about waking all of Ernie's children and his wife.

"Weren't no way we was gonna get it in there without wakin' 'em up, the piano was so big and that little place so small."

Ernie's family got up from their beds and lit an oil lamp while the drunken men hoisted the piano over the stoop and carried it inside.

"That Ernie," my uncle said, laughing. "He's as crazy as a shithouse rat. He sets down at the piano, starts banging on it like he knows how to play the thing, and this awful racket comes out of it, like cats screwing, or something."

"Just gotta learn me some chords, fellas," Ernie said to those gathered around the stolen piano. "That's all I gotta do, learn me the chords, and I'll have it made."

"Those poor kids," my Uncle Joe said, sobering and shaking his head. "Bad enough they gotta live all crowded like that together, then on top of it old Ernie making such a racket with that piana every time he gets drunk."

It was Ernie Slowen's ambition to be the second Hank Snow of his generation. The first Hank Snow, the country singer, had been born and raised in Oldsport. He was something of a local hero in our part of the province, as the singer Anne Murray was in the northern part when she became famous years later. But Hank Snow was a true blue country singer — his whine was famous all over North America, and long ago he'd moved to a mansion, it was said, in Nashville. Every visitor to our part of the province was loudly reminded that Hank Snow was from there and had sung at the Grand Ole Opry at least fifty times. This information, if you couldn't get it anywhere else, was most readily available from Ernie Slowens. But far from idolizing the man, though he knew every available fact of his life, including which room of which house he'd been born in in Oldsport, Ernie seethed with resentment.

"Ain't nothing ol' Hank got that I don't have," he was fond of saying. Except that Hank Snow might have known a few chords. But the inability to sing or play an instrument wasn't enough to stop Ernie from trying to become a famous country and western singer. Part of the battle, he thought, was looking the part, so he began to dress accordingly. He wore a vest cut from deerhide with bright silver buttons, jeans, and leather boots. To complete the outfit he donned a Stetson cowboy hat he'd picked up somewhere, and to see Ernie on the street without this outfit was as likely as seeing him naked. He wore it so often the buttons dropped off the vest, and the hat frayed around the edges from constantly being swept off his head. In a false Southern accent, he would say, "Good day ma'am," to every woman that passed. No one paid him any attention. Most thought him crazy. He couldn't keep a job. The mill had fired and rehired him so many times that eventually they or Ernie or both just gave up. The same went for the fishing boats. Uncle Joe got him work several times on the day trawlers, but Ernie couldn't be trusted to come to work or to stay sober or attentive if he did. His family lived on what work Ernie could get and keep — bottle collecting and odd jobs. Of course, most people had no money to give away, but they did what they could. They gave food when they could afford it. Each winter, Tad Morton, the foreman at the mill, 'lent' the Slowens wood for their stove. Everyone remembered the year they ran out. It was January and the trees were too frozen to cut. The story goes that Ernie chopped up his kitchen table and chairs and burnt them so his family wouldn't freeze to death at night. After that Tad decided he'd help the Slowens out if he could.

"Might as well," I heard him say once. "If I didn't they'd just steal wood from the mill." This was Tad's way of being charitable without making it seem so. My mother's ideas about charity didn't just spring whole out of her forehead, although she was more extreme than most.

The Cape Heritage Society made many visits to the Slowens' with leftover foodstuffs from box socials and tea parties. At Christmas they carried them what they could by way of food and a few toys for the children, who, it was understood, would be receiving no others. Irene Slowens accepted these offerings silently, without a word of thanks and without offering even a cup of tea. Etta described her as a short, overweight woman with greasy black hair and a desperate look.

"She was cleaning out the stove when we came," Etta said. "Sweating from the heat of a bucket of hot coals she was carrying to dump in the snow. Her face was streaked with soot so I couldn't tell if she kept herself clean or not. But by God those children were dirty. Hair like rats' nests. You could hardly see faces for the grit. I tell you, it's a sin. A black sin."

A black sin, Etta said. And so it was. Whenever we thought we had it hard at home, whenever one of us complained that we didn't want to live with our family anymore, all we had to do was to think of the Slowens' children sleeping on the floor of the little shack without enough to eat — cold in the winter, hot and itchy in the summer, living with a drunk father and a silent, desperate mother. Our troubles seemed light by comparison. We should be grateful to the desperate. It is their imagined plight that makes our own lives bearable.

Yet, even in a village such as ours, the Slowens couldn't remain as they were. People would have let it go on forever if they could have. They cared, I think, or most of them did, but they also believed that God took care of those who took care of themselves. They didn't want to interfere. But the family was interfered with anyway, from the inside. One night Ernie came to my Uncle Joe's having just gone home after a bout of drinking. He was near hysterics.

"She's gone," he told my uncle, who stood in his white long johns at the door, peering out at the man in the Stetson hat.

"Who's gone?" Uncle Joe said groggily. He'd been asleep for an hour or so, and wasn't entirely awake, or sober.

"Irene!" cried Ernie. "I think she's left me."

My Uncle Joe turned on the overhead light, switched out his bedside lamp, and invited Ernie in. The liquor was gone, as it usually was after one of their evenings together, and my uncle poured Ernie coffee from a pot sitting on the stove. Ernie took the cup, still shaking, perhaps as much due to distress as liquor, and said that when he'd got home that night his children were waiting for him. Apparently his wife had just up and left without a word to anybody. She hadn't even taken a jacket, and it was cold that September.

"The kids said she looked upset when she went," Ernie said mournfully. "I think she's gone for good, Joe. She just couldn't take it anymore." Ernie sat in my uncle's kitchen and cried. My Uncle Joe said later he was surprised. He never suspected Ernie actually loved his wife because he never mentioned her.

"I'm sure," he said, "that she'll turn up in the morning. She can't have gone far. She don't have a car or nothing."

Ernie believed my uncle, and went home. In the morning the two of them looked for her, hoping she'd gone to stay with a friend. The problem was Irene Slowens didn't have friends, at least none that Ernie and my uncle could think of. They searched the town over twice, then got the kids in on it. They went to every door and knocked to see if someone had seen her. Eventually, everyone got in the spirit and began searching for Irene, though for most it was halfhearted. They all thought what Ernie did. Irene Slowens had just had enough. My mother was ecstatic.

"I'm glad she finally got some sense into that thick head of hers," she said, when no one had heard from Irene for three days and the town had pretty much stopped looking. A week later her body floated in off the wharf. Some fishermen getting ready to go out for the day spotted it, and pulled it in with their nets. They knew who it was right away. The Oldsport newspaper reported it as an accidental drowning. She had fallen, they wrote, off Stone Mountain Bluff while out on a moonlight walk.

"Hah!" my mother said when she read it. "When did that woman ever take a moonlight walk, I want to know?"

"I guess she really did have enough," said my Uncle Joe solemnly.

Everyone, even my mother, felt the shock of Irene's death. The entire town turned out to her funeral, perhaps more out of guilt at the hopeless neglect than any real mourning. The children were all present. A few of the boys sported ties and the girls wore ragged hand-me-down dresses supplied by none other than the Cape Heritage Society. Ernie didn't wear his outfit. No one ever saw it on him again.

The kids left. The eldest took the youngest to Oldsport to make better lives for themselves. Ernie put the piano outside as a centrepiece in the graveyard of junk behind his house. Then he dedicated himself to his real calling — drink. He no longer talked of being a country music star. The Baptist and Anglican ministers, in turn, dedicated themselves to his salvation, perhaps making up for the lack of interest they'd shown when his wife was alive. The Baptist minister, Reverend McCall, even let him stay at the parsonage with the proviso that he didn't drink.

Ernie could manage to stay sober for a few days, and once, with the minister's help, he did it for a month, but the story goes that one night he just up and left the clean, sparse room the minister and his wife had prepared for him. He opened the window, climbed out onto the lower roof, and down the ivy trellis. Later that night, roaring drunk, he tried to climb back in again, but the minister was waiting for him in the little room. He was sitting on the neatly made single bed, still wearing his white collar though it was almost eleven o'clock.

"I'm disappointed," he said to Ernie, who had one leg inside the room and was staring at his would-be saviour through the paned top half of the open window. "I really thought you were gonna make it this time."

"I'm sorry, preach," said Ernie. "Can I stay the night?"

"Go home, Ernie," the minister said. "Go home and pray to the Lord to save you."

But Ernie did not like to go home, perhaps because even in a tiny shack there was too much room without his wife and children. He would only sleep there in the coldest winter months. In the summer you'd find him passed out on the grass between the post office and the town hall. Sometimes he'd lie under the porch at Robichaud's grocery. He became, like my mother's yellow rug, a shadow of his former self. He begged for change on the street when it was payday at the mill and on Fridays when the cod plant handed out their wages. He was our town's first vagabond, though he wasn't very successful. Everyone ignored him. He died in August of 1968 and wasn't found until a week later when someone finally thought about him and paid his shack a visit. Even my Uncle Joe had stopped chumming with him. My uncle was one of the very few people who attended his funeral, in a town where a funeral was an event. Usually everyone went to everyone's funeral. But Ernie was ignored then too, perhaps because in many ways the entire town still blamed him for the death of his wife.

It was the death of Irene Slowens that eventually brought the Cape Heritage Society into conflict with my mother. Etta was present at the town meeting when the Society decided to change their mandate. Instead of fixing up an old house and preserving history, they would 'preserve lives.' It was their new intent to stamp out poverty everywhere. In their naïveté, they began looking around for other 'needy' families, and the first one they settled on was ours.

"There's no husband there," one of them said. "Poor Harold's been dead two years."

"I know Dora doesn't have much of a pension," said another. "And the boys are too young to work. Harold didn't have any insurance or anything like that."

"Christmas is coming. Maybe they could use a little something extra."

Etta stopped them before they could go any further. "If you

go marching into Dora's house with charities," she said, "you'll all be out on the toe of her shoe in less than a minute flat."

"Oh come on now, Etta. You know she could use the help."

"Maybe she could," said Etta. "But she won't take it. I can tell you that as sure as the sun will rise tomorrow."

"Perhaps we could appeal to the children," said Freeda Wilson. "She couldn't deny her children a few small gifts at Christmas time." Besides old Robichaud, Freeda was perhaps the one exception to the relative poverty in the Cape. Her husband owned the Sea Cottage Inn and the cod plant. They were not, as most called them, stinking rich (alluding to the money the cod plant brought in and the smell it gave off) but they were comfortable. Their house was larger than most, and it was said that Freeda had furnished it nicely.

Freeda was the real driving force behind the Cape Heritage Society. Her word usually carried the day, and she now looked to Etta (who had caused her more than enough opposition in the past) with a somewhat set expression on her face. "Come on now Etta," she said. "You wouldn't be the one to deny those poor children a nice Christmas, would you?"

"There isn't anything wrong with their Christmas. Rolly and I always give them a gift or two."

"And what does their mother give them?" asked Freeda slyly. Everyone knew my mother no longer believed in Christmas. She kept the tradition alive when my father was alive, if only for his sake. But she now believed we were all too old for it. Her only concession was a bag of fresh oranges (hard enough to get in the Cape at that time of year) on Christmas Day, and a partridge dinner with all the trimmings if Tom could manage to shoot us a bird. We received no gifts — money didn't allow for that — although my mother let Etta buy us all one small thing as a symbol of their friendship. The Christmas before the Cape

Heritage Society got us in their sights with their philanthropic cannon, Tom got a pair of wool socks and two coils of bronze rabbit wire. Billy got a new shirt and a plastic comb of his own, and I got a set of drawing pencils. This Etta told the Society, adding that it was a damn sight more than some kids got at Christmas, alluding in her way to the Slowens who had probably got nothing at all in their time in the Cape. But Freeda wasn't satisfied by this.

"I can't think Dora would be opposed to a little gift box," she said finally. "No matter how stubborn the woman may be."

The group of women voted that this should be so, but not before Etta gave them an earful to take home with them.

"You've got no right," she said, standing in front of them all, "to force your goodwill on anybody, especially Dora Conrad. You all know what she thinks of charity, and you wouldn't do it to anybody else in this town, so I don't see why you're doing it to her. As for 'preserving lives' there isn't any amount of goodwill boxes going to make up for poor Irene Slowens, and nobody will ease any of your guilty consciences until you're in front of the Lord-almighty yourself. And Freeda," said Etta, turning to that woman. "I think you're the biggest bitch ever to walk down the streets of this town. Dora Conrad, as stubborn as she is, would make three of you when it comes to character."

A shocked gasp came from the women, though I'm sure not a few secret smiles were hidden behind hands. Many of the Cape Heritage Society felt Freeda Wilson was too big for her britches anyway. Many of them told the story, I'm certain, to their husbands that night with a great sense of satisfaction that someone finally had the nerve to tell Freeda what everybody thought of her. Yet they did not oppose the woman when she insisted they come to our house the day after Christmas and offer us their charity. Etta quit the Society that afternoon, walking out after her speech.

"It was silly anyway," she told us, echoing my mother. "Just a bunch of women pretending they're something they're not."

Etta didn't tell my mother what the Cape Heritage Society had planned for her on Boxing Day. It was better, she said, that she not be prepared.

"Forewarned is forearmed," she told us. "I'm afraid your mother would wait for them at the door with Tom's loaded shotgun." Of course, none of us really believed my mother would resort to murder, but Etta was taking no chances. We all knew how Mom felt about the Society as it was. She wasn't given to pretension in any of its forms. If they offered such an insult as saying she couldn't take care of her own children (Etta was sure this was how she would see it), we were afraid she might say or do things she couldn't be responsible for. Etta told us boys on Christmas Day, when we went over in the afternoon to receive our gifts, an event we looked forward to more than the oranges at my mother's dinner.

"I've got a plan," she said, picking up the newspaper we had thrown onto the kitchen floor in our excitement to unwrap. That year she gave more expensive gifts than usual. I received a pair of leather gloves because Etta said I was almost ten now and would soon be wanting to look sharp. Billy was cradling a new book by T. H. Raddall — a rare gift and valuable. Tom got a gun-cleaning kit, with a real barrel wire.

"No more coat hangers with a piece of rag tied on the end," he told us proudly.

"Now listen to me," said Etta, throwing the last of the paper in the stove and pulling up a chair before us. "I've decided I can't sit idly by and watch this go on."

"Are you gonna tell Mom?" asked Billy. "She'll be wild, you know."

"Well now," said Etta thoughtfully. "Telling your mother would be the honest thing to do, and I always say that honesty's best."

"I don't wanna be around when you do it," said Tom, shaking his head. "There'll be hell to pay."

Etta looked at us all for a long moment before speaking again. "Can I trust you boys?" she asked. We gave her an enthusiastic chorus of consent, and she smiled. None of us said it aloud, but we would have done anything for this woman, and I think she knew it.

"I've decided," she said, "that in this case I'm not going to do the honest thing. Now I don't mean," she added sternly, "for you kids to run about telling lies. That's not right. But I think in some cases a little dishonesty goes a long way in smoothing over a situation. Do you know what I mean?" We nodded, though I for one did not exactly see her point. Tom may not have either, but perhaps Billy did. Billy wasn't the most truthful boy I've ever met.

"When the Heritage Society comes tomorrow I want you boys to do something for me."

"What's that, Etta?"

"I want," said Etta, "for you to intercept them. I don't want your mother to know they were ever here."

We could barely hide our surprise. Etta always made it a point to love us, but didn't interfere if she could help it. She let my mother take care of us in her own way, and only said anything when she felt it absolutely necessary. This was something entirely different. She was now intent on deceiving our mother and she wanted our help. The three of us discussed it later that night in our room when our mother was asleep.

"I don't think it can be done," Tom said. "She'll find out somehow. If not tomorrow then later, when one of them old bags calls her up and asks her how she liked the gifts."

"Etta said she'd make sure they didn't call," said Billy. "But the thing I don't understand is why Etta just doesn't stop them from doing it?"

"I think she tried," I said. "They wouldn't listen to her."

"Stupid bitches," hissed Tom. "They can just take their gift boxes and shove 'em, far as I'm concerned."

"Will we get in trouble, you think, if Mom finds out what Etta wants us to do?" I was scared we'd be named as accomplices if my mother discovered Etta's plan. I thought we should just let well enough alone. The worst that could happen was a screaming match. There would be a few days of being especially careful around her, and she surely would not stop talking about it for a year. But at least we wouldn't be involved. Tom and Billy were pretty much of a similar opinion, though none of us questioned Etta when she told us what she intended to do.

"Maybe Etta's right," Billy suggested. "Maybe she'd shoot one of them with your shotgun, Tom, and Etta's just trying to save her from prison."

"Naw," said Tom. "She don't even know how to load it. Besides, if it came to that, I'd just take it out hunting around the time the Heritage Society is supposed to come." The conversation started to drag, and I was just beginning to drift off, when Tom's voice woke me up again. "Maybe we shouldn't help," he said. "She couldn't pull it off without us."

"Why wouldn't we help?" asked Billy. "Etta needs us."

"But it don't make any sense," said Tom. "It's stupid, is what it is."

"Doesn't matter," Billy said. He rolled away from us and pulled the quilts firmly up over his shoulder. "Sense or no sense," he repeated. "Etta needs us."

We awoke early the next morning and came downstairs all

three together. My mother was already at the stove. "All of you up at the same time," she said. "Miracles never cease!"

She was frying dough in the pan, and when we took our seats at the table she served us — three pieces of dough each, the thickness and shape of a pancake, fried in vegetable oil. Wordlessly we smeared them with butter and waited our turn for the carton of molasses. We ate silently and were nearly finished when our mother sat down with us, the stove filled with wood for the morning, a cup of tea in her hand.

"I'm going into town this morning," she said. "I want you boys to have your chores done by the time I get back."

"What are you going for?" asked Billy innocently, and Tom raised his head and shot him a glance. My mother didn't seem to notice.

"That crazy old Scot across the Cape wants me to come in with her. She said she got some errands to run. Don't know what errands you can run on Boxing Day with all the stores closed, but I said I'd go. Be good to get out of the house for a few hours. Roland's driving us."

"Is there any left?" asked Billy. He'd finished his fried dough, and was looking greedily towards the stove for more. My mother told him there wasn't any. "Can you fry some up?" he asked.

"What do you think I am?" she said. "Your personal chef?"

"I'm still hungry," complained Billy.

"You're always hungry," she said. "There's three oranges left from yesterday. You can have those after you bring in the wood." My mother was in one of her rare good humours, and we were beginning to think maybe Etta's idea wasn't a bad one after all. We didn't know until later that her mood was mostly due to Etta's scheming. Just before supper the night before, Etta had caught my mother alone and asked her to go into town the following day. At first she'd refused. Sometimes, when Roland was home with the car (a second-hand Oldsmobile he'd purchased just the year before) my mother would go into town with Etta and run errands herself instead of sending us. But on Boxing Day she didn't see any good reason to go until Etta said she was taking her out for dinner at the little restaurant in town, and then for a game of Boxing Day bingo at the church. Initially, my mother even fought that.

"You old fool," she said. "What would you want to give me a present for?"

"Because you're my friend," replied Etta. "Isn't that a good enough reason?"

"No," said my mother. "It ain't, when you've never done it before."

"Come on now, Dora. Let's go out and have us a little fun. It wouldn't hurt, would it? After all, it's Christmas."

"Now you know I don't hold with any of that foolishness," my mother said. "Christmas is the same as any other day to me, except you can't buy a loaf of bread or a bottle of milk because of some one else's convictions."

But my mother was won over almost from the first, and Etta knew it. The two of them had been to town together before, but never just to eat out (something my mother never did anyway) and play bingo. There had always been some practical purpose to it. Etta later said she'd felt guilty when she saw my mother actually approved of the idea.

"Honestly," she said. "It was a Christmas present. That wasn't part of the plan. I just thought since I had to get her out of the house it would be a good time for the two of us to go out on the town."

Roland didn't go to dinner with them, or to bingo. Instead he went to Carson's tavern, and said he would meet them later.

"Don't get drunk," Etta warned, and she and my mother

went into the little diner to eat. It was something of a tradition in our town to go to the Cape diner on Boxing Day, and Etta had to call ahead to make reservations. On any other day of the year, you could waltz in and take a seat at practically any table. The owner of the diner was a woman named Maude Sanders. A widow like my mother, her husband had died in an accident on his fishing boat, and since then she'd operated the diner alone and lived above it in a small apartment. She kept her diner running from her summer business when the boys from the boats would occasionally eat there, and from Boxing Days, when most of the town would turn out over the course of the afternoon. She made enough on that one day to keep her going the rest of the winter, if she shut down the diner for the coldest winter months, as she always did. That Boxing Day was no exception. Maude had hired two serving girls to help her out, and still the wait was long. My mother and Etta didn't mind. They took a seat by a window overlooking Main Street. Everyone in the restaurant said hello to them, and Maude wasn't the only one surprised at seeing my mother out. There was some whispering, but the two of them paid no attention. They ordered coffee and waited for their food — hamburgers and fries, a simple meal, but one rarely made at either of their homes. My mother was cautious about the food, mostly because she didn't cook it. She complained the bread was dry and the fries overdone. But her complaints were surprisingly good natured, and she ate every bit of her meal, even ordering a second cup of coffee.

Etta pointed to a few people in the restaurant, and she and my mother in low voices pried what secrets they could out of that person's past. I'd heard them go at it many times. They could be malicious if they wanted, but it was for their own amusement and I suppose they did no harm. When Etta told us how they'd enjoyed the day I realized why our neighbour wanted to save my mother the trouble of the Cape Heritage Society. It wasn't because she was afraid of what my mother might do, but because she wanted to spare her the pain of such an insult.

After dinner the two of them walked from the diner to the church and sat down at the bingo tables with the same crowd that had been eating at the diner, except, of course, for the men, who were congregating at Carson's tavern.

Boxing Day bingo was held in the Baptist church, though both Anglicans and Baptists attended. The minister of the Anglican church thought gambling was sinful, and would not give permission for one to be held in his church. But he was new, and the tradition of bingo on Boxing Day was old, so it moved from the Anglican church where it had always been held to the basement of the Baptist church right beside it, along with, I'm sad to say, not a small portion of the Anglican congregation — those who were willing to sacrifice the denomination of their faith in favour of a yearly bingo game. No one said anything the first time the Anglican minister's wife showed up with the Baptist minister's wife and bought her cards to play.

"I guess it isn't as wrong as some would believe," it was said later. "I guess we know who wears the pants in that family."

It was all in a good cause — but not for the Heritage Society, representatives of whom were at that moment sitting unbeknownst to my mother in her kitchen. The proceeds went to the Ladies' Auxiliary.

No cash prizes were given at the Boxing Day bingo (a fact that was pointed out several times to the new Anglican minister to no avail). Prizes consisted of foodstuffs and other small items. Cooked ducks, bags of potatoes and carrots (courtesy of old Robichaud), a fruit basket, an old iron someone had cleaned up and donated, a brand new washboard, and the grand prize — two face-cords of wood to be delivered by representatives of Mackay's mill next fall to the winner. A woman from Oldsport, visiting her sister, won it.

"Lucky she wasn't from Cape Breton," one of the women at my mother's table laughed. "Mackay would have a hell of a delivery on his hands."

Etta won nothing. My mother won the fruit basket. They found Roland waiting in front of the church, on time, and sober. They got in the car to go home. Etta sat in front; my mother sat in the back with the basket of fruit carefully balanced on her lap.

"I had a good time," my mother said, and even Roland told Etta later he was surprised she said it. Etta, of course, was beginning to feel guilty. She'd had a good time too, except for the gnawing realization that if Dora ever found out why she'd taken her out that day it might ruin the friendship. She hoped like hell that the women from the Heritage Society had come and gone, that there hadn't been some delay that kept them at our house. Her heart jumped into her throat when they turned onto the Cape road and saw Freeda Wilson's car coming down it.

"Now what's she doing up here?" my mother asked, ruining Etta's hopes that she hadn't recognized the vehicle or the driver. "And with a carload of people too!"

"Don't know," said Etta, trying to hide her nervousness. "Out for a drive, I guess." Etta held her breath, wondering if my mother would accept that. She stole a glance into the rear view mirror and saw my mother staring thoughtfully out the side window while they drove.

"What you doing tomorrow, Dora?" asked Etta, thinking if my mother suspected anything, the question would draw her out.

"Oh, nothing," my mother said casually. "If the store's open I might send the boys for milk and a few things. And I got some washing to do."

Etta relaxed, and they drove the last few minutes in silence. Roland took my mother directly to her door and when she got out he turned the car around and drove back down Cape Road to their own driveway.

"You shouldn'a done it," said Roland, speaking of the matter for the first time since Etta had mentioned her plan.

"I was only trying to protect her and the kids," said Etta. "I didn't want those old bags sending Dora on a rampage and ruining the boys' Christmas."

"I know," said Roland. "But still you shouldn'a done it."

Etta said nothing while they parked the car. She got out and went into the house. But as she looked out her kitchen window across the smaller cape towards our house she knew she should not have done it, and wondered what in the world had made her.

⌒

The day that the Cape Heritage Society women descended on our house like a prim battalion of angels we made ourselves busy. Quickly we performed our morning chores, washed our faces and hands, put on clean shirts, and nervously awaited their arrival. Tom took control, telling us how we must act.

"We'll have to get rid of them fast," he said. "In case Mom gets home early. And don't say anything about whatever they bring. We don't want to pretend we like them or anything, then they might call back to see how we're doing. Just take the stuff, thank 'em, then get 'em the hell out of here."

"Jeez," Billy said. "You'd think they were terrorists instead of a goodwill society."

65

"Doesn't matter," Tom said adamantly. "They shouldn't be sticking their noses in where they don't belong."

"Then why don't we tell them that," I said. "Maybe they'd just go away."

"I agree with Luke," Billy said. "I don't see what all the fuss is about."

"It's too late for that now," argued Tom. "We'll just make sure they're not here when Mom comes back, otherwise we'll be picking dead women up off our kitchen floor."

We went on like this for fifteen minutes or so, arguing about a course that was already decided, when we heard the car coming up the lane. Tom ran out to check, and soon reappeared back inside.

"It's them," he said. "Now remember. Don't talk to them. Just make them feel uncomfortable, so they'll leave."

The three of us lined up at the door. There was a last minute smoothing down of hair and tucking in of shirts, none of us questioning why we wanted to look good for people we didn't want there. To dress up for company was ingrained in us, even though we'd never really had any. We didn't care about the promised gifts. We looked on them more as a nuisance that we'd have to get rid of.

Three of them came to the door. There was Freeda, Caroline Morton, the wife of Tad Morton, the mill foreman, and Eileen Hunt, no relation to Etta, who was our town's postmistress and Freeda's sister-in-law. We knew them by reputation only, and so were more than usually shy when they came into the house carrying the goodwill box. Once Tom allowed them onto the porch, we just stood before them in the doorway to the kitchen. Tom stared them down. Billy smiled widely at them and I stole an occasional furtive glimpse but kept my eyes mostly averted to the floor.

"Is your mother home?" asked Freeda, while the other two looked curiously on from behind. Tom shook his head no.

"Where is she?" asked Freeda politely.

"She's out," Tom said. "What can we do for you?"

"I would have thought," said Freeda, "that Etta would have told your mother we were coming."

"She did, but Mom had to go out anyway. She just said to leave whatever you brought and go."

Freeda pursed her lips together, as if she wished to say what she thought of such a lack of hospitality. The two women behind her fidgeted nervously. The woman carrying the box tried to set it down on the porch, but Freeda caught the movement out of the corner of her eye.

"Bring that in, Eileen. We'll just wait until Dora gets back."

"You can't do that," Tom said firmly. "She won't be back for a long while."

Freeda smiled kindly at us. "That's all right, Tom. We don't have any more deliveries today, do we girls?"

Without being asked, Freeda came into our kitchen and took a seat in my father's rocking chair. The other two women inched inside the door, but came no further than the shoe mat. Eileen still cradled the wooden tea box in her arms.

"Set that down," Freeda repeated, "and come in. I'm sure you boys don't mind if we stick around awhile, do you Tom?"

"Yes," Tom said. "We do."

Freeda laughed lightly at Tom's impertinence. "I guess we know who takes after your mother in this family." Freeda urged the other women to sit, which they did reluctantly. They seemed to be waiting for something, perhaps my mother's unannounced return, upon which they would fly out of their seats and beat it for our front door. But Freeda didn't seem at all nervous. In fact, she asked Tom if he'd been raised to offer visitors a cup of tea.

"No," Tom said. "I wasn't."

"I'll make your tea," Billy said eagerly. Billy and I had only been watching the confrontation, unsure of what to do. We knew Tom didn't want our guests to stay, but we had no idea he would get so rude about it. When Billy offered to make the tea Tom whirled on him.

"What are you doing?" he said. "What did I tell you?"

"It's only a cup of tea, Tom. What can it hurt?"

Billy was enjoying both Tom's nervousness and the rarity of having guests in our house, even if they were uninvited. He marched into the pantry and got the tea bags, the sugar, and the cups. Tom and I watched anxiously as he prepared the pot, stopping to ask each lady what she would like in her cup. The women noticed but said nothing when Billy, after getting the bottle of milk from the icebox and whitening the tea, replaced what he'd used with water from the dipper. They may have noticed the grease mark on the bottle, and realized my mother monitored the amount in it. We were not allowed to drink it except at meal times, for it was expensive. Freeda thanked him when he presented her with her cup of tea.

"You're a real gentleman, Billy," she said. "I hope you know that we're only here to help you. Caroline, bring over the box and we'll show the boys what we brought for them."

Caroline started out of her chair towards the box, still sitting beside the kitchen door, but Tom stopped her. "We don't want your stupid presents," he said. "We already got presents for Christmas."

"Now Tom," said Freeda, as if speaking to a five-year-old instead of a fifteen-year-old boy. "I told you, we are only trying to help, and you should be more considerate of people trying to help your family."

"We don't want your help!" shouted Tom.

"Freeda," said Caroline Morton quietly. "Maybe we should just go."

"Nonsense," Freeda answered. "I don't understand, Tom, why you're being so resistant. Now your mother, I can understand, but you —"

"You leave my mother out of this," Tom warned. "My mother would make three of you."

Freeda's face flushed with embarrassment. Tom had been talking to Etta, and knew what had been said at the famous meeting when Etta quit the Society. She recovered quickly, however, and choosing a different tactic, turned to Billy and me.

"You boys," she said kindly, "wouldn't be opposed to a few presents, now would you?" Billy and I looked uncertainly between Tom and Freeda. But Tom had grown sullen, perhaps embarrassed by his lack of control. He was no longer looking at any of us. Choosing a seat by the stove, he sat staring moodily at the wall. Cautiously, we edged closer to Freeda and the gifts. She took the things out one by one and handed them to us.

"They're not much," she said, "but it's the least we could do."

Not wanting the fruits and sweets in the box to go to waste, yet with an unspoken agreement that none of it should remain for our mother to see, Billy and I immediately began to consume it all in front of our guests. Tom would not take any, but we acted as if we were starving.

"Want some?" Billy asked, his mouth stuffed with banana bread, holding a piece out to Tom. Tom did not respond, and Billy shrugged and went back to the feast. The women watched us, horrified.

"Do you boys get enough to eat?" Freeda asked, throwing a concerned glance at the other two women.

"Yes ma'am," Billy said, his mouth half full. "We just don't want any to be left for when Mom gets home."

"Does your mother deny you food, dear?" Eileen Hunt asked me.

"Well," I said, "this morning Billy was still hungry, but Mom said she wasn't his personal cook, so he didn't get any more."

"Except oranges," Billy said.

"Except oranges," echoed Freeda. "Well, I'm glad we could be of some use after all." She shot Tom a triumphant look, though I'm not even sure he saw it. Without glancing away from the position he had fixed on the wall somewhere above Caroline Morton's head he said, "We get plenty to eat. We don't need your food. Why are you here, anyway? You know we don't want you."

"I'm sure your father wouldn't have treated us this way, Tom."

"You never even knew my father," Tom grumbled.

"I most certainly did," said Freeda. "I knew him well. Your father was a good man. I talked to him whenever he was in town and I happened to see him."

"It must have been hard on you boys," Caroline said to us. "Losing him that way."

Tom looked at Caroline as if he was about to say something mean to her, then decided against it. "We do okay," he mumbled, and looked back to his spot on the wall.

"I know," said Freeda, "that if your father was alive, he wouldn't be ashamed of taking a few things from neighbours if he was in need. After all, he believed in Christian charity as much as we do." Freeda was speaking to Billy and me, but in the middle of her speech Tom got up and stormed out of the house. "I swear," she said, "that boy is the spitting image of your mother."

"You should see him when he gets really mad," I told her.

"I saw him beat up a boy once, 'cause he called us names."

"Really?" said Freeda, and nodded. None of us noticed Caroline Morton, though I'm sure at that moment her expression must have been unusual. Though I didn't remember, it was Caroline's boy Tom beat up, though she chose not to say anything about it at the moment.

The three women sipped their tea, and Freeda pointedly drained her cup in front of Billy and me, perhaps waiting for an offer of more. She didn't get it. Billy was suddenly nervous, and continually glanced up at the clock, the hands now moving towards three.

"Maybe you should leave now," Billy said to her. "We've got some things to do."

"I'd like to wait for your mother," Freeda said, unperturbed. "If you think she'll be home soon." At that moment Tom came storming back into the house. His hair was wet, and he was panting heavily, as if he'd been exerting himself.

"You better leave now," he said grimly.

Faced with such opposition, Freeda's goodwill mission was over, and she knew it. She set aside her teacup and stood to announce it was time to go, as if she hadn't heard Tom's demand and had made the decision for herself. The other two women stood up with her, eager to leave.

When Freeda reached the door, the other women already ahead of her, she turned and said as gracefully as she could: "Thank you for the lovely tea. And Tom, I'm sorry if we upset you, but you have to remember that we were only trying to help."

"We don't need your help," Tom repeated stubbornly for perhaps the fifth time. Freeda considered him briefly, then gathering herself, turned and followed the others out of doors.

"Tell your mother we'll call," she called back to us, "just to make sure she appreciated the gifts." Billy, still shovelling in the food the women had brought, stopped long enough to look questioningly at Tom. "What if she does call?"

"Etta will make sure she won't," Tom muttered.

Just then we heard Freeda's voice from outside. "Good gracious! What happened to the car?"

Billy and I ran to the kitchen window and looked out. Freeda's car, a blue Chevrolet Charger, new that year, had rolled to the edge of the Cape, only three feet from the drop off onto the shore and the Atlantic Ocean. Caroline had opened the front door and stood looking inside.

"It's in neutral," she shouted to Freeda. "You must have left it and it moved."

"My God," said Freeda. "We're awfully lucky it didn't go over."

We watched as Freeda carefully got in and started the car. The other women stood at a safe distance and waited until she had backed it well away from the edge of the Cape before they got in with her. They turned the car around and drove away. Billy turned back to our brother, who was sitting in my father's rocker, staring out over the water.

"You did that?" he said. "All by yourself?"

"I had to find some way of getting them out 'a here before Mom came home. I was gonna tell 'em if they didn't go I'd push the car over."

"What if they didn't go?" asked Billy quietly.

Tom shrugged. "I guess I would'a pushed it," he said.

"Jesus Tom! Like they said, they were only trying to help!"

Tom shook his head, slowly, stubbornly. "And like I said, they should know we don't need their help."

That was all Tom would say. Billy and I stared at him with a new-found respect, and not a little fear. Freeda was right. Tom was like my mother in many ways. In fact, I think she would have been proud of Tom's escapade with the car, had he ever told her about it.

"Well," Billy said, "we should eat this stuff before Mom comes home. Tom, you gonna help us?"

"No," he said. "Just throw it out."

We ate what we could, and eventually Tom, drawn by our satisfied expressions, ate as well. We threw the leftovers over the edge of the Cape for the seagulls to eat, and carried the box of gifts into the barn. Tom wanted to throw them away as well, but Billy wouldn't hear of it. We hid them under some loose boards in the floor, and when my mother came home we were sitting at the kitchen table playing crazy eights and acting as if we'd spent a boring, unproductive afternoon.

"Did you have a good time?" Tom asked her.

My mother shrugged, and showed us the fruit basket. She put it away in the pantry, but not before she reached into it and presented us with a stalk of purple grapes, placed on a saucer and set down in the middle of the table amidst our slush pile of cards.

"Here," she said. "You can have these."

We thanked her, but after my mother put her things away and came back out into the kitchen the grapes still sat on their saucer, untouched.

"What's wrong with them?" she said. "Are they sour?"

"No," Billy said. "We're just taking our time."

My mother looked at us strangely. She knew that all of us, especially Billy, loved grapes. They were such a rare treat, she'd expected we would eat them all right away. We couldn't tell her that among the gifts the Heritage Society had brought us there were many fruits and sweets, all of which we'd eaten. We were stuffed, and our appetite for grapes greatly diminished. My mother shrugged it off, and went upstairs to take a nap. The next day, Billy had diarrhea from all the unusual foods he'd eaten the day before, and spent a good portion of every hour in the bathroom.

"Goodness, Billy!" my mother said. "What on earth were you eating?"

Billy couldn't say, but later on when he got Billy alone Tom said, "I know what you've been eating. You've got the Heritage Trots."

From then on, whenever anyone got the diarrhea in our family, it was known as the Heritage Trots. My mother didn't know where the phrase came from, for that part of the story she never got out of us. But the association of human waste and the Heritage Society was in some way satisfying to her, so she began to use it too. "God, I had a terrible night," she might say. "The Heritage Trots got me." It was a small revenge, and perhaps not as satisfying as pushing Freeda's car into the Atlantic would have been, but it was lasting. The phrase is still in use in our family, which is more than I can say for the Cape Heritage Society.

⁓

It took my mother two weeks to discover the trick that had been played on her. Etta had asked the members of the Cape Heritage Society not to mention the gifts to my mother. "To save on embarrassment," Etta said. They agreed, but Freeda Wilson, when my mother had not called up personally to thank her, ignored Etta's warning and telephoned her the Monday we returned to school from Christmas break.

"I just wanted to make sure the kids enjoyed the gifts we gave them," Freeda told her over the phone. "I realize they weren't much, but it was the least we could do."

"The least we could do!" my mother raged. "The least that woman could do would be to jump off Stone Mountain Bluff and save us all a lifetime of trouble!"

Etta was even more incensed than my mother, and called Freeda up personally. "I have half a mind," she told her, "to come down there and tell you what I think of you in person."

"You were the one that hid this from Dora," Freeda answered. "You made your own bed, Etta."

"I'll make her bed!" Etta ranted. "Out of rocks and poison ivy, if I could. Out of rusty spikes and hobnails!" Etta even wrote a letter condemning the Society to the *Oldsport Advocate*. The letter appeared the following week in the Opinion section titled "Local Charity Under Attack."

An anonymous answer appeared the week after. It began rather high-handedly with: "The world's greatest problem is that some people just don't seem to care about other people. It is in the face of great difficulty that we set out to help the less fortunate, and nothing, including the biased opinions of some of our own members, will stop us from doing what should be done."

Etta did not respond with a letter in kind. By that time she'd calmed somewhat, but without even meaning to she had started an editorial argument. Each week for two months someone had something to say about the Cape Heritage Society. The *Oldsport Advocate*, dedicated as it was to covering the news of its satellite village, printed all the letters. Wrote one contributor: "I wonder what they do with all those nickels they've been making for all these years at the socials? Seems to me, ain't very much of it was spent on anything useful. If we've been giving them money, it's about time they showed us what they've been doing with it." This particular letter, though not eloquent, put its finger on the very heart of the matter. A barrage of letters followed, demanding to know what the Heritage Society did with all the money. Finally, a letter came to the paper from the

Society itself stating that, "All the money is safe and sound in Oldsport bank, nearly five hundred dollars. Anyone wanting to check the bank book can do so at the yearly elections meeting to be held in April of this year." It was this piece of information that dealt the death blow to the Cape Heritage Society. Five hundred dollars was a hell of a lot of money. It seemed a crime that it should sit in a bank in another town and draw interest. There were many suggestions about what could be done with it. "A townwide picnic," said one. "Donate it to the Ladies' Auxiliary," said another. "Or the fire department." "Put a statue of Hank Snow on the town hall lawn," drew a lot of support. Eventually, when the society disbanded, the fire department and the Auxiliary were the beneficiaries. The department needed a new truck, and the Heritage Society's money eventually helped buy them one. But by that time, Freeda Wilson had quit.

When Etta discovered my mother had found out about the visit, she went right over to see her. My mother greeted her in the kitchen, but didn't offer a cup of tea. Etta sat down anyway and looked openly at her. "I'm sorry, Dora," she said. "But I had my reasons."

"You were in on it then," said my mother quietly.

"I knew about it, but I wasn't a part of it, if that's what you mean."

"You know I don't take anything from anyone," my mother said, so mildly that at first Etta thought she wasn't taking it all that hard.

"I know you don't," Etta said. "I tried to tell them. But you know what Freeda Wilson is like when she gets an idea in her head. I just thought it might be better if you weren't around to see it."

"Those women," my mother said softly. "What right do they

have, I'd like to know? Have I ever denied my boys something to eat, Etta? Don't I take care of them like I should?"

"Sure you do," Etta said. "You might be a little hard on them sometimes, but sure you do."

"It hasn't been an easy road without Harold. He might not have been much, but he was something. When he died I told myself there, that's it. He's gone. He's been taken away and there isn't anything I can do about it. So I struggled on. But there's one thing I always told myself. That I'd never take nothing from nobody, as long as I lived. And even that they try to deny me. You can't trust them, any of them. When it comes right down to it, you can't even trust that God Harold was talking about. You've got to do for yourself. I always said that. Don't be dependent on anyone for anything, and you'll get by. Isn't that right?"

Etta nodded, though she told us later she had never seen my mother like this. We had a few times. Her morose silences and introspective moods always came after one of her rages, like the aftermath of a bad storm. You couldn't call it a calm exactly, more like an absence of mood. In these periods my mother was always the most unpredictable. She could flare up again, or just stay quiet for days, until her natural aggressiveness came back. I suppose Etta was just fortunate enough to have never been around when my mother felt like this, or perhaps she'd just never noticed the extent of my mother's despair.

"Dora," Etta said gently. "You mustn't take any of this out on the boys. It was all my fault. I was the one that planned it. Maybe I shouldn't have. But I just wanted to spare you the insult of it. Do you understand that?"

"Yes," my mother said. "I understand. But the boys lied to me. I didn't raise them to be liars, and they lied to me. They hid the fact, and there's nothing I like less than a liar. My father was

DARREN GREER

a liar. My brother Joe is too, and what good came out of them, I ask you? I came out of a family of liars. I swore I'd never be one, and I'll be damned if I'm gonna raise a pack of them."

"Did the boys get home yet?" Etta asked.

"No," my mother answered. "But I'll deal their punishment when they do."

"Well, don't be too hard on them. Just remember, it isn't their fault. It's the fault of those damn women, thinking they're better'n everyone else. Remember that."

Etta got up to leave, and my mother lapsed back into silence. She bid her goodbye and was on her way out the door when my mother called her back.

"What did the boys do with it?" she asked.

"Do with what?" Etta said.

"The box the Heritage Society brought. The gifts."

Etta shrugged. "I don't know," she said. "I never asked."

"Alright," said my mother.

Etta turned to go then thought better of it. "Don't think," she said, turning back, "that the dinner and the bingo was part of the plan, Dora. I meant what I said. It was your Christmas gift."

"Thanks," my mother said absently, and since there was nothing left to do, Etta left, although she felt uneasy. She said she would rather have had my mother scream and yell at her than be so distant.

In the days after the arrival of the gifts from the Cape Heritage Society into our house, and before my mother found out about them, Billy and I secretly used them when my mother wasn't about. As Freeda had said, they weren't much: a homemade bamboo fishing rod, a few pairs of wool socks that we didn't dare wear for fear my mother would notice, a couple of tin soldiers, and a prize possession — a second-hand pair of ice skates. None of us owned a pair in those days. When Tom played hockey he borrowed from whatever boy stood his size and didn't want to play anymore. Tom was the best hockey player around, and if one team was down, the boys on that team would pick a player to sit out and lend his skates to my brother until the scores equalled out again. Tom was careful never to score too many goals, or put his team too far ahead, or they might decide they didn't need him anymore. The boy who had lent his skates might ask for them back. Billy and I never got to play — no one wanted to lend us their skates.

The skates the Cape Heritage Society sent us were white figure skates. Girl skates. And they fit only Billy. Billy doubted the wisdom of going to play hockey in figure skates until he struck on an idea. He stole the shoe polish my mother kept in the pantry and polished the skates black. During the course of the day they would wear white again, and he might have to stop and add more polish, but at least he could play hockey with the other boys. He wasn't a great hockey player like Tom. His ankles were weak. They bowed when he stood, and he couldn't handle the stick at all. But he could be vicious. If the action wasn't too fast, he'd be in there, fighting for the puck. More than once Billy ended up in some full-fisted brawl in the centre of the frozen pond, with me on the sidelines cheering him on. Usually the argument started when another boy, angry at my brother's aggressiveness, made a snide reference to the colour of his skates. Billy started coming home with bruises and black eyes. He learned his fighting skills on the hockey rink, and all because he didn't own a pair of skates more suited to boys.

When my mother asked us to show her the things the Cape

Heritage Society brought, it was Billy who ran out to the barn and brought in the small box of items. He set them down in front of her. Wordlessly she took the things, one by one, and dropped them into the lighted stove. When she'd burned the entire contents of the box, she turned back to Billy.

"Is that everything?"

"Yes ma'am."

My mother turned to Tom and me. "He's not holding anything back, is he?"

"No ma'am," we said in unison. My mother nodded and asked Billy to go out, take the axe, and smash up the wooden gift box. "We'll use it for firewood," she said.

Tom and I followed Billy outside with the box, and watched while he lifted the axe and brought it down on the wooden crate, splintering it.

"That was stupid," Tom said to him. "What if Freeda told her what was in the box?" Billy laid aside the axe, and kicked the remaining pieces apart with his foot.

"She didn't, did she?" he said. "Luke, grab some of these pieces and take them inside." I started gathering the broken slats from the box, while Billy went into the rear of the barn, and returned with the skates.

"You better hide those well," Tom said. "If she finds them, you'll be in trouble."

"Don't worry," Billy said. "She'll never find them."

Sure enough, the next day my mother went out and searched the barn while we were eating breakfast. Tom was immediately on the alert.

"She must know," he said. "Freeda must have told her what was in the box."

"Don't worry," Billy repeated. "She won't find them."

A half hour later my mother returned, empty handed.

Wordlessly, she took our plates from us, started the dishes, and chased us off to school. On our walk, our lunch pails under one arm, our books under the other, we begged Billy to tell us where he'd hidden the skates.

"I won't tell you," he said. "You might say something in your sleep."

No matter what we said, Billy wouldn't give away his hiding place for the skates. But at each hockey game, he produced them, and then they'd disappear again. I believe my mother always knew Billy had those skates somewhere, but wherever he'd chosen to hide them, she never discovered the hiding place, and neither did we.

Some memories of childhood we carry around with us like snapshots in a wallet, ready to tell them whenever we're called upon. Others, when considered, leave us confused and grasping for meaning. The story of the Heritage Trots and the skates I tell readily, but one I have never told is the story of what happened the day our mother discovered there had been a plot against her. We came home from school that day, unsuspecting, the three of us tired from our half hour walk, our arms dragging with the weight of our books, our empty lunch pails dangling from one hand, beating a staccato rhythm against our thighs. We didn't always return from school at the same time. Tom might stay to play hockey until dinnertime, and Billy sometimes went to the library, or was kept after in detention. That day we all came home together, and I can't imagine it any other way. We'd barely got inside the door, our coats and boots taken off and placed in the proper places on the porch, our books deposited on the kitchen table, our lunch pails left beside the sink for my mother to clean out for the next day's packing, when she got up from her rocking chair brandishing a piece of kindling wood.

"I never raised a pack of liars," she said to us evenly. "That's something I never did."

The three of us froze. I was bending over to pull up one drooping sock. I'm not sure what Tom and Billy were doing, but perhaps we looked quite comical then, caught in the web of my mother's words, the tone of which we'd heard so many times before.

"What's wrong, Mom?" asked Billy, and though he tried to make his voice light, you couldn't mistake the fear in it. We knew what was wrong. Only a crime of the gravest sort would cause my mother to bring the kindling stick *into* the house, instead of leading us all in turn out to the woodpile, even in the cold of January.

"Don't 'what's wrong' me!" my mother said. "I don't want any more lying, I told you!"

"We're sorry, Mom," Tom said, his voice shaking. "We're sorry. We won't do it again."

"If I ever thought I'd bring up a group of boys to let a pack of strange women in my house when I'm gone, then lie to me about what they did, I never would have bothered with any of you at all."

"It was Etta's doing!" shouted Billy, his loyalty to our neighbour gone in his sudden panic. "She was the one who planned it all."

"I'll deal with her," my mother said. "Now which one of you wants to go first?" There were no takers, of course, and my mother waded in, knowing that none of us would stand still for the beating. I remember very little of these times, though they were present all throughout my childhood. I remember only the determined yet passive set of my mother's face, the scrambling, frantic efforts of our legs to bear our bodies away, even though we knew the beating was inevitable, as if instinct cried out against such punishment while at the same time our hearts, conditioned as they were, told us we deserved it. My mother didn't go for any single one of us. She clutched at the nearest shoulder. The kindling stick she held in the other hand, already bringing it around in a wide arc. She happened on Tom, though he managed to pull away. But the kindling stick was already moving, and though I'm sure she meant to hit Tom elsewhere, by moving he changed the target and the wood connected with the back of his head. He fell to the floor, but my mother never stopped in the midst of her battles to count casualties. She reached for Billy and brought the stick with all her strength across his hip. Billy screamed, and pulled away from her grip. Then she turned to me, now the closest, and the youngest, and too stricken with fear to move away. I was hit once, across the chest, and fell backwards, the air escaping with suffocating swiftness out of my lungs and leaving me gasping for breath on the floor. My mother bent over me.

"Don't you dare lie to me!" she shouted, bringing the stick down across my legs with every second word. "Don't you ever dare lie to me again!" I cried out with each stroke of the kindling stick, but still my mother didn't stop. Eventually the pain, the shouting, the noise receded, and I slipped into unconsciousness. I don't know how long I was out. I only know that when I opened my eyes I saw both Billy and Tom beside me. They sat me up. Blood from a cut on Tom's neck had soaked the collar of his shirt. Both my older brothers were crying. When Tom saw I was alive, but groggy, he stood up and faced my mother, who during my brief hiatus from the world had taken a seat in my father's rocker and stared silently out the window at the ocean as if nothing had happened.

"You could have killed him!" Tom screamed. "You're crazy! You're a murderer! You could have killed him!"

"Take him upstairs," my mother said quietly. "Take him upstairs, and don't you come down until I tell you."

Tom and Billy took me upstairs as they were ordered to do, and left my mother sitting where she was, in the same place she'd been when Etta had come over earlier that day. I remember very little after that. Pain in my legs, as if parts of them were on fire. A throbbing ache in my head. The muted sobbing of Billy and Tom as they carried me to our room.

They laid me on my bed. Billy lay down beside me, and Tom pushed his bed closer so there was no gap between, and they held me. They covered me with their bodies, their arms, their legs, as if somehow they could protect me from the pain of something that had already happened.

"We love you, Luke," Tom whispered in my ear. "We love you, and we won't let her hurt you anymore."

"We hate her, remember that," said Billy. "We'll get out of here, the three of us, and we'll never have to see her again."

They whispered these things and others to me, and somehow we fell asleep that way, in the sunlight pouring in through our small bedroom window. And while for days my arms and legs ached from the severity of the beating my mother had administered, my soul sang for much longer afterward with the whispered confessions of my brothers' love.

THE HOUSE ON GASTON ROAD

Tyler's Cape was rarely called by its full name. Even on some local maps it was shortened to the Cape. Tyler had been a farmer from Oldsport who, on a journey up the coast to Farmer's Mill, another small town fifteen miles south of us, died in our part of the world and left the then unsettled town as part of his legacy. The story goes that the road from Oldsport to Farmer's Mill had washed out only five miles from the larger town, almost exactly where the Oldsport road now meets the Cape road, though at the time the Oldsport road was little more than a cattle and horse trail and the Cape road didn't exist. The young farmer had decided to bypass the flooded area and take his oxen and cart along the beach until he could rejoin the road on the other side. No one has ever said why Tyler was in such a rush to get to Farmer's Mill, though occasionally it's been suggested that because Tyler was a bachelor he was on his way to propose to a woman. This, however, is only speculation. It makes the genesis of our town's name romantic. No one knew what girl Tyler was intent on proposing to, or why he was taking a lumbering oxcart to Farmer's Mill when a horse and cart, or horse alone, would have been a far more ready means of transportation. Some have proposed the theory that he was going there on business, perhaps to bring back a load of feed for his oxen. But feed for animals isn't so romantic as young girls and dying for love, so the first version is preferred. Anyway, Tyler made it up a good stretch of the beach before coming upon a sinkhole. This short finger of ocean, perhaps no more than nine feet across and five feet deep, pushed its way onto the beach at high tide. As boys we sometimes swam in it when the tide was in, for the sun heated it and made it more bearable than the ocean. Tyler, that day over a hundred and fifty years ago, must have been quite anxious to get where he was going for he decided to cross the sinkhole at high tide instead of going around. He guessed rightly that the hole wasn't deep and wrongly that his oxen would not be immersed. His mistake lay in not testing the sand. Even as a boy I remember that when the beach flooded at high tide the sand around that hole turned to mud and could suck the boots right off your feet if you weren't careful. Tyler soon found this out, for when he drove his oxen forward they immediately began to sink. In no time at all both cart and oxen were being sucked helplessly under, and Tyler, that sturdy soul, went with them. From then on the sinkhole was called Tyler's Hole, and by association the entire town, when Collier the lumber baron decided to settle there, was named after him as well. Although Tyler's Hole didn't fall on our property it wasn't far, and Billy, Tom, and I spent much time there in the summer. Besides being a good place to swim, the soft sand made it easy to dig clams which we'd bring home in tin buckets for our mother to steam. We thought the place haunted by Tyler's ghost and the ghosts of drowned oxen and avoided it at night. When swimming I could never quite forget that buried somewhere below me were the bones of Tyler and his beasts, though Tom always assured us they would have rotted long ago. Billy was especially fascinated by the place.

"Can't you hear them screaming?" he'd say to me, on his knees, his ear pressed to the soft sand beside the sinkhole. "They're buried alive down there."

Billy did this purposely to scare me, though if Tom was around he'd immediately deflate the narrative. "That was a hell of a long time ago," he'd say. "There ain't nothing down there now but sand, crab shells, and rocks." Tom, the realist, didn't often indulge in the suspension of disbelief. In the rare cases he wasn't around, Billy would continue until he succeeded in scaring me enough to want to go home.

"Baby," he'd say walking back. "Scared of a dead farmer and a few fat cows."

But Billy would never tease me for long. Part of his talent was the ability to scare the hell out of himself as well as his listeners. We'd go home together. Billy's first story, the one he wrote and published in the school magazine, was about Tyler and his oxen. And if Tom was our realist, Billy was our romantic. In his written version of the story Tyler was on his way to Farmer's Mill for love.

My mother didn't believe in allowing boys to roam widely. She often warned us to stay within earshot, and while this might have been restricting to children with parents of normal powers of voice, with my mother it was not so. I remember being with my brothers half a mile down the coast, playing hide-and-seek or kick-the-can among the tall skinny pines of Tyler's Woods, and hearing our names carried faintly, but distinctly, on the wind. "Tooommmmm! Billeeee! Luuuuuuke!" Our mother calling us home for supper. But for all her vocal range, and the freedom it afforded, we didn't stray far from our home. A trip to town alone was like a trip to a forbidden city.

For years a lively fishing industry existed in the Cape. Some men, like Roland, worked on the deep sea freezer trawlers, and would be away for weeks at a time during scallop and lobster season at Grand Banks, off the shore of Newfoundland, or at Browns' and Georges' Banks closer to home. Others, like my Uncle Joe, worked on the day trawlers that hunted ground fish along the coast — haddock, halibut, Boston blue, and, of course, cod. All this fish was brought to and sold at the plant near the wharf, where those women and the few men who preferred not to make their living at sea dewormed, filleted, salted, and wrapped the fish in the processing plant. Yet, despite this activity, the one main street of the Cape never teemed with commerce. Most of the deep sea fishermen, when they came back from weeks at sea with their pockets full, went to Oldsport to spend their money, and sometimes even to Halifax. The few small clothing shops hiding behind brightly painted false fronts on Main Street made their money, what little of it there was, from day fisherman and mill workers. Sometimes Robichaud the grocer saw some deep sea money, when the family of some long absent fisherman ran out of cash and bought on credit. He would wait until the husband or father returned to pay the bill.

Other than these — Robichaud's grocery, Milo's Second Hand Shop, the small Stedman's department store — a few municipal buildings and a post office sat on Main Street. The town hall, which doubled as a community center and was where the fire department stored their one pumper truck, was built in the early 1900s at the corner of Main and Collier streets. In 1956 a flag pole was erected on its front lawn. It stood only a measly six feet, and on windless days the hem of its Nova Scotian coat of arms brushed the grass. Next to the town hall sat the Masonic Hall, with a large bronze Masonic symbol, the hammer and cross, nailed above each door and a smaller one above each window. We'd never been in that hall. It was used exclusively by our town's small chapter of Freemasons. Billy entertained us with stories of masonic rites, the sacrificing of cows at midnight and plans for world domination concealed behind the building's innocent white-painted shingles. Billy's plan was to infiltrate the secret society when he came of age and expose it on the front page of every newspaper in the world.

"But won't they get mad?" I asked him nervously. "Won't they try to hurt you?"

"Probably," he answered, unconcerned. "They might try something."

"But they wouldn't do anything to your family, would they?" I had fears of retaliation. Billy in Toronto, and us here at home on the day the news came out, our house surrounded by a group of large men in black robes . . . Freemasons in a murderous rage over their betrayal.

"Don't worry," Billy always said magnanimously. "I'll protect you."

He never explained how he'd protect us, and I had no idea that the Freemasons were about as dangerous as, if a little more secretive than, the Ladies' Auxiliary.

Tom, as usual, had little time for our brother's fevered imaginings. "Forget the Freemasons," he'd tell us. "We'll have our own secret rites to face if we don't get our groceries done and take them home so Mom can make supper."

The grocery store lay past the town hall, set back off the road directly across the street from the collected buildings of the fish plant. Saul Robichaud, out of some deeply rooted Anglophilia, had named his store Smith's Grocery in hopes of attracting English customers, though everyone called it Robichaud's Grocery anyway. Besides, anyone who hated the French wouldn't be fooled by the store's name. Robichaud's nieces and daughters served as cashiers. They spoke to customers in English (for some of them it was badly broken), but to each other they rattled off in French. They spoke loudly, yelling across the cashier stations to each other, and inevitably Saul would thrust his head out of the little window in the manager's office in the back of the store and roar out some unintelligible comment to them. To us it sounded like for years the Robichauds had been having a family argument that had never been resolved. We didn't consider that they were just an extremely loud French family, nor did we notice the way the girls, all of whom were overweight but pretty, smiled at each other when the old man yelled at them. Though I still don't understand the language, I understand now that Saul Robichaud was what would be called in English "a pushover," though exactly what these girls were getting away with was never clear to me.

On each of these trips into the grocery store there was a routine to be followed. Tom gathered the more esoteric items on the list, things my mother didn't order every week and that had to be hunted down. We could rarely afford meat, and what fish we ate was caught or purchased at one of the plants. Billy was assigned the task of buying meats when we had the money. He also collected a small sack of flour from the bin each week, heeding my mother's warning to check for weevils. She was convinced Robichaud sold poor quality food, based only upon her experience of having once purchased a cabbage that was rotten at the heart, for which Saul apologetically refunded her money. But Billy was always told to be alert and choose carefully the flour, the carton of fresh eggs, the butter. I was left to gather the vegetables. I learned the first time I was given this responsibility not to take it lightly. That first time I grabbed tomatoes willy nilly, threw just any old potato into the cart. Tom didn't bother to check them, even though I was only seven. My mother took one look at the bruised tomatoes and potatoes with soft spots and eyes and started cursing. Not at me, but at Tom, for his negligence. After that he showed me what to look for, and it was many months before I was allowed to shop for vegetables alone. When everything was gathered we met at the front and one of the cashiers would ring us through. Then we'd begin the long trek home.

It was during one of these return trips, just after the spring thaw, when Billy had his first episode. We were taking our time that day. It was early afternoon and the sun was directly overhead. We had removed our sweaters and stuffed them into the open tops of the grocery bags. We plucked long thin stalks of wild wheat from bunches growing on the side of the road and put them in our mouths, sucked the raw sweetness from them and chewed them down to nothing as we walked. Billy, the pedant, was telling us about Port Royal.

"First of all," he was saying. "The winters were very harsh. At least half the people froze to death in the winter, or died of scurvy."

"What's scurvy?" Tom asked him. We were walking the road slowly, taking care not to let the mud pull the boots off our feet and leave us in our socks.

"Scurvy," Billy said, "is when you get sick because you don't have any fruit. Didn't you learn any of this in school, Tom?"

"No," Tom answered, apparently unconcerned about the

holes in his education. "But we don't have any fruit and we don't die."

"That's because we eat other things with the things that fruit have in 'em," Billy answered smartly. "If we didn't, we'd die too."

"What things?" asked Tom. But he had Billy there. He didn't know what things you ate to avoid scurvy beside fruit. But he continued to describe the horrors the first settlers at Port Royal suffered in the name of colonialism. He'd just learned about the fort and that part of Acadian history that winter. He often shared the exciting parts of his lessons with us, and later, when I reached the same grades he'd completed, I didn't have to work very hard to pass. But my brother always made his version of Nova Scotia history much more interesting than my teachers did.

"The best thing about it," he told us, "were the punishments. If you stole, they cut your hand off. Simple as that. No questions asked. If you murdered someone they murdered you. You didn't want to mess around when you were in Port Royal!"

He began to tell us about an instrument of torture the early settlers devised for people who broke the law. It was called a 'Whirly-gig' — a round wooden cage, like a human bird cage, Billy explained, with a flat top and mounted on some kind of gear box. The authorities would place the criminal in it and turn a lever at the base of the cage to spin him or her around and around at dizzying speeds.

"Sounds like fun," Tom said, and even Billy admitted it did. But, he told us, the criminal would emerge, many minutes or hours later, deathly sick, covered in his own vomit, and unable to stand up. "Sometimes," Billy explained, "they would spin you so long you'd die. Your brains would just leak like water out of your ears."

At that moment Billy decided to give us an impromptu

performance of 'Whirly-gigging.' He stepped off the road into the grass and began spinning about in circles. Tom called out a half-hearted warning not to drop the groceries, though we were both laughing at the strange antics of our brother. Suddenly Billy stopped, and staggered forward in self-inflicted dizziness. Tom and I laughed harder, thinking he was about to fall over. Suddenly, his head jerked back violently on his shoulders, and he let out a grunt. His arms jerked upward, and the two bags of groceries went sailing into the air. Fortunately, the sweater stuffed in the top of one of them kept anything from falling out. The contents of the second scattered everywhere. In the excitement I stepped on a box of baking powder, driving it down deep into the mud where we never found it. But we didn't think to gather the groceries then. We watched as Billy fell, his arms and legs held stiffly like a toy soldier, onto his back. Almost immediately his body began to buck violently. His eyes rolled back in his head to the whites, and the heels of his boots, still in the road, beat a tattoo into the mud.

"Billy!" Tom screamed, and dropped his groceries where he stood. I held on to mine, too frightened to move. I didn't know what was happening, and I could only watch this sudden possession of my brother. Tom jumped on Billy without hesitation, straddling his chest. But it wasn't enough. He was thrown up and down, like a boy on a wild horse, with the force of the convulsions. Tom shouted, slapped Billy in the face, grabbed him by the collar of his shirt and tried to pull him up, all to no avail. Finally, of their own accord, the convulsions ceased, and Billy lay motionless on the side of the road. Both Tom and I were sobbing.

"Billy," Tom cried. "Get up, you fucker. Get up!"

I still couldn't move. I could only call out to Tom, "What's happening to Billy?"

"I don't know what's happening!" Tom shouted back. "He's having some kind of fit, for Christ's sake!"

Tom crawled off Billy's chest and tried to pull him to his feet. Eventually, after what seemed like hours, he started to come around. Blood trickled from one corner of his mouth. He'd brought his teeth together with such force that he damaged his gums and caused them to bleed. When he awoke, he told us later, he had no clear idea of where he was. He saw Tom, a shadowy figure with the sun behind him. Tom was shouting "Wake up! Wake up, you fucker!"

Billy sat up slowly, looking at Tom and then me with what, under other circumstances, would have been a comically stupid expression on his face. "What happened," he said groggily.

"What happened!" Tom shouted. "You had a goddamned fit! You threw a fit right here on the road!"

Billy looked up at Tom in total confusion. "A fit?"

"Yes," Tom said excitedly. "A motherfucking fit."

There was a long silence. We nervously waited for our confused and disoriented brother to say something. He held out his arm, and Tom helped him to his feet. Tom kept ahold of him, supported him, while Billy looked around.

"Did anyone see?" he said slowly.

I shook my head. "No one but us, Billy." It sounded like a stupid question. On one side of us lay a wide swath of snake grass and alders, beyond that the shore and the ocean. On the other was nothing but the overgrown field running all the way back to the woods. There was no one around to see anything.

Billy gave his head a shake to clear it, and pulled himself roughly away from Tom's grip. He stood on his own, though he swayed back and forth unsteadily on his feet.

"A fit," he said finally. "Neat!"

The three of us searched a half hour for the missing groceries. Tom had thrown away the list, so we had to try and remember what we'd bought. We searched without speaking, picking up whatever we could find and placing it back in the empty bag. Some of the groceries were dripping in mud. We wiped them off the best we could, and hoped Mom wouldn't be too mad. We didn't find the baking soda, though at the time we didn't notice it missing. It was only later, when she asked for it, that we remembered. A few other items couldn't be found either. The half bag of flour had spilled, mixing with the dark wet soil of the road.

"Don't worry," Tom said, as the three of us walked slowly home. We were being unusually quiet. Billy was quietest of all. He wouldn't look up from his boots as he walked. "When we tell Mom about it, she won't get mad at us," Tom finished.

"What was that, Tom?" Billy said, looking up at our older brother.

"When we tell Mom you had a fit, she won't beat us for the groceries," Tom repeated.

Billy stopped in his tracks, and started to slowly shake his head. "We're not telling Mom anything."

Tom and I turned back to him. "What do you mean? We gotta tell her, Billy."

"Uh-uh," said our brother, shaking his head. "We're not saying anything about this."

"Why not, Billy?" I asked.

"Because," he told me. "They'll send me away."

Tom looked confused. "What do you mean send you away?"

"You remember Davis Keating?" Both Tom and I nodded uncertainly. The Keatings were a large family that lived on the other side of town. They had a retarded boy named Davis. His parents had sent him to an institution in Dartmouth when he was ten.

"But Billy," argued Tom. "Davis was retarded. That's why Mrs. Keating sent him away."

It was true. We'd all heard the story of how Davis got out of bed one night and played with his father's matches. He started a fire in the kitchen and nearly burned them all in their beds. After that, his mother decided she couldn't handle him anymore and sent him away to an institution in Trenton to live. We never heard from Davis again. But neither Tom nor I could see what that had to do with Billy, and we told him so.

"Doesn't matter," Billy said determinedly. "They'll send me away, Tom. I know it."

"Billy," Tom said taking a step towards him, "you're being foolish. You only had a fit. They're not gonna send you away 'cause you had one little fit. Why, lots of people have fits."

"Oh yeah?" Billy said. "Name one."

Tom couldn't. We didn't know anybody who had fits. He'd made it up. "Come on, Billy," he said finally. "Mom wouldn't send you away anywhere. You're her kid. She doesn't send Luke away 'cause he still pisses the bed sometimes, does she?"

Billy looked straight at me and said drily, "It's not the same thing." It was always an issue between us, him having to sleep in the same bed with me. But he didn't complain now, and looked defiantly back at Tom. "Don't say anything, Tom. You better swear it."

Tom shrugged, and turned away from him. "I'm sorry, Billy, but Mom has to know about this. Besides, what would we tell her about the missing groceries, and the mud all over your pants?"

Tom started to walk away. We were within sight of Etta's house now, travelling the last uphill stretch of the road that led to our house. I turned, intent on following Tom. I thought the argument was over. Tom always had the last word. Billy and I rarely questioned him. But before I turned the whole way around I saw Billy move from the corner of my eye. The next thing I knew Tom was face down in the the road with Billy flailing on his brother's back, pounding him with both fists. "Don't you dare tell Mom about this, you son of a bitch!" he cried. "They'll send me away, and I don't wanna go there! Don't you dare tell her, Tom! I'll kill you if you do!"

Tom, indignant, managed to throw Billy off and struggle to his feet. Billy landed them both in the wettest part of the road, and they were both covered in mud. Billy had again thrown his bags of groceries aside. Tom, despite his best efforts, hadn't been able to hold onto his, and so four bags of groceries were fallen and scattered in the mud. Tom ignored this for the moment, and fought to control Billy's wildly swinging arms. Finally Billy gave up, and collapsed against Tom's chest.

"Don't let them take me," he sobbed. "Don't let them take me."

"I won't," Tom said, and held Billy close. Billy allowed himself to be held, still crying, then pushed Tom away for the second time, and tried to gather himself. He stood off to the side, his back to us, and wiped tears away with his filthy hands, smearing more mud across his face. Tom and I wordlessly gathered up the fallen groceries for the second time that day. When finished we silently began the last leg of our journey home. Tom wouldn't tell, and neither would I. There was that understanding between us, though nothing was said.

Of course, when we couldn't come up with a satisfactory explanation for the missing groceries or the mud on our clothes, our mother beat us. Tom gave her a story about getting into a fight, but he knew it was hopeless. She led us, one by one, out to the wood pile, and brought the kindling across our legs. Even through our pants, the slim pieces of wood cut deep, leaving red welts on our skin that didn't fade for a day. I cried, even though I received only one to Tom and Billy's three. Tom, as usual, stood still for the beating, his face contorted in an effort not to cry. Billy skittered away after each stroke, though our mother held him firmly by the arm, and only had to turn where she stood to beat him more.

Billy assured us the fit was an isolated episode, although years later he mentioned it in a letter he wrote to Tom from Toronto. He said the city was so big, and the thousands of people on the street every day so indifferent, that you could "throw a fit on the sidewalk" and no one would notice. We thought at the time it was a figure of speech.

My Grandfather Conrad died that year, in the spring of 1966, three years after our father's death. He was no great loss to us. I remember my father's father little from when I was a child. On a rare Sunday he would drive down from the house in Trenton when my father was alive. His wife, my grandmother, died when my father was a teenager, and my grandfather never remarried. When my grandfather came to visit us, he always came in a mint green 1946 Ford Thunderbird. The car had been given to him new as a gift from his wealthy congregation many years before, and though he had often preached about the dangers of material possessions, he loved that car. While my grandfather was in the house talking to our parents, my brothers and I circled the Thunderbird parked behind the barn, admiring it. There were few cars in the Cape, and even fewer cars like this. Billy knew all about it, from an advertisement for one in an old *National Geographic* he had found in the Cape Heritage Library at the back of Saul Robichaud's store.

"198 horsepower," he would tell us, quoting directly from

the advertisement. "Twin exhaust. Chrome mufflers, and a v-8 engine with a four barrel carb. An 8:5:1 gasoline conversion ratio with a road-ruling, trigger-torque 'Go!'"

Eventually, when Billy had expounded all he knew about the Ford Thunderbird, we would ask my grandfather to take us for a ride. "Stuffed leather seats," Billy would quote to him confidently from the adverstisement. "With a comfort and spacious sleekness that makes even routine driving the most thrilling entertainment."

Without a smile, my grandfather would quietly refuse us. We waited for the day he'd relent and take us for a drive in his grand machine, but that day never came. Instead he would come out of the house, bid us each in turn a stern goodbye, then get into the car and drive away. My mother was sometimes in a rage for days after his visits, though she'd never say exactly why. We'd learned from my father that before any of us were born he and our mother lived in my grandfather's town and went to his church. Then something happened, and they moved away to the Cape where my father landed a job with the power company. Now there were only these occasional visits, which, for some reason we could never divine, made my mother angrier than if he'd never come at all.

When my father died, my grandfather came to the funeral and left without going to the cemetery. He never came back to our house again — which proved, as if further proof were needed, that there was something amiss between him and my mother. Even my father, when he was alive, expressed an uncharacteristic bitterness when he spoke of our grandfather.

"He believes in God," he said. "But it isn't the same kind of God I believe in. It's the kind of God your mother especially doesn't like." This was the closest we ever got to solving this little mystery, and it was many years before we found out the full truth. But whatever my grandfather had done to my mother, he must have regretted it, for in his will he left us his house and the mint green Thunderbird with the stuffed leather seats. This was, I suppose, a way of apologizing to my mother for whatever had happened between them. At least that's how we saw it. She chose to see the house and car as further evidence of his spite against her, a way of humbling her from beyond the grave. She shouted obscenities for half an hour the day the lawyer called, and refused even to attend the funeral.

"Does he think I should be grateful?" she screamed. "What does he think we live in now, a box? What does he think we drive, a bicycle?"

In fact, we didn't own a car *or* a bicycle, and so my grandfather's gift was not only appropriate but needed. My mother, however, wasn't prepared to listen to this kind of logic, and so Tom, Billy, and I said nothing while we dressed for the funeral. To engage with her while she was in one of these moods was asking for trouble, so we only did what we had to do — add the finishing touches to our funeral dress while she stood there and preached to us about our grandfather. Etta and Roland had agreed to drive us down to Trenton to attend the service, though neither she nor her husband had ever met the Reverend Conrad. But according to Etta, having us attend the funeral was "only right." She had offered to take my mother too, but that was out of the question. Our mother sullenly watched us get ready, leaning against the doorjamb of our bedroom, her arms crossed over her bosom. We climbed over each other in our tiny bedroom in an effort to steal glimpses of ourselves in the small mirror fastened to one wall, to make sure we were respectable. When we asked where any of the accessories to our suits might be — ties or black shoe polish, hardly ever used and so lost to my mother's habit of putting things away — she refused to answer us. Instead, she fired bitter questions.

"What do you remember of your grandfather?" she said when Billy asked her if his tie was on straight, after having to find it himself. "What good memories do you have of that old bastard, anyway?"

"Jeez, Mom," Billy said, nudging me out of the way to check his own tie in the mirror. "I don't know."

"He gave us money once," Tom offered. "Twenty-five cents apiece. Just after Dad died, remember?"

"No," said my mother firmly. "I gave you that money."

"You?" questioned Tom. "He was the one who handed it to us."

My mother stubbornly shook her head. "I gave it back to him."

"Oh," replied Tom, and continued to dress. It surprised none of us that my mother would rather put herself out seventy-five cents than accept what she considered charity from anyone, especially our grandfather. "Why should I let him give you kids money?" my mother continued. "He never gave you anything else. As a matter of fact, he never gave your father anything either, except a head full of religion and what good did that do any of us, I ask you? Where did that New Testament of his get him? Nowhere!"

She kept up her tirade. I don't think it would have mattered if we were there or not. On our way downstairs she told us not to associate with anyone at the funeral.

"They'll just be prying their noses into our business to find out what we're all up to. You keep to yourselves, you hear?"

"Yes, Mom."

The three of us, scrubbed and starched in our best dress, walked stiffly across the Cape to Etta's house, where she and Roland were waiting for us at the door. As we piled into

Roland's Ford, Tom asked Etta what in the world had got into our mother.

"I guess she just doesn't like your grandfather," Etta said.

"Don't like him!" answered Tom. "Sounds to me like she hates his guts!"

Etta said, "I don't think your grandfather ever approved of your mother. I think he wanted your father to be a minister, and somehow he blamed your mother for his not being one."

This surprised us, because none of us had ever considered the fact that someone out there had wanted our father to be something he wasn't. But now that we'd heard it, Billy asked the question that suddenly occurred to all three of us.

"Why wasn't he a minister, Etta? He loved God enough."

"Well," said Etta thoughtfully. "I don't think just loving God is enough of a reason to become a preacher. Your father told me once that being a minister was more about people than it was about God, and that he was never very good with people."

This caused all three of us sitting in the back seat to stop and think for a few minutes. Etta, when we had driven halfway out of the Cape, decided we should all sing something. We joined in a chorus of "She'll Be Coming Round the Mountain," with Roland, and even Tom, joining in. It didn't dawn on any of us that we weren't behaving like a group of people heading to a funeral. But none of us had known the man very well, and a trip to Trenton was so rare that we treated the coming event as an adventure rather than with the solemnity it called for.

Out of curiosity, though nominally for our sakes, Etta and Roland took us the long way to Trenton so we could go down Gaston Road and see the house our grandfather had left us. None of us, not even Etta or Roland, had seen it before. It was set far back off the road, in the centre of a pasture, and Roland didn't turn into the drive but simply slowed the car as we passed to get a better look. But even at that distance and speed we could see it was much bigger and well cared for than the house we lived in. It was white, with two solid stories, and many windows. Tom said it would be nice to go to bed at night and not have to bend down to avoid hitting his head on the sloped ceiling in our bedroom. Tom was sixteen that year, and already he was five foot eleven and still growing. My mother always said that when he hit six feet she wouldn't be able to afford to feed him anymore and would have to kick him out.

"Do you suppose she'll let us use it?" Tom asked Etta. Etta didn't answer, and Roland hit the accelerator and we shot past. Billy said the house looked like it was worth a lot of money, and then grew quiet. He was waiting for an opportunity to get enough money to go to college and move out of the Cape. Perhaps he was expecting my mother to sell the house and give him a share, which, Etta could have told him, was about as likely as Tom's dream of moving into it. But Etta, who knew more about the situation than we did, said nothing to us as Roland drove the remaining distance into Trenton and to my grandfather's awaiting ceremony.

My mother didn't have to worry about us talking to anyone at the funeral. Perhaps we would have liked to, but we came late, and slipped into the rear of the packed church while the service was already in progress. The minister claimed to be an old acquaintance of our grandfather's, and he spoke of all the good our grandfather had done in the little community outside of Trenton where he'd lived and presided over the small Baptist church. We wondered why the ceremony hadn't been held there, in my grandfather's church, until the minister explained to the congregation that the Gaston Community Church was small, and the expected numbers at the funeral so big, that they'd decided to hold the funeral in Trenton where there was more room.

Tom and I and Billy listened in fascination as our grandfather was endlessly praised, and a short biography of our long dead grandmother was given. We were particularly surprised when our own family was mentioned. We were named, one after the other, as the "loving relations" of the deceased. We'd hardly ever seen the man, let alone loved him, but that didn't stop a few of those in the church turning about in their pews and nodding their condolences when our names were called. It surprised us that the turnout was so large, and that my grandfather seemed so well respected. We had heard him run down so often by my mother we couldn't imagine that anyone, especially an entire town full of people, could think differently about him.

We left the church as soon as the service was over, the first out as we'd been the last in. No one bothered or even spoke to us as we stood on the church steps in the sunshine, trying to make up our minds whether to go to the graveside service.

"It's way on the other side of town," said Roland cautiously. "It'll be late by the time we get back."

"Doesn't matter," said Etta, who was determined as always to do the right thing. "If the boys want to go, we'll go."

Uncertain ourselves, we stood and looked around at the people who filed out of church and milled around in small groups on the steps. Many of them were older, and most seemed to have no idea who we were. A few, however, we caught staring at us and whispering to each other when they thought we weren't looking. Tom and Billy voiced the suspicion that they knew who we were but for some reason were afraid to approach us.

"They probably think you're our mother," Tom said to Etta. "They wouldn't remember what she looked like, would they?"

Etta stared back at a group of old women who'd been peering intently at us from under black straw hats for some minutes, and said, "I suspect you're right, Tom." The women turned away from Etta's challenge, though we got the feeling we were still the focus of their conversation, if not their eyesight. Finally Roland settled it, and said if we didn't go to the graveside he would buy us all an ice cream. The three of us, even Tom, who must have considered himself too old for such a bribe, agreed almost instantly. The idea of something cool to eat out of sight of all these strangers immediately won out over respect for a man we hardly knew. We had started up the sidewalk, away from the church and back towards the car, when a woman approached us. She was perhaps a few years older than my mother or Etta, and wore a black dress, matching straw hat, and glasses. I recognized her as the organist at the service, though there was something even more familiar about her.

"You must be the Conrads," she said, putting herself between our party and the route to Roland's car. She held out her hand to Etta. "I'm Dolores Whynot, Reverend Conrad's secretary."

Etta took her proffered hand and shook it, while Roland stepped behind her, under an attack of his usual shyness, and only nodded slightly at the introduction. "I'm Mrs. Hunt," said Etta. "The boys' neighbour."

Mrs. Whynot was caught off guard for a minute, though she quickly recovered. "Oh, I thought you were Harold's wife."

"No," said Etta. "But these are her boys."

Mrs. Whynot appraised us, looking up at Tom, levelly at Billy, who stood her height, and down at me. "Hello," she said. "I recognize you."

"Recognize us?" said Tom. "You've seen us before?"

Mrs. Whynot nodded. "Many a time, though you were much

younger. I used to sit in the car and wait while your grandfather visited your father when he was alive. You boys used to play out in the yard while your grandfather was visiting. I used to watch you. Do you remember?" She was looking straight at me.

I nodded. Occasionally, when my grandfather came for his visits, a woman came with him and sat outside in the passenger seat of the Thunderbird and waited for him. We never had the nerve to go up to the car and talk to her. Billy made up a story about her, saying that she was actually the wife of a high Nazi official who'd escaped from Germany just after the war and lived now in my grandfather's community trying to pass herself off as Canadian. He had nicknamed her Eva after Hitler's mistress, Eva Braun.

"So," said Mrs. Whynot to Etta, "where is Dora this afternoon?"

"She couldn't come," Tom said quickly. "She was busy."

Dolores Whynot again looked surprised, and perhaps shocked, that the daughter-in-law of her boss had thought it best not to attend his funeral. "It's too bad," she said, "that you boys couldn't have known your grandfather better. He really was a wonderful man."

"I'm sure that he was," said Etta politely.

"Well," Dolores added optimistically, "at least we'll get to see more of you when you move into your grandfather's house. I live only just down the road from you a bit."

"There's no guarantee that we'll be moving into my grand-father's house," said Tom.

"Yes," Billy piped up cheerfully. "We might sell it!"

"Sell it!" exclaimed Mrs. Whynot. "The Reverend would never approve of that. What on earth for?"

Billy shrugged. "For money, I guess."

Dolores Whynot looked horrified. "But that house is so

much bigger than where you live now. I just thought that . . . wouldn't you like to live in such a big house?" She said this to me alone, as if I were the one, at nine years old, who made decisions for all the family. I only nodded uncertainly, but the woman took that as confirmation of our intent.

"Of course you won't sell it," she said confidently. "Why, we'd love to have you as neighbours after all these years. I'm sure your mother would settle in after awhile. I mean, Reverend Conrad only wanted to do something for the boys, and . . ."

"There is no guarantee," Etta interrupted, "that Dora will want to sell the house either." She threw a warning glance in Billy's direction. "But whatever she does with it, I'm sure she is grateful for Reverend Conrad leaving it to her."

"Yes," said Mrs. Whynot, though she looked as if she doubted it herself, and for good reason. The fact that my mother hadn't even bothered to come to her father-in-law's funeral proved she wasn't grateful. But Etta had decided we owed this woman nothing, and taking my hand, with a word to the rest to follow, brushed past my grandfather's secretary.

"Take care now," she said to her briskly.

"You too," Mrs. Whynot echoed, although she appeared somewhat bewildered. Perhaps she expected something more from us, some idolatrous words about our dead grandfather, or a promise we wouldn't sell the house he'd so generously left us. More likely, she only wished to speak to us further, to find out more about the Reverend's extended family. Our mother would have been satisfied. Dolores Whynot learned no more about us than she had from the visits she'd made to the outside of our house with her employer. Billy, of course, couldn't resist a reference to those days as he passed her, even though she had no idea what he was saying.

"See ya, Eva," he said. She nodded at him, not hearing, or

ignoring, the nickname. We were all surprised, however, to see her climb into our grandfather's green Ford on the other side of the street.

"I thought he left that car to us," said Tom.

"Yeah," said Billy. "Shouldn't we go say something to her, Etta?"

"No," Etta said. "We shouldn't. Your mother hasn't accepted that car yet, and I don't see any reason why Mrs. Whynot shouldn't be driving it until she does."

"I bet she's spitting nails because she didn't get the house either," said Billy. Tom was too affronted by the fact that somebody was now driving the car that ostensibly belonged to our family to say anything.

"Don't always think the worst of people, Billy," Etta admonished. "You'll get what's coming to you, if it's meant to be."

Billy only shook his head, not listening. "I only hope that when we sell the house, a bunch of long-haired hippies move in. That would sure teach old Mrs. Whynot for stealing our car, wouldn't it?"

Roland and I laughed at Billy's joke. Tom and Etta did not. In fact, Tom stayed unusually quiet the entire drive home, even refusing an ice cream when Roland offered him one. He was already working out in his mind what he would tell our mother when he got home. Etta was quiet for other reasons. She already understood that my mother had different plans for the wonderful things our grandfather had left us.

We came trailing back into the house in the late afternoon, somewhat more rumpled than when we'd left. My mother was waiting for us at the kitchen table. We didn't even get to tell her the events of the funeral before she started right in again, as if our conversation had not been interrupted by the funeral and the subsequent burial of her father-in-law.

"I only hope," she said to us, "that none of you expect us to pack up and move to that old man's house. You might as well get that out of your mind right now."

On the drive home from Trenton we hadn't been talking about the house, or even my grandfather, but Tom was ready. He said to her without hesitation, "It's only a house, Mom. It was a gift. He didn't mean anything by it."

My mother nodded, but Tom knew better than to think it was in agreement. She'd wanted someone to say it was "only a house." She needed a rational voice to repudiate, and Tom nearly always supplied it for her. "Maybe if I hire someone to burn it down? Can you hire someone for that sort of thing? Burning down a house?"

But Tom only shrugged, and went upstairs to change back out of his suit. Billy and I followed. We knew she would not burn down the house. She was only talking. But still, with my mother, it was better not to take chances and challenge her on anything. Before long she followed us up, and stood in the doorway to watch us change out of our clothes as she'd watched us change into them. At one point, Tom, bare-chested and ready to take off his pants, said to her, "Mom, would you mind?"

"Why? You haven't got anything I haven't seen before." She did turn away, however, but she didn't stop talking. "If the old bastard had any relatives who were still alive, or anyone who even gave a shit about him, I'd call them up and tell them to take the goddamned house. And that ugly car too."

Even less than my brothers was I able to talk to my mother in these moods. Sometimes, I think, she enjoyed the challenge of Billy and Tom. The two of them together could meet her head on, if only occasionally, but my mother rarely bothered to argue with me. She knew she could win hands down. But possessed by some courage I didn't even know I had, fuelled by Billy's idea, I turned and said: "Why don't you sell it all, Mom?"

She spun around again and looked directly at me, even though Tom hadn't quite finished dressing and was scrambling to fit himself into his jeans. For a second, I thought she was considering my suggestion. I'm sure she'd thought of it before. We all had. Since my father had died money had been a problem. The Nova Scotia Light and Power pension left to my mother hadn't been much, and though we got by, we did so meagrely. The only other recourse for a single mother with children in those days was to go on welfare, and we all knew my mother would have chosen death, literally, over that. But I also know that she saw the proceeds of the sale of my grandfather's house and car as a kind of welfare in its own right, and so was torn. Billy, of course, became excited again at my suggestion, as if he hadn't thought of it before.

"That's a great idea, Mom!"

I knew by the look on my mother's face that I'd made a mistake, and was glad of the interruption. I had already changed, so I moved over to the mirror to search my face for signs of emerging stubble. The need to shave was a long way off for me, but I couldn't wait until it came. I often spent mornings watching the ritual of Tom with his straight razor in front of the bathroom mirror. By the time the biological privilege came to me, it had been so slow in coming, with single hairs appearing here and there on my otherwise smooth face, and I'd practised so often in secret with Tom's razor, strop, and shaving lather, that I was no longer excited by the prospect. Shaving became a chore that to this day I absolutely hate. Had Billy noticed me checking, he might have made fun, but he was waiting for our mother to answer his question.

"So?" he said, when she didn't immediately respond. "Why don't you sell the place, Mom?"

"Because," she said slowly, "your grandfather was a miserable son of a bitch, and I wouldn't take anything he gave me, including a million dollars right here and now." Respectfully, none of us stated the obvious: that it was unlikely our grandfather would give us anything right here and now. Dead, the only thing our grandfather could give us was memories, and not very good ones at that.

"But Mom," said Billy, "wouldn't it be kind of like shysting the old guy, if you did sell everything? It would sure put him in his place." Billy broke into his most winning smile, but it did no good.

"Forget it," my mother said. "I know what you're after, Billy, but we're not selling anything. We're not living in it, and we're not driving it. As far as I'm concerned that house and car can sit out there on Gaston Road and rot." With that she left us. We heard the clump of her shoes on the stairs, then the banging of pots and pans in the kitchen as she began preparing supper. Our moods became, if anything, more sombre. Our little room looked so small now. We were sure our grandfather's house would have much bigger bedrooms, and probably enough so we could each have our own. We had dreams, foolish ones considering none of us had a driver's licence, of riding to school every day in the mint green Thunderbird. Tom sat heavily on the edge of his bed. He pulled his T-shirt on over his head and said, "She's fucking crazy."

"Shhh," I said. "She'll hear you."

"I don't care," said Tom angrily. "There's that beautiful old house out there, with no one in it, and here we are living in this dump!"

I'd never thought of our house as a dump before. My mother

kept things exceptionally clean, and I told Tom so.

"You know what I mean," Tom said. "What has she got against Granddad anyway? Billy, do you know?"

Billy only shook his head. He had stopped dressing, and half in and half out of his suit, sat on the end of his bed staring dumbly at the wall. "I don't care about the house," he said. "Or the car. I just want her to sell it all."

Tom and I knew what Billy was thinking. No one, least of all my mother, had imagined that any of us would even *want* to go to college. My father had left school in Grade Ten, and didn't much believe in any education other than the Bible anyway. Perhaps that would have changed as we got older, but he died before he could decide whether or not we should have a shot at higher education. My mother made her theories on education clear: up until Grade Ten we should go to school and do our homework. After that we could do what we wanted. For Billy this was a bitter pill. He saw the proceeds of the sale of the house and car as a means to furthering his dreams of becoming a writer and eventually moving to Toronto. Tom and I couldn't understand why he wanted to go to such a big place so far away from home. By Billy's own admission two million people lived there. Two million people living in one area was as unimaginable to Billy as it was to us, living with only one close neighbour in a village of one hundred and fifty. Even Halifax, smaller than Toronto, was daunting to anyone from the Cape. It was a hundred miles away. When you didn't own a car a hundred miles might as well be a thousand, and Halifax became as exotic and remote to us as Istanbul. Tom and I had never been there. Billy had, four years before on a school trip with the honour students of his class. (Unlike Tom, Billy had been a good student until his interest waned. I fell somewhere in the middle, which always seemed to be the case between me and my brothers.) From that one trip Billy talked as if he'd been born and raised in Halifax. He spent endless hours describing it to us.

"They got everything," he'd tell us. "Shops, and airports, and two big bridges that span the harbour." Phrases like 'span the harbour' were typical of Billy's conversation. He talked as if he was writing everything down.

"I saw a whore," he whispered to us once. "You should have seen her. She wore a blue dress, this shiny blue material, and thigh-high black leather boots. Her face was painted as bright as an Indian's."

"Where did you see her?" I'd asked him excitedly.

"Yeah," Tom said. "You didn't tell us anything about no whore." Billy had been to Halifax only that one time and he was still trotting out remarkable stories we'd never heard.

"I saved it," he answered proudly. "I saved the story for a rainy day."

It was Billy's theory of writing. What made good writers good, he told us, was discipline. What constituted discipline was not telling too much too soon, to save some good stuff for later. "If you tell the whole story right away," he said confidently, "no one's gonna read more than the first page."

It's my opinion that Billy, despite what happened to him, could have been a writer. He didn't read a lot because frankly there weren't that many books available in the Cape. But he was using words as a boy that I never understood until I was an adult. I don't think he was any smarter than Tom and me. I just think he was more focused, or he looked at the world in an entirely different way. I'm not sure how much good it ever did him. I'm inclined to think now it might have done him harm. Tom, echoing my father's judgement of the Old Testament, thought Billy was 'impractical.'

"That's what got him into so much trouble," he told me once.

"Billy just doesn't have any idea of the true value of things."

I think Tom was wrong. Billy had an idea of the value of some things, namely his education, and his need to get out of the Cape. When my mother refused to sell, and he could see no other way to get the money he needed, he began to see his dreams slipping away. Tom suggested he work at the mill for a few years and save money, but Billy wouldn't hear of it. He saw the mill as a trap.

"Sure," he told us. "You start out trying to save money. Next thing you know you're down at Carson's pool hall on a Saturday night drinking the money you're supposed to save, and the next thing you know you've fallen for some girl from town. Then comes the baby. After that you're doomed."

Tom only shrugged when Billy said this, perhaps knowing that his younger brother meant no disrespect. Tom could see no further than the mill and, one day, my grandfather's house. In fact, Tom ended up marrying a girl because she got pregnant, just as Billy had predicted. Tom wanted less out of life than Billy did, and it's ironic — though usually the way — that Tom ended up with more.

But Billy still wouldn't give up. He said he'd find the money somewhere. "Even if I don't," he said, "you don't think I'm staying around this place forever, do you? I'd rather be broke in a big city than rich in the Cape." That day in the bedroom after my grandfather's funeral Billy swore he'd get my mother to sell the house and give him the car to boot, though Tom confided that evening while we were chopping wood that Billy was wasting his time.

"Mom will never sell that house," he said, splitting a piece of wood cleanly down the middle and waiting for me to carry the fallen pieces away. I set up a new piece on the block and stood back, expecting him to lift the axe again. But it stayed at his side. He looked thoughtfully up at me. "I want that house, Luke. I want us to live in it."

This time it was my turn to argue. "Mom won't have it."

"That's what I don't understand," said Tom, looking pained. "What in the hell could he ever have said to her, to make her so mad?"

I shrugged. "I don't know. You know Mom. Could'a been anything. But one thing's for sure. The house will rot before she'll let anyone move into it."

"Well," Tom said, sighing, "whatever she does, she won't sell it." He was about to say something else when she thrust her head out the porch door.

"Tom, you done with that wood? I need it."

"Coming," he said to her, and the two of us hurriedly gathered the remaining pieces and carried them into the house so she could bake bread. Tom told me not to mention the house or the Thunderbird.

"You'll just get her riled up again," he said.

THE SUNBEAM

Of my two older brothers, my mother was always for some reason hardest on Tom. Perhaps this was because he was the eldest, and my mother believed he should receive the lion's share of responsibility. She always shouted at him more. Whenever any of us did something she disliked, Tom wouldn't escape punishment, either with us, or if he'd been put in charge, on our behalf. He bore it well. It was difficult for my mother to get him to cry. She'd have to beat him long and hard for that to happen.

Once my mother sent Tom out with the axe to chop down a lilac bush in the back field. It was a windy day and she complained the strong sweet smell of them was carrying into the house and making her feel nauseated. Tom didn't question her, and ten minutes later came back with the job completed —

the lilac tree cut down, dragged away and left to rot in Tyler's Woods.

"Go change out of your clothes," she said to him. "You smell like lilacs. I can't stand the smell of those goddamned things."

Billy asked Tom why on earth our mother would want to cut down an innocent lilac tree harming no one in the back field. Tom only shrugged.

"I guess it's like she says," he answered. "She doesn't like the smell of them."

"It's because she's crazy," pronounced Billy finally. "No one but a crazy person would do something like that."

But Tom wouldn't admit our mother was crazy or anything else, and he did everything that was asked of him. He accepted my mother's verbal and physical abuse like a true stoic. If he ever felt, like Billy did, that our mother's demands were sometimes unreasonable, he never once showed it.

In school Tom was considered to be a solid student. Not because of his marks, which had always been abysmal, but because of the vigour with which he played our town's two sports, baseball in the summer and hockey in the winter. Tom liked these sports, and was widely acknowledged to be the best hitter in school. But he didn't live for them. They were part of the curriculum, and constituted the bulk of our physical education program in those days. He put no more into them than he did his studies. He just happened to be better at one than the other.

I never played on any teams with my brothers for I was always a school behind them. When I first went into elementary, at Grade Primary, Billy moved on to Grade Six in the high school next door and Tom to Grade Seven. By the time I got to the bigger school both Tom and Billy had quit. But I watched them play many times. Tom especially was a sure-footed baseball player. He beat the ball to every corner of the field, and always seemed to be chasing some other, slower runner on his team around the bases. Billy was slightly less athletic. He could catch a ball, and once on base he could run. But he'd rarely hit. Where Tom swung at the ball, almost lazily, and never failed to connect, Billy would bring the bat around with every ounce of weight in his body. Usually he fanned, or if he did hit, the ball wouldn't roll much further than the infield. The only great hits I ever saw Billy make were foul balls. Tom suggested to Billy once that he turn his body more towards right field. "That way those wicked foul balls you hit will land in fair territory." But they never landed anywhere but in foul, and Tom was to retain the title of our family's best athlete. On the hockey rink, the frozen man-made pond at the Mackay mill, Tom was nearly as successful. Once he scored seven goals in one scrub game. It remains as far as I know the Cape record. The old-timers of our town, fishermen living on unemployment during the winter months, would come out and sit on half-piled stacks of lumber to watch Tom play. It was unanimously agreed that he should try out for the National Hockey League.

"He's got what it takes," an old man told me once. I had unthinkingly chosen to sit next to this old fellow, not bothering to note that he was chewing what seemed to be several plugs of tobacco at once, and was more than usually careless about where he spit the juice. I moved away from him after he blindly deposited some on my shoe.

"I don't think Tom wants to play professional hockey," I shouted to the old guy in case he was deaf.

"What do ya mean?" he shouted back. "Don't want to play? What would hockey be if Bobby Orr had said that, I ask you?"

But Tom wasn't good enough, and he knew it. "How many little towns you think there are in this country?" he asked me once. "And how many guys in those little towns think they can play in the NHL?" He finished by saying, "Sure, I'm the best here, but there's better somewhere. You can bet your life on that."

"But how do you know?" I asked him. "Shouldn't you try out at least?"

"Oh yeah?" said Tom flatly. "And where am I supposed to try out? You ever see any scouts from the NHL sitting around Mackay's pond on a Saturday afternoon?"

I admitted I hadn't, but I didn't see any reason why he couldn't go to Trenton or Halifax and try out. "There must be scouts out there somewhere," I said. Tom shook his head. "Besides," he added, "to play hockey you gotta live in the city. And there ain't no deer to shoot in the city."

Hunting was Tom's truest passion. Even before he was old enough to carry a gun you could find him in Tyler's Woods, stalking animals, perhaps marking them for the day he could bring them down. The glory of Tom's childhood was the days my father asked him to accompany him on the fall deer-hunting expeditions. Even then Tom was disgusted by my father's habit of not shooting any deer deemed too small or helpless for his gun. The does and the smaller deer provided the freshest meat, and though a rack of buck antlers proved the mark of a sportsman, Tom was of the mind that any deer, short of a fawn, was fair game. My mother agreed with him. We were always the last to have deer meat on our table. By the time my father got the buck he wanted, everyone else had either laid up their rifles for the year or were hunting illegally. And the meat from those big bucks, she claimed, was as tough as shoe leather.

"You won't have any qualms about shooting us a tender young doe when the time comes, will you Tom?" she often asked him.

"No ma'am," he would answer.

It was Tom's monkey paw, that wish that he could be the provider in the family. Suddenly my father was dead and the gauntlet was passed to my oldest brother. He took it, even though he was not old enough to carry a rifle by himself. But my mother, and our town's only game warden, turned a blind eye. We needed the meat, and Tom as the oldest had to supply it now that my father was gone.

I'll never forget the first deer Tom shot. He came running home one Saturday morning, excited and barely able to form sentences properly. "I got one," he shouted. My mother, Etta and Roland went with him to drag the small spike horn buck back to the house, and then helped him skin and dress it. It became an unplanned party, with Etta, Roland, my mother, Billy, and myself in attendance and Tom in the centre. For weeks he virtually beamed whenever anyone talked to him about it. He'd describe the scene over and over again. It became such a hot topic that Billy and I fell asleep at night with Tom telling us the details. After awhile we got so bored with the story that Billy and I began making jokes.

"Guess what," Billy would shout, pretending to be Tom when Tom wasn't around. "I just murdered a poor, defenceless forest animal. Blam! Shot his head right off. Aren't I terrific!"

"Jeez, Tom," I'd say to Billy. "That's wonderful. What are you going to do tomorrow?"

"Well, I dunno," Billy would say, scratching his head in a very Tom-like manner. "Maybe I'll just crawl up the ass of a bear and kill it from the inside out."

We made sure never to say these things when Tom was in earshot, and eventually, as killing became a part of his life, the excitement wore off. The enthusiasm, however, did not. He began to spend more time in the woods than he did on the hockey rink or at home. Billy and I rarely hunted with him, for there was only the one gun in our house — a Winchester twelve gauge.

My father had had a healthy fear of guns, but no respect for them. As a result he cleaned the weapon only when necessary, and the rest of the time it had stayed hidden under his bed. When it was passed on to Tom it was in poor condition. Brown microdots of rust had bloomed on the metal barrel. Tom immediately cleaned it, and from then on cared for it like a baby. The antiseptic odours of Tom's cleaning fluids often lingered in our kitchen. He'd sit in my father's rocking chair and gently rub down the barrel with a rag soaked in oil. A wire brush on a bendable rod was inserted down the inside of the barrel to clean it out. He bought linseed oil for the pine stock. Then he'd carry it, cradled carefully in his arms, up to his room, ready for the next day's hunting. Billy and I were forbidden to touch it unless we were in his presence. Tom was especially nervous when Billy asked to hold it.

"Always treat a gun like it's loaded" he'd say, while Billy held the stock to his shoulder and tried to get a bead on our kitchen clock.

"But it's *not* loaded," Billy would complain.

"That's not the point. You always have to pretend it is."

"But if it's not loaded," Billy always asked, "why should you pretend it is?"

"Because," Tom explained patiently, "you don't want to kill anyone."

Billy looked at Tom without taking the gun down from his shoulder. "Has anyone ever been shot by a gun that ain't got a bullet in it, Tom?"

Tom then carefully took the gun from Billy, shaking his head.

"You're crazy, Billy. I don't want to be around when you're old enough to hunt."

"Why not?" Billy would say. "I'd be just as careful as you. Carefuler, maybe."

But no one was as careful as my brother Tom with guns. With anything. And no one in our family was as good at anything as Tom was at hunting. Before he got his first deer at fourteen he was already supplying our table with plenty of small game. He brought home rabbits and partridge regularly. Once Uncle Joe mentioned that porcupines were good to eat. Tom marched into Tyler's Woods and emerged with a dead porcupine. It hadn't taken him long to find one. The woods were crawling with them. He brought it home mounted on a stick like a gruesome lollipop. Skinning it, he said, was "one helluva job." Several times he stuck himself with the sharp quills. Finally with gloves he managed it, and brought the skinned carcass inside for my mother to cook. She did so, all the time saying he was as crazy as our Uncle Joe. When she finished, now in the spirit of the thing herself, she spruced it up with some spices and a side of sliced boiled carrots and set it down in front of him. We all gathered around to watch. Fearlessly, Tom drove his fork into a piece of the meat and brought it up to his mouth. We grimaced when he finally put it in and began chewing.

"How does it taste?" my mother asked him.

Tom nodded enthusiastically. "Good. Real good. Want to try some?"

"No thanks," said my mother drily.

"What does it taste *like*?" Billy asked him.

Tom chewed thoughtfully on the same piece, savouring it. "I'm not sure," he said. "It's tender. A bit like chicken, only wilder."

We all stood around, waiting for him to swallow and go on to the next piece. But despite his favourable response Tom just went on chewing. The more we watched, the more he chewed that first piece.

"Well, go on!" my mother said, suddenly smiling. "Eat the rest."

"I will," Tom said, and continued chewing, slowly, then faster. But he couldn't swallow it. He kept trying to swallow, then amidst our laughter, spit the piece, mulched into formlessness, onto his plate, and sheepishly scraped the remainder into the garbage. From then on, porcupines were forever safe from Tom's gun.

I went hunting with Tom many times. He was the most patient hunter I ever knew. We'd walk perhaps thirty yards into Tyler's Woods, then he'd stop, and motion for me to stop also. We would stand there, with Tom carefully looking around for prey, until he deemed it safe to move on again. His theory was that human beings were no longer natural to the forest.

"Once we were," he often told me, "but that's all done now. We're noisy. The animals can hear us a mile off." Tom stopped and waited for suspicious deer, which he imagined stood stock still at the sounds of intrusion, to lower their heads and go on feeding.

"If we're lucky," Tom said, "we'll walk right up to them."

When I was with him this happened only once. We'd just begun another thirty-yard trek, being careful to snap as few twigs and crunch as few leaves under the heels of our boots as possible, when Tom gave the signal to stop. Often I was bored during these excursions. I shuffled, fidgeted, transferred my weight from foot to foot. I looked at Tom, at trees, at the sky, but was careful not to make noise and bring Tom's wrath down on my head. Tom was never ordinarily quick to anger, but in the forest he flared up in an instant if you spoiled his chance to shoot an animal.

That particular day patches of snow lay on the ground and had begun to melt in the mild October weather. The leaves were wet and didn't crackle underfoot. We were so silent I began to believe we belonged to the forest again. We must have, for at one point, bored, I looked up to see a doe feeding only twenty feet away on the far side of an old knarled oak. Her neck was bent and she was nosing for food in the snow. She sensed me, drew her head up suddenly and turned to look. There was no panic in her eyes, only a faint curiosity. She lifted her nose higher, nostrils flaring slightly. I thought she'd run then, having identified me with her sense of smell as a stranger to the forest. Instead she dropped her head again and continued snuffling through the snow.

"Tom," I whispered. My voice startled her. She took a few tentative steps away, but still showed no signs of running. "Tom," I whispered again, "there she is."

I'd begun to turn around, to see if Tom was still beside me, for he made no response. The gun went off not five feet from my left ear. When I turned back to the deer, she was down, and Tom had brushed by me and was running toward his kill. I followed, my ears still ringing from the shot, my heart beating fast from the excitement. When I got to the clearing Tom was already kneeling down over the deer, drawing his knife from a sheath attached to his belt.

"Is she dead?" I asked excitedly.

"Not yet," Tom answered.

The doe had been feeding in a small snow-covered clearing. I knew from Tom's instruction to look for deer where there was snow that they preferred the fresher grass there than what could be found rotted under a carpet of wet leaves. Yet my finding her first had been entirely luck, and I was beginning to think it wasn't necessarily good luck. Blood, brilliant red against the snow, splattered the clearing. The doe lay on her side, uselessly struggling to get back on her feet. It wasn't a clean kill, and later Tom would profess disappointment in it. He'd hit her with the shotgun blast dead on the nose as she'd looked toward us. Much of her snout had disappeared. What was left was a mangled horror. Her teeth, tiny and brown, were exposed and bleeding from a partially opened mouth. Her eyes rolled up in terror and pain to the whites as Tom bent closer. My excitement left me, replaced by a sudden sick remorse. I felt like throwing up.

"Kill it, Tom," I said shakily. "Kill it now!"

Tom did, but he didn't shoot. Another shotgun blast, even to the head, might spray lead pellets into the carcass and spoil the meat. He drew the sharp edge of his knife quickly across her throat. Slowly her eyes deadened, but not before the life I'd seen in them imprinted on my mind to haunt me later that night in the dark of my room.

Tom was oblivious to my silent suffering. He'd done this many times, and was shaking only with the excitement of the kill. I didn't tell him how I felt. Not that Tom would have judged me for it, but still, I didn't want him thinking I was weak. I watched as he cleaned the deer. Assuming I possessed an interest I truly did not feel, he explained what he was doing and why.

"You slit the throat to bleed it," he told me. I watched in disgust as more blood from the doe's slashed neck poured onto the snow. "Otherwise, the blood will stay in the veins and ruin the meat. It's important to get out as much blood as you can right away. We could always clean and dress it at home, but if we do it now it'll be lighter for us to carry."

He pushed the deer over on its back, stood up, and straddled her chest. Kneeling down over her, and pinching his knees together to hold her in place, he drove his knife with all his strength into the doe's white underbelly. He then dragged the sharp edge of the knife down the length of her guts, splitting her open cleanly. He turned the doe back over on her side and asked me to fetch him a short stick. I looked around for one on the ground, then finally, at Tom's urging, broke one off an alder bush and stripped it. Tom took the stick from me, and set it temporarily aside. I felt the bile rise in my throat as I watched him reach into the guts of the doe with both hands. Minutes later, Tom had pulled the innards out and left them lying in a steaming pile on the snow. His hands and the sleeves of his jacket were soaked and glistening with blood and flecks of tissue from the doe's innards.

"You've got to be careful not to puncture the shit bag," Tom said casually. "Dad did it once, and boy does it stink." He laughed, and I walked to the edge of the clearing, my own guts heaving and threatening to come up as violently, if a little more naturally, as the doe's. Tom rattled on about what he was doing. I placed my hot cheek on the cool bark of a tree, and wrapped my arms tightly around it to keep from falling down. When he was finished he called to me, and, feeling a little better, I went back.

"Now," he said, "I need your help."

The stick I'd found was too small, but Tom had found another and as I watched, still unable to ask any questions, he whittled it down with his knife to a point on each end, then handed it to me and grabbed one of the deer's hind legs.

"This part is easy," he told me. He took his knife and just below the doe's hoof separated fur and tendon from bone with its tip. He repeated the operation on the other leg, again just below the hoof, then taking the stick from me drove its sharp ends into the little slits he'd created.

"The tendons are strong," he told me. "They'll hold."

The two of us laid hold of the stick with a hand each and dragged the deer along by its hind legs through the snow and leaves. The tendons, strong as Tom had said, did not break away. By the time we got to the barn my arms were aching. I kept asking Tom to stop so I could switch hands. I tried not to look at the dead animal as we dragged it.

When we had it in the barn, Tom stopped and extracted two pieces of meat from inside the deer where its guts had been. I hadn't seen him place them there.

"I saved them," he said, holding them out towards me. It was the heart and liver. Blood from the organs stained his bare hands and ran in rivulets down his wrists and into the sleeves of his coat. He didn't seem to mind.

"Which do you want?" he asked me. "It's your first kill. You get to choose."

I didn't want either of them. The idea of eating anything at all, especially any part of that deer, made me sick, but I also didn't want to disappoint my brother. I chose the heart, because it was smaller.

"Run it into the house, and ask Mom to cook it up for supper."

I did as he asked, carrying the bloody heart in both hands, horrified at its wetness and warmth and not wanting to look at it in case it was still beating. My mother wasn't in the least fazed by the bloody organ I carried into her kitchen like a sacrifice.

"Throw it in the sink," she said. "I'll get to it when I can."

That night my mother cooked the heart and liver of the deer. Tom related the details of the hunt, proudly slapping me on the back when he told my mother and Billy how I'd seen it first. I didn't say a word. Everyone was nearly finished before Mom looked over at my plate.

"Luke," she said. "You haven't touched a thing!"

"I'm not hungry," I told her.

"But you always loved deer meat," my mother said.

I shook my head. "I'm just not hungry."

After that, Tom would ask me to go hunting with him, and I could always find a reason not to. If he had any small disappointment in this, it didn't show. Nothing could spoil his hunting for him. One of the reasons Tom wanted us to move into my grandfather's house on Gaston Road was, he admitted, because of the superior hunting. "There's more forest," he told us. "I could shoot deer out the back door."

Yet my mother saw Tom's even wanting to move into her father-in-law's house as a sort of betrayal. It became a sore point between them. "A few little deer ain't the reason you want to live in that house," she answered. "I don't know what the reason is." She went on to say that as long as she lived no one would live there, not if all the deer in the world came out and did the polka on the front lawn.

"Deer don't polka," Tom said grimly.

❧

My grandfather's house sat unused for four years. My mother heard rumours that my grandfather's old secretary Dolores, the woman we'd met at the funeral, was taking care of the property and driving the car occasionally to keep fuel in the carburetor and the brakes from seizing. My mother promptly called her up and told her and her husband to kindly keep their feet off her property and leave the car in the garage. This was the only time she admitted ownership over any of it, and this only to keep someone from doing work on the house.

"You have to keep it up," complained Dolores to my mother. "A house that size is in constant need of repair."

"Let it rot," said my mother and hung up the phone.

Billy worked on our mother for three of those years to get her to sell the place. He tried every tactic he could think of. Once, when my mother was in town, he searched the house from top to bottom for the deed and the keys to the car. He knew Dolores Whynot had sent them to my mother not long after our grandfather was buried. "She'll never know," he told us as he rooted through her dresser drawers and looked under her bed. "I could sell the house and retire on the proceeds and she'd still think she owned the goddamned place. I could also take the car and use it to get away. Where do you think she hides it, Tom?"

My mother had never trusted banks. She cashed her pension checks at Robichaud's grocery and hid the cash somewhere in the house. Wherever the cash was, Billy suspected the deed was there too, and perhaps the keys. He looked in every place he could think of — through her room, in the pantry, under the cushions of the chesterfield, even in the barn. He finally gave up.

"Maybe she hides it in her brassiere," Tom joked.

"That and half the King's Army," retorted Billy sourly. My mother had a sizable bosom.

"So what are you gonna do, Billy?" I asked him finally.

He only shook his head. He knew as well as we did that his dreams of college were dead. And since high school was only a means to that end, he came home less than a week later with his incomplete report card and tossed it on the table in front of my mother.

"I ain't going back," he said.

"Suit yourself," she answered. "But you'll have to find work. There are no free rides around here!"

My mother's proviso was that if you quit school you went to work instead. From each working son she required a living allowance of fifty dollars. Tom, never the best of students, had quit the year before and taken a job at the mill. He dutifully handed over fifty dollars each pay day. Accepting money from a working son wasn't in my mother's endless book of what constituted charity. It was only natural for Tom to put back what he had for all those years taken. Billy defied her, however, by refusing to look for work. "I'm not getting locked into some job at the mill for the rest of my life," he stated flatly.

She was furious. "I'm not supporting you," she told him. "You'll work your way like Tom or you won't live here at all!"

"Don't worry," Billy said calmly. "I'll get money." My mother expected all that month to have to kick Billy out when he couldn't come up with his share. But somehow, come month's end, and each month after that, he brought her the money, which my mother squirrelled away with the rest of her hidden stash. We endlessly speculated about where Billy, jobless, at sixteen, could come up with fifty dollars each month — more, if you counted the money he drank with. My mother was convinced he was doing something illegal, but she could never figure out what. Nothing illegal went on in the Cape as far as any of us knew. Apart from robbing the grocery or the post office, of which we surely would have heard, ill-gotten gains were as hard to come by as honest earnings, perhaps harder. Billy only laughed when she suggested his means of getting money were shady.

"Sure Mom," he'd say. "I got a prostitution ring down at the wharf. I sell girls to the trawlermen for a dollar apiece."

"Well, you're doing something," she'd say dubiously. "Money doesn't come into your hands out of thin air, does it?"

Billy only laughed again. He never told us where he was getting his share. Tom thought he had a job somewhere, but Billy wouldn't admit to that either. "Where would I get a job in this town that you all wouldn't know about in five minutes? The only place to work is in the cod plant or at the mill. You ain't seen me ducking into the mill lately, have you, Tom?"

Tom admitted he hadn't, and Billy went on enjoying the little mysteries he created. It was only when Tom started going out with Billy that we questioned our brother's income no longer.

As they got older both my brothers fell into the habit of spending Saturday nights at Carson's pool hall in town. For Billy it was but one night out of the many in the week he spent there. For Tom it was only the one, and even this my mother begrudged him. All day Sunday he'd fight a hangover *and* my mother, who couldn't stop talking about what a waste of money drinking was. But even she knew teenage boys needed some freedoms. Besides, the money Tom spent was his own. He never dipped into the money he gave her to support the house. So she complained — it was not in her nature to do anything else — but she didn't insist upon his not going. After a while it got so she would not ask him to do anything on Sunday mornings. On those days I got the lion's share of work, which I resented greatly. Tom and Billy would be laid up inside while I shovelled snowfall or split wood. What bothered me most was that the tavern was the first place they could go and I couldn't. It seemed just days before the three of us had been playing cowboys and Indians in Tyler's Woods or fishing for snapper off the docks downtown. Now Tom and Billy were living the lives of adults. They still treated me kindly, but the essence of manhood, the sudden inflation that results from an assumed responsibility in the world, was present in them and not in me. It became apparent in the ways we talked to each other. We still shared the same room, but the late night bull sessions were drawing to a close.

Often Billy wouldn't come home at all, and though Tom went to bed when I did on weeknights, he was too tired from a day's work at the mill to keep up conversation for long. I'd be talking to Tom the way we used to, about anything at all, and he would interrupt me with his snores. During the rare times all three of us were home and in the room together, Tom and Billy talked about girls. Both my brothers were broad-shouldered and handsome. Tom was the taller of the two though Billy had a slightly better build. Tom's hair was light brown and cut short. Billy's hair was darker, and once he became a fan of John Lennon he no longer allowed my mother to give him the customary bowl-cut. She fought him on this because, she said, hair growing almost down to his shoulders would block him from getting a job.

"John, Paul, George, and Ringo make about a million dollars a year," he told her. "Long hair doesn't seem to hurt them any. Besides," he'd say as an aside to Tom and me, "the chicks like it."

Though neither Tom nor Billy mentioned the names of girls they slept with, they gladly related the incidents themselves. And there were so many incidents, in such a variety of places, that I thought hardly a girl or a location existed that hadn't been screwed or screwed in by one or the other of them. I never doubted the veracity of their stories. Neither of them ran about town bragging about their sexual exploits. They only told each other, in the awed voices of young men who still couldn't believe the fantastic gifts God had bestowed on them. Occasionally they'd politely ask if there was any girl I was interested in. I'd name a few from school, and try to explain what it was I liked about them. But my heart wasn't in it, and I think Billy and Tom sensed this, though probably not consciously. Eventually they gave up trying to find out who and what I was

interested in and continued on with their own stories. Billy was
of the mind that the more girls he slept with the better. Tom
was more likely to find one willing girl and practise until one
or the other of them wanted a change. Neither Tom nor Billy
ever brought their girlfriends home. My mother never expressly
forbade it, but I think that no girl, given the reputation of my
mother's tongue, would have agreed to come with them. For her
part, my mother called their women "wharf whores" — a fact
that seemed to be confirmed when Billy came down with a
nasty bout of gonorrhea. Even Tom had something to say
about that.

"Didn't you use a condom?" he asked.

Billy laughed. "Why in the hell would I use one of those?"

Tom shrugged. "For protection."

"Christ," Billy said, "I don't even know where you'd get
condoms."

"I can get them for you," Tom said.

"Nah. Don't bother. I don't need them."

"Alright," answered Tom. "But you're the one always saying
you don't want to get some girl knocked up."

"Keep your condoms, Tom. I got better methods."

"Just warning you," said Tom. "You've got to be careful."

Tom kept his condoms hidden underneath his mattress. My
mother knew they were there. Even as we got older, our room
wasn't forbidden to her. She cleaned and scrubbed and looked
through our things as she'd always done. Nothing we wanted
to keep secret from her was hidden in the house. But Tom must
have decided the barn was too far to run for a condom, or
perhaps he thought they'd rot outside. Whatever the reason,
we all knew they were there, though Billy never used them.
Sometimes, alone in my room on Saturday nights with Billy and
Tom gone off to Carson's, I'd slide one from its foil wrapper

and fit it over my small erect penis. Although I was still too young to be having sex, I'd been inadvertently instructed in the art of masturbation. Many nights I'd awoken in a creaking bed to find Billy in the dark beside me moaning softly to himself. At first I couldn't figure out what he was doing.

"Shut up," he whispered one night when I innocently interrupted him to find out. "I'm jerking off."

Tom too would sometimes make strange noises through the night when he thought everyone was asleep. Eventually I discovered on my own what they were up to, but by the time I was able to perform this act successfully on myself both Tom and Billy had stopped. They were getting enough sex. They didn't need the additional release. I indulged when they were gone, though grimly, with nothing in my mind but the idea of the coming climax. I tried to summon images of girls, naked, in the positions I'd heard Tom and Billy describe so often. Yet these were mechanical and uninspired fantasies. It was only when, one night alone in the room, with Tom and Billy at Carson's and my mother already in bed, I pictured an older boy from my school. In my fantasy he was in his underwear and kissing me. The climax was immediate and as sweet as any I've ever felt, though the oceans of guilt that followed immediately afterward were almost more than I could bear. Never once had Billy or Tom mentioned kissing boys. I knew from their talk of "faggots" and "queers" that what I was doing was grossly abnormal, and under no circumstances would I mention it to them. I suffered in silence over something I didn't want and couldn't control.

One Saturday morning, when Billy hadn't come home the night before, Tom and I were sitting at the breakfast table listening to my mother's threats to kick him out. "I don't stand for any gallivanting," she told us. "You boys know that. If Billy wants to stay out all night and drink, or do whatever it is he wants to do, he can do it somewhere else."

Gallivanting was my mother's word for whatever it was Billy did when he was not at home. She got it from her brother, my Uncle Joe, who used it as a euphemism for drinking. Whenever we met him on the street, his clothes dirty, his eyes bloodshot from a night of boozing, we'd ask out of courtesy what he'd been up to lately.

"Ah, ya know," he'd tell us, "I been out gallivanting."

Billy, my mother insisted, took after my Uncle Joe in more ways than one. "Your Uncle Joe is no good," she told us, "and your brother's turning out just like him."

It was true Billy adored our uncle, while Tom and I had never been as close to him. When Billy was a boy he'd spend hours in the old man's shack, unbeknownst to our mother, sitting beside the potbelly stove. Joe would drink cheap red wine directly out of the bottle and tell Billy fishing stories. When drunk enough he'd sing sea shanties in a loud rough voice. The drunker he became the better his singing voice got. In fact it was at Uncle Joe's, my mother guessed, that Billy might have stayed the night. Wherever he was, she swore it was the last straw. "I've had enough. I can't handle him anymore."

Tom and I ate quietly, throwing doubtful glances at each other and nodding only when what she said seemed to require a response. We waited in unspoken agreement for Billy to come whistling into the yard, when we'd both draw back and allow the by now familiar confrontation to take place. But before that could happen, Tom said he heard the sound of an engine coming up Cape Road.

"I don't hear anything," I told him.

But Tom's ears were sharp. Sure enough, after another few seconds we all heard it.

"Who's that now," my mother grumbled. Tom went outside to see. My mother retrieved her shawl and followed. It was an overcast morning and a chill wind was blowing in off the Atlantic. She pulled the shawl tightly about her shoulders and I followed her out between the barn and house to see who had come. There was never much traffic on the Cape road. Roland's car sat in his driveway where we could see it plainly. Whatever vehicle was racing up the road was too loud and blasting to be any old car. To our astonishment a motorcycle appeared around the final bend in the road and raced at high speed toward us, stirring up dust. We covered our ears with our hands to block out the unholy roar of its engine. The machine flew into the yard and skidded to a stop. Billy shut it off. The silence was sudden and deep.

"Hey folks," he said, climbing unhelmeted off it. He kicked down the metal stand and leaned the bike upright. His hair, his face, his clothes were streaked with mud. He looked a fright. "Breakfast ready?" he called cheerfully.

"Hey, Billy," I said, "where'd you get it?"

Billy shrugged. "I bought it."

"From who?"

"Doesn't matter."

Tom and I circled the motorcycle while Billy stood off to one side, smiling. "It's a beauty, isn't it?"

"What kind is it?" Tom asked. "I ain't never seen one like it."

"It's British," Billy said. "They call it a Sunbeam. It's old, but it works fine."

It wasn't like any motorcycle we'd ever seen — low-slung,

yellow and heavy like a wasp, with a long black leather seat and two stubby handlebars like cow horns, each with a leather handle grip and metal handbrake.

"Real cool, Billy," I said admiringly.

"Yeah," my mother mocked. "Real cool." She'd been looking back and forth between Billy and the motorcycle, and she could not keep to herself any longer. We might have known she'd be angry. "How did you afford to pay for this, young man?"

Billy shrugged. "I had some money."

My mother turned on him. "You had twenty dollars the last I heard. Are you tellin' me you paid twenty dollars for this?"

"That, and a little more."

"Where did you get the 'more'?"

"Don't worry about where I got it," Billy said, unwilling to meet my mother's eye. "I just got it."

"Did you steal it, Billy?"

"No," he said, defiantly shoving his hands deep into his front pockets. He looked over at the bike as if it could give him answers. "I didn't steal it."

"Then where'd you get it?"

"I don't figure that's anybody's business but mine," he stubbornly insisted.

My mother stamped her foot once, hard, on the grass. "Don't tell me it ain't none of my business," she shouted. "You live under my roof and anything you do is my business!"

"Aw Jesus, Mom," said Billy. "Can't you just give it a rest for an hour or two?"

"Don't you be telling me what to give a rest!" Her voice took on an hysterical edge. "I'll be the one saying around here what gets a rest and what doesn't. Now I want you to tell me where you got the money to buy this thing!"

"What does it matter?" shouted Billy. "It's bought now!"

"It matters plenty. If you don't tell me," she said, "you can just run it out of here right now!"

Billy stepped back, vehemently kicked a stone lying in the yard. It ricocheted off the side of the barn and barely missed my mother, though she didn't seem to notice.

"So," she said, "I'm waiting."

"I paid Tad Morton thirty dollars cash for it," he answered. "And I owe another fifty."

"You owe?" Those words to my mother were anathema and Billy knew it. No doubt, she'd rather he had stolen it.

"Take it back," she half whispered, half spoke. "Go get your money back right now."

"Mom!"

"Ain't no son of mine gonna run himself into debt before he's twenty. I'd rather see you dead than owing anyone."

"I'll pay him," insisted Billy. "I'll go to work at the mill."

"No, you won't. You'll take it back, or you won't be living in this house."

Billy finally faced my mother, and we could see by his face that we were in for another of their matches. "There's no way in hell I'm taking this motorcycle back. I bought it. It's mine!"

"Get it out of here, Billy. I mean it."

"Alright," he said, and with exaggerated, furious motions jumped back on the bike and kick-started it to life. They kept shouting at each other, but the words were lost over the roar of the muffler. Billy turned the bike around. With a flick of his wrist on the handle grip accelerator he raced it forward on its hind wheel. It looked as if he might lose control of it, that it would take off underneath him or fall over on its side. But the front wheel touched back down and he sped off, churning up dust as he went. When the dust settled he was gone, though we still heard the steady whine of the Sunbeam's engine long after he'd disappeared from sight around the first bend.

"I'll be damned if you boys are going to run this family into debt," my mother said angrily, as if we were the ones who'd got the bike on credit. With that she turned and, pulling her shawl more tightly over her shoulders, marched back into the house.

"Is Billy coming back?" I asked. Tom shook his head. "I don't know." He was looking down the road the way Billy had gone. "He'll kill himself on that thing," he said finally.

"You think he'd take me for a drive on it?"

Tom looked at me. "You wanna go for a drive with Billy? Are you crazy?"

I shrugged. "It looks like fun."

"Fun," Tom scoffed. "Well, one thing's for sure. Mom isn't gonna let him keep it here, if he does come back."

Billy didn't come back — not for three days. It was the same as when my mother got in an argument with Etta. We weren't allowed to discuss him. Any mention of his name met with her disapproval. When he finally turned up she didn't speak to him as he limped into the house. Billy told us he'd had an accident with the Sunbeam. The bike wasn't hurt, but Billy was. He'd been riding through a field, probably drunk, and didn't see the log hidden in long grass. When his front tire encountered the log the bike stopped dead and pitched him headlong into a patch of alders. His hands and arms and face suffered scrapes, and he bruised one knee badly on an upturned stone, which gave him a limp for several weeks afterward. My mother said nothing about this either, and he didn't tell her what had happened, though he told Tom and me. But neither did she refuse him entry into the house, as we knew she wouldn't. Somehow she always had more tolerance for Billy than she did for me or Tom.

It seemed the more he defied her, the more she was willing to let him get away with. Perhaps she knew that with Billy she wouldn't have to worry about him for long. In fact, none of us were surprised when Billy came home, less than two months after he bought the Sunbeam, and told us he was leaving. He waited until we'd sat down to supper. Tom had just got home from work, a half-hour's walk from town, and was so hungry he hadn't even stopped to wash his hands or change out of his stained coveralls.

"You stink of oil," our mother told him. "You better give me those so I can wash 'em this evening."

"What for?" Tom said. "They'll just stink again when I get home tomorrow."

Our mother was about to make some answer when we heard the Sunbeam coming up the road. Minutes later Billy strolled into the kitchen. My mother stood up to fetch him a plate. It no longer bothered her when he was late for meals. She had given up on him years ago for that, though Tom and I got a talking to if we were even five minutes late. But Billy told her that he wasn't hungry and not to bother.

"Suit yourself," she said, sitting back down to the table. "It's not like you've been working enough to work up an appetite anyway."

She still couldn't resist the occasional jab at our brother's lack of work, though Billy, for his part, had stopped taking her bait. He only sat down in a chair by the door, pulled off his boots, and looked up at us. "I'm going," he said finally. "I made up my mind."

My mother barely looked up from her plate, though she asked him where he thought he was going. Of course she knew. Billy had been talking about it so long he didn't need to tell her.

"To Toronto," he said. "I'm leaving in a couple of weeks."

Tom and I continued to eat our food, waiting for my mother to react. She surprised us when she didn't, though Billy had warned us not to expect much from her. "She'll be glad to get rid of me," he'd said. And so it seemed. She only asked where he planned on getting the money for such a venture.

"I got some saved," he told her. "Whatever I don't have I'll have to do without."

"Well," she said, looking at him for the first time. "Don't expect anything from me. You're a man now. You'll have to make your own way."

"I'll make it," Billy said. "Don't worry."

"I'm not," said my mother firmly, and went back to her food. That was the end of the discussion. No more was said about it by either of them.

Two nights before Billy left, Tom gave him a parting lecture in the usual place — our bedroom at night. "Don't you dare take anything off any of those city people. And don't let them think they're better than you. Remember, there isn't one of them that knows how to clean a fish, or skin a deer, or find his way by the moss that grows on the trees, and the North Star."

Billy laughed aloud. "What good is skinning a deer gonna do me up there, Tom? They haven't got any deer."

"That's what I mean," said Tom. "Why do you want to live in a place where there ain't no deer, Billy? You're a country boy. Hell, you could go to Halifax and live in the city if you wanted to. At least you don't have to go very far to shoot a rabbit."

Billy waited a long while before answering. He lay on top of the covers in nothing but his underwear, thinking. His disinclination for work wasn't due to lack of strength. The muscles in his arms bulged as he lay there, hands placed behind his head. Finally he said, "I guess I'm going there because there isn't anything here."

"What do you mean?" said Tom. "There's everything here!"

"Like what?"

"All the things you like. Women, booze, money, your family, your friends. There isn't anything in Toronto that isn't here, except us."

"You don't understand," said Billy finally.

"No," Tom said, turning his face to the wall and his back to us. "I don't understand, Billy. There isn't anything in Toronto but a bunch of stuck-up people, and I sure hope you don't become one of them."

"Don't worry. I won't." There was determination in Billy's voice, both against Tom's telling him not to go, and in support of not becoming 'stuck-up.' But Billy was right. Tom didn't understand, and neither did I, at least not then.

The next night, Billy's last, was a Thursday in August. He had turned seventeen in July, the age of consent in our part of the world, and nothing my mother, Tom, myself, or even Uncle Joe could say would hold him back. I was eleven years old. It was 1968. Nothing in the Cape had changed, but Etta's new television told us that the world was busy reorganizing itself around us. We'd heard of hippies and Woodstock. And although most of it was taking place south of us in the United States, we were assured that in some of our own cities change was underfoot. Billy wanted to be part of this change. The Cape and its stubborn resistance to change could no longer contain him. He convinced my mother to let him take me out on the town for one last hurrah. At first she refused.

"You'll get him drunk," she said. "Or you'll kill him on that motorcycle of yours." Billy told her this was to be his last night in town for a long while, and he wanted to spend it with me. Finally she agreed, if we were back early. Tom begged off. He had to work in the morning, but he swore to Billy that he'd be up early to see him away. Before we left for town, Billy took me with him to say his goodbyes to Etta.

"You take it easy up there," said Etta. "Don't get in any trouble." Etta sat us down at her kitchen table. Roland, as usual, stayed in the living room and watched television. They were the second house in the Cape to have one, and Roland was already addicted to it. He appeared only for a second to wish Billy luck.

"Don't worry about me," Billy said. "I'll have plenty to do when I'm there."

"How's your mother with you going?" Etta asked.

Billy shrugged. "She's fine with it, I guess. She doesn't say much."

"She wouldn't," Etta replied with a smile.

Before we left, Etta handed Billy an envelope. He opened it in front of her and pulled out a thin packet of dollar bills, bound with a wide white elastic. "Now don't be acting like your mother and say you'll be taking no charity," said Etta firmly. "You'll be needing every red cent you can get up there."

"Jeez Etta," Billy said, and I could see he was genuinely touched. "Thanks a lot."

"You're welcome." Etta surprised both of us by giving Billy a big bear hug at the door, and as well as he could, unused to such displays of affection, my brother returned it. We had turned away when Billy suddenly turned back to her again. "Can I see the caul one more time before I go?"

Etta couldn't keep herself from smiling. "There's more of the boy in you than you know," she said.

Roland liked to watch TV in the dark, so Etta excused herself and turned on a lamp. She lead us to the window and parted the faded yellow curtains. There the caul sat, undisturbed after all these years, in its pickle jar on the window sill. It had been a long while since any of us had asked to see it. Long ago it had ceased to be solely mine and was, as always for us, a symbol of the things we wanted.

"Go ahead," said Etta, in a familiar refrain. "Touch it." Billy put his hand out and lightly drew his fingers over the glass. Whether out of a forgotten sense of fear, or some new reluctance, I still couldn't bring myself to touch the jar. But Etta didn't urge me. This was Billy's moment.

"So," she said finally. "What do you see?"

Billy pulled his hand away from the glass and turned back to Etta and me, smiling.

"I see me getting the hell out of this place as soon as possible."

Etta, myself, and even Roland laughed along with Billy, though for my part I did so a little sadly. I didn't want Billy to go, and I knew the prediction he'd just made was one that would surely come true. Hastily Billy repeated his goodbyes, and only a minute later we were out in the salt-smelling air of the Cape, walking back towards our own house. The stars were out in numbers, shining fiercely down on us. Billy stopped for a minute, halfway between the two houses, to stare up at them.

"Don't they have stars in Toronto?" I asked him, thinking of what Tom had said the night before. If they had no deer, perhaps they didn't have anything else there either.

"Of course they do," he said. "But the lights from the city make them kind of hard to see."

I couldn't understand why anyone would want to live where you couldn't see the stars, and I told Billy so.

"You'll understand eventually, Luke," he said.

But I didn't understand. And I wanted that moment, with Billy and me standing in the darkness staring up at the night sky, to last forever if it meant Billy would stay home. But I was old enough to know that he wouldn't, and it wouldn't take me too much longer to realize that it was the stars that Billy was after when he left us — though, as he admitted to me later on in life, he never found them.

"Come on," he told me, and started towards home again. "We've got stuff to do tonight."

"What stuff?" I called, struggling to keep up.

"You'll see," he said, running now. "Just come on."

I'd been on Billy's bike before, unbeknownst to my mother, but that night I felt wild, my arms fastened tightly around Billy's waist as the Sunbeam carried us into town. Occasionally Billy twisted around and shouted something to me, but his words were lost in a rush of wind. I only held on tighter, closing my eyes each time we hit a bump and the bike jarred underneath me. The wind tore at my clothes and hair and roared in my ears like a living thing. The Sunbeam and wind drowned out all else, and several times I found myself screaming for joy, revelling in the violence of our ride. Billy didn't even slow as we tore down the main street, and the lights of shops and houses streaked by. I heard one or two angry shouts as we passed, but he didn't slow or pay any notice, if he even heard over the noise of the wind and the engine. By the time he slowed the bike, my hands, locked around his waist, ached from the cold, and I was so busy blowing hot breath to thaw them that I hardly noticed where we'd stopped. Billy shut off the engine and told me to get off. Standing on firm ground my legs still tingled from the vibration of the Sunbeam's engine. We'd pulled into a parking lot in front of a low, grey, and windowless building with a sagging tar-papered roof. A few beat-up cars and pick-ups sat here and there in the lot. Billy ordered me away from the bike and parked between a blue Dodge and a tomato red Ford pick-up truck.

"What are we doing here?" I asked warily.

"First stop," he said. "Come on."

I watched Billy walk towards the door. Loud, drunken voices and the sounds of a jukebox playing country music carried faintly outside to us. I made no move to follow. "Billy," I said quietly. "I don't want to."

He stopped and turned back towards me. "I thought you wanted to come out with me tonight."

"I do," I said. "But I didn't know we were going to Carson's."

"What's wrong with Carson's?"

"Mom will kill you if she finds out this is where you took me."

Billy laughed. "I ain't gonna tell. Are you?"

I shook my head. "But I'm only a kid. What if they won't let me in?"

"Come on," he said, turning and motioning for me to follow. "They'll let you in. Don't worry about it."

He walked up the three wooden steps to the front door. I still couldn't make up my mind. Billy was leaving tomorrow. If my mother found out I'd been at Carson's, she'd kill me, and I had to stick around to take the killing. Billy put his hand on the door handle and called to me: "Are you coming or what? You can stay out here all night if you want. I'll send some of the boys out later to keep you company."

"I'm coming," I said, running up behind him. I didn't know what kind of people hung out at Carson's pool hall, but I had my ideas. I'd heard of the fights that took place there, and I figured it was better to be inside with Billy than outside alone. Billy laughed, and pulled open the door.

Inside was the loudest, smokiest, dirtiest place I'd ever been in. It looked like the interior of our barn, only bigger, with long tables cut from old wharf boards standing in long narrow rows. Without windows there was no place for the cigarette and pipe smoke to go, and it hung in thick clouds just below the ceiling. Perhaps a dozen customers, mostly fishermen still in their oil-skins, sat at tables, alone and in groups of two and three. They all were drinking beer directly from the bottle. A few stood near a pool table in the far corner. A young woman in tight jean shorts with long skinny legs was leaning over the table prepar-ing to take a shot as we entered. She held off, and looked over at Billy and me just as we came in.

I thought at first, because everyone just looked at us without smiling, that they would kick us out. But when Billy raised his hand in greeting, a few men sitting around tables called his name in return. Two of them, older men with beards sitting alone in the far corner of them room, did not wave and eyed us both suspiciously. Billy called out a greeting to them anyway.

"Come on," he said. "Let's get a drink."

We took a seat near the pool table, beside three boys who looked not much older than Billy. One of the boys changed the song on the jukebox to "I'm Moving On" by Hank Snow, and dramatically dedicated it to Billy. Billy smiled and nodded thanks. The young woman shooting pool completed her shot and came strolling over to our table.

"Hey Billy," she said. "I didn't think you was coming in tonight."

"Hi Carla. Sure I'm coming in. Where did you think I'd spend my last night, at church?"

"So you're going then?"

"Yup," Billy said, and pounded a fist on a table. "Where's Carson? I want a drink."

Carla leaned forward on her pool cue and motioned with her

head towards the back of the bar. "He's in the kitchen. He ain't none too happy you're leaving, Billy."

Billy shrugged. "Too bad."

Carla butted the end of the cue once on the floor. "Hey Carson!" she called. "Billy out here wants a drink!"

A voice came drifting faintly out from a small dark doorway in the back of the hall. "I'm coming!"

Carla looked down at me, and smiled. "This Luke?"

"Yup," answered Billy. "Haven't you ever met my little brother?"

"No," Carla said, and offered me her hand. "Nice to meet you, Luke." I shook it, shyly, without looking into her face.

"Hey Billy!" One of the boys at the other table turned towards our table. "You gonna let me win my money back tonight?"

"Not tonight, Ron," Billy said. "I'm not playing tonight."

"Ah come on," Ron said. "I ain't got but three dollars in my pocket. You gotta give me a chance at least. You took half my week's pay last Saturday."

"Whose fault is that?" said Billy. "If you're stupid enough to bet your food money, I can't help it!"

"Hey!" said the boy. "I don't mind the food money. It's the drinking money that bothers the fuck outta me."

The three boys at the table laughed out loud at the joke. Billy laughed for a moment with them, then turned back to us. Carla said to him, "You ain't playing tonight?"

Billy shook his head. "I need all my money for the trip."

"Hey," Carla said, looking down at me. "I bet you didn't know your brother's the biggest hustler in the province, did you?"

I shook my head no. I didn't even know what a hustler was, but Billy shushed her before she could say more.

"Doesn't matter, anyway," she said. "He's gonna be a writer.

148

You gonna send us all a copy of your first book, Billy?"

"Damn right I am," Billy said proudly.

"Don't forget to dedicate it to me."

"I won't," Billy said, and winked at me, though I didn't understand why. Before I could ask, one of the men standing at the pool table called out, "Carla. It's your shot!"

"I'll be back," she said. "You're cute, Luke."

She went back to the table and leaned over to take her shot. I said to Billy, "Is that your girlfriend?"

Billy shook his head. "Just a friend. You like her?"

I couldn't answer, and Billy laughed. An older man wandered up to our table and, ignoring me, involved Billy in a conversation about my Uncle Joe. Nothing about what they were saying interested me, so I turned to watch Carla and the other man play pool. I had never seen a pool game before, and I watched in fascination as the brightly coloured balls glided smoothly across the table. Carla winked at me once, and I turned away, embarrassed. Before long, a corpulent, red-faced man in dirty cook's whites appeared at our table. The fisherman left again, wandering off with beer in hand to talk to someone else.

"What do you want?" said the new man gruffly. This, I presumed, was Carson.

"Two beers, Derrick," Billy ordered.

Derrick Carson squinted at us through the cigarette smoke, and pointed one fat finger accusingly at me. "He ain't old enough to drink."

"I don't want any," I said nervously.

"I wasn't old enough to drink when I first came in here either," he said. "Matter of fact," he laughed, as if it had just occurred to him, "I'm still not. I just turned seventeen this summer."

"Not the same thing," said Carson. "I made an exception for

you, Billy, but I won't have your mother in here after me if he
gets drunk."

"Ah come on," Billy said. "I'll see he only has one. Give him
a beer, will you?"

"Can't do it, Billy. I'll lose my license if the inspector comes
around."

"When's the last time the liquor inspector came to this shit-
hole, twenty years ago?"

But Carson stuck to his guns. "He ain't old enough, and I
ain't serving him."

"Alright," said Billy finally. "Bring him a Pepsi, and bring me
a beer." Carson moved away, weaving his considerable bulk
back around the tables and customers, and disappeared the way
he had come. Billy glanced over at me.

"Sorry," he said. "I wanted to treat you to your first beer."

"That's okay."

"He's just pissed off 'cause I won't be playing for him
anymore."

"What you mean, 'playing for him'?"

Billy looked quickly away. "Never mind."

Carson brought back Billy's beer and my Pepsi. I noticed that
Billy didn't pay him for it. He left us again and we sipped our
drinks in silence. Billy studied the pool table and the game taking place in front of us. After about ten minutes, before the
game with Carla and the other man was over, Carson came up
to our table once more.

"What do you want?" Billy said, not taking his eyes from
Carla's game.

"Two guys over there want to play you."

"I told you, I'm not playing tonight."

"There's fifty dollars in it."

"I haven't got fifty dollars to spare," Billy said.

"I'll front you," said Carson.

Billy seemed to think this over carefully. I was dying to know what 'fronting' was, but I was afraid to ask with Derrick Carson standing right there.

"Come on Billy," Carson said finally. "For old times' sake. I'll front you, I said."

"What if I lose?"

"You won't," Carson answered.

"What's my cut if I win?"

Carson seemed to think about it carefully himself. "Ten dollars," he said finally.

"Thirty," countered Billy.

Carson agreed so easily it surprised me, though I still wasn't sure what he was agreeing to. "Alright. Thirty."

Billy, Carson, and I looked over at the two men sitting in the far corner of the room, the same ones who hadn't smiled or greeted Billy when we'd come in. "Where they from?" asked Billy.

"Oldsport."

"They any good?"

"Never seen 'em play," said Carson. "But they heard about you. That's why they came out."

"Alright. Send them over after this game."

Billy watched Carla play out her game, and when she was done, quietly got up from his chair. Carson came out with another cue stick from the back room and handed it to Billy. It was thicker than the others, and inlaid with an intricate pattern of silver at the base. The two men from the far corner got up and walked over to meet Billy. One of them carried a cue of his own. Everyone in the bar got up and wandered over to the pool table. The boys next to us stopped talking and turned in their seats. Carla deposited her plain wood cue back in the rack and came over to keep me company in Billy's chair, carrying her beer with her.

"You ever seen your brother play?" she asked.

"I didn't even know he did play," I told her.

Carla smiled. "Oh, he plays alright. Just watch."

The first man from Oldsport broke apart the triangulated nest of pool balls, and sunk two right away, followed by two more. He missed the third, and it was Billy's shot.

I haven't spent a lot of time in bars and pool halls. But to this day, Billy is the best pool player I've ever seen. I've often thought if he was half as good a writer as he was a pool player he would have made it. Pool playing and writing have things in common, Billy has told me. They both require finesse, confidence, balance. And in a limited space there's an infinite number of combinations to choose from. From the first Billy had what it took. I'd never felt so proud of my brother. His manner as he shot each ball straight into its pocket was one of cool detachment. He shot neither too quickly nor too slowly, circling the table like a man who's done this many times before and is confident of himself. The shots he made never came off as too difficult or showy. After each shot the next seemed to line itself up perfectly. Like all masters, he made what is difficult seem very, very easy. The Oldsport man didn't get to shoot before Billy had cleared his own balls from the table. Begrudgingly, the man handed the fifty dollars over to Carson, and incredibly, asked Billy to play again.

Billy played five games of pool with those men, winning each time. I'd never seen so much money change hands, and I could not imagine, in this part of the province where money was scarce as moose, how they managed to have so much to begin with. But Billy took it all from them, and I understood then where he'd got the money to pay my mother and to drink with.

I understood something else that night as well. After the last game, one of the men who lost got frustrated enough to grab my brother by the shirt collar and throw him roughly against the pool table. Billy showed little surprise, and only waited for three of the Capers watching the game, signalled by Carson, to pull the man away from him.

"Don't worry," the older man said, pulling himself indignantly away from those who restrained him. "I wouldn'a hurt the punk."

Billy motioned for me to head towards the door. His goodbyes to all, except for Carla, were brief, and before the two men had taken their places again at their table, Billy and I were out the door.

"Sore losers," was all Billy said as he jumped back on the motorcycle and started it up. He motioned impatiently for me to climb on, and I did. I realized why Billy came home so often with black eyes and torn clothes. He wasn't always so lucky as tonight. There wasn't always somebody to pull those he humiliated at the pool table off him. Suddenly, as Billy turned us around in the parking lot, I was glad he was going to Toronto. The Cape, and the boredom it held for him, made him a danger to himself. I didn't realize that Billy carried the danger around inside of him, and that Toronto, if one wanted to escape bar fights and gambling and pool tables, was the last place you should go.

We got home much later than my mother had demanded, but the lights were off and the house was as silent as a tomb. Billy made me swear I'd never tell where we had ended up, for he would never be able to come home again, he said, if Mom found out he'd taken me to Carson's. We walked the bike the last half mile to the barn so we wouldn't wake anyone, then crept quietly into the house and up the stairs. Tom didn't stir as we silently undressed in the dark and climbed into our shared bed.

"Remember, Luke," Billy whispered. "Not a soul."

"I won't tell," I whispered back.

"Goodnight, little brother."

"Goodnight, Billy."

We slept without covers, because in summer we were used to that, though for August it wasn't especially warm. I turned away towards the door, and Billy threw his arm across me the way he used to do. I moved a little closer to him. Though I'd see him in the morning I felt that I'd lost him already. I even entertained thoughts of asking Billy if I could go with him, though I knew he'd never take me. It was the last night the three of us would ever spend together in that room, and I was sad we would not spend it talking to each other like we used to do. I heard Tom get up during the night to use the bathroom. When he came back to bed, sensing I was awake, he whispered, "What did you guys do tonight?"

"Nothing much."

"Did you go to Carson's?"

"Yes."

Tom chuckled quietly to himself, and we both drifted off to sleep. When I awoke in the morning, Billy's place in bed beside me was empty.

Billy's first idea had been to take the Sunbeam to Toronto. He only told Tom about it, knowing my mother would never stand for it. Even Tom thought the idea bad.

"It'll never make it, Billy. That's a nine-hundred-mile trip."

"Might make it part of the way," said Billy. "Then I'll junk it and take the train the rest."

Tom was more afraid that Billy would never make it even part of the way. The idea of Billy opening up the Sunbeam on a busy highway, he said, gave him the shivers.

"He'll wrap himself around a transport truck," he told me. "He'll end up as roadkill on the Trans-Canada."

Tom badgered Billy about the bike so often that finally he agreed to leave it behind and take the train. Tom even offered to pay the train fare. At first Billy refused to take money from our brother, though he'd no qualms about taking it from half the province at the pool table. But Tom insisted, saying that paying for the train would be like buying the Sunbeam from him. Reluctantly Billy agreed. But in the morning of the day he left, he must have changed his mind. I don't think he intended to cheat Tom. He knew Tom didn't really want the bike and was only giving him money for the train so he'd leave the Sunbeam safely behind. He got up early, took his bag, already packed, and crept out of the house while it was still dark.

Tom told me later he heard him get up. He waited quietly in bed for sounds of the motorcycle. He'd thought, he told us later, of going out and warning Billy, but something had prevented him. He was angry our brother was leaving without saying goodbye, and going back on the deal they'd struck.

Tom lay awake in the half light of our bedroom, the sun just beginning to rise out of the Atlantic, and waited. He thought that maybe Billy would wheel it out, but our brother had other ideas. Through the open bedroom window Tom heard the Sunbeam revving in the barn. The engine screamed as Billy gave it gas, and threw it into gear. A loud crash woke us all. The Sunbeam gave a terrific whine, shut itself off, and Tom got moving. When I opened my eyes, startled by the noise, he was rushing around the bedroom, trying to fit himself into jeans and a T-shirt.

"What in the world was that?" shouted our mother from her bedroom.

"It's Billy," Tom called out. "He tried to take the bike."

"I knew it," cried mother angrily. "Leave it to that boy!"

"What's going on, Tom?" I asked, with only one eye open.

"Get up and see," Tom said grimly. "Billy's leaving."

I jumped out of bed, jumped into the same jeans I'd worn the night before and followed Tom out of the room. Our mother met us at the head of the stairs and we all clamoured down, half dressed, and ran outside into the cool summer morning.

Billy was nowhere to be seen. A heavy mist covered the ground. We ran between the barn and house and stood to look for the shape of Billy's back on the Cape road, but saw nothing. When my mother started cursing Billy, Tom held one finger to his lips. "Shhhh," he said. "Listen."

We strained to hear, and from far off, deep in the mist, we heard someone whistling.

"Billy!" I called out. "Billy, come back!" There was no response. The whistling stopped.

"We should go after him," I said to my mother.

"What for?"

"He didn't say goodbye!"

"Doesn't matter," Tom said. "Come on."

Tom led us into the barn. When our eyes adjusted to the gloom, we saw the Sunbeam lying on its side on the barn floor, a chain tangled up around it. Tom had fastened the rear wheel of the bike to a wall joist at the rear of the barn and secured the chain with a padlock. Billy, unable to see the danger in the early morning gloom inside the barn, had attempted to drive the bike out. The Sunbeam had stopped short, and Billy was probably thrown.

"Well," my mother said in satisfaction. "He couldn't have been hurt too badly."

"No," Tom said. "I guess he wasn't."

I looked in wonder at Tom and my mother. I found out later they'd cooked it up together. My mother paid for the chain and lock, and Tom had crept out in the night to secure the bike. As we watched he bent down and righted the fallen motorcycle, kicked down its stand. He produced a key from his pocket and unlocked the padlock, drew the chain from behind the joist and through the spokes of the Sunbeam and tossed it aside.

"Come on" our mother said, looking extremely pleased with herself. "We'll get some breakfast."

Tom glanced at me as he passed by. "I didn't want him to kill himself on that thing," he said simply, and followed my mother into the house. I stood without a T-shirt, shivering in the cold, and stared at the motorcycle. Then I went outside and looked down the road the way Billy had gone. It would be days before my mother realized Billy had the last laugh. He'd wanted the Sunbeam not to go to Toronto but only to drive to Trenton. Billy never found her hiding place for the keys to the Thunderbird and the deed to the house and land left us by my grandfather. Still, he hadn't grown up in the Cape and spent all that time in Carson's tavern without learning a few shady tricks besides playing pool and drinking beer. He hitchhiked to Gaston Road and hot-wired my grandfather's Thunderbird. He drove it like that all the way to Toronto. Tom discovered this when my mother sent him down one weekend on the train to have a look at the place and make sure Dolores Whynot wasn't "putting her oar in where it didn't belong." My mother swore that was it, that no matter what happened in Toronto, Billy would not be returning. She had half a mind to call the police on him and have him thrown in jail for grand theft auto. As always, she didn't call the police and Billy got away with it, though he admitted years later that he'd sold the car shortly after reaching Toronto for far less than what it was worth.

From the very first Billy didn't keep in touch, perhaps because he knew that my mother for months was waiting to call him a liar and a thief over the phone. Tom and I had a few letters, though even these stopped coming eventually. We got a call from him one Christmas, though on this occasion my mother didn't mention the fact that he'd robbed her. He didn't leave a number or an address where he could be reached, and after that he didn't call anymore. Once, after years of silence, my mother, in her detached manner, suggested the possibility of his death.

"Knowing that boy, he got himself wrapped up in some kind of trouble and got himself killed over it." But none of us really thought he was dead. We would have heard if he was. All we knew was for some reason he had stopped talking to us. Tom and I talked about him often.

"Remember what he said in the first letter," Tom said to me during one of our reminiscing sessions. "How Toronto was so big no one cared what you did in it?"

"Yes," I said, smiling. "He said he could have thrown a fit right in the middle of the street and everyone would have just walked right by him."

"As different from the Cape as you could get," said Tom, sighing. "Billy always did hate this part of the world."

"That's no reason not to call," I said, admonishing Tom in place of our mother. "Does that mean he hates us too?"

Tom shrugged. "He's in trouble I guess. That's the only thing I can think of. Maybe's he's been in jail or something and is too ashamed to let us know."

"For this long?" I said. "He would have had to kill somebody to get that much time!"

"Doesn't matter Luke," Tom said finally. "There isn't anything we can do."

"There must be a way to get ahold of him. To help him somehow."

Tom only shook his head.

It would be more than twenty years before we would hear from our brother again. Still, whenever I thought of him, it would be Billy on the day he left home that I would picture. Billy as a dark, muscular, wild-eyed boy of seventeen and not as the man he must have grown to be. People, my brother the failed writer would one day get around to telling me, only grow in our presence, and even then we fight it.

THE WEDDING

❧

*T*om bought a car less than a year after Billy left for Toronto, a 1962 blue Dodge Charger. He paid two hundred dollars for it to an Oldsport man who had owned it for years and practically ran it into the ground. My mother thought even that was too much money. She asked him why he didn't just use the Sunbeam since he now owned it. Tom had tried the bike a few times, taking it to work one day and hunting another. But as a means of transport, he said it was impractical. I was dying to use it. My mother wouldn't hear of it. "You'll get yourself killed," she said. "I can't afford to pay for any more funerals."

We saw less and less of Tom that year, and where he spent the majority of his time we couldn't fathom. To my mother's questions he was evasive, adopting the time-honoured methods of our absent brother. She didn't press him. I think my mother already knew before Tom brought Suzanne home that he'd met a girl.

My oldest brother met his future wife while pheasant hunting in the Annapolis Valley. Tom loved to hunt pheasant, but because there were none in our part of the province he had to make the three-hour trip to the wild orchards outside of Kentville to do so. He had one friend at the mill, a young man his age named Mike, and sometimes the two of them drove to the Valley for the weekend to go hunting. This had been one of those times. It was a Saturday, and Tom was in some woods near an orchard where pheasants sought shade at noon. Suzanne was picking apples for ten dollars a bushel at the far end of the field. Tom shot at a pheasant in flight and this seventeen-year-old girl came marching fearlessly back into the woods, claiming some pellet from his gun had almost hit her.

"Boy, was she mad," Tom said when he eventually told us the story. "She came flying back through the woods, apples falling this way and that out of her apron, screaming that I'd almost killed her." He laughed. "She was so worked up she grabbed an apple out of her apron and threw it at me."

Tom, the former baseball player, picked the flying apple out of the air and took a big bite. Suzanne laughed, went back to work, and Tom was smitten. He stayed in Kentville for two extra days, taking one of them off work to go hunting in the same area, hoping to get a glimpse of her again. Finally he just walked out of the woods on the second day, the barrel of his gun broken open in case she thought he would shoot her, and asked her out. She was standing on the top plank of a picking ladder when he came and stood shyly beneath her.

"Why would I want to go out with you?" she said, continuing to comb through the branches above her for ripe apples. "You might shoot me."

"Naw. I wouldn't," Tom swore to her, and laid his gun over the top of the apple barrel, already almost full with a quarter of a day's work. "I just want to see if you'll go out to dinner with me."

"We'll see," she said shortly. "Now get out of here and let me finish working."

"I'm not going nowhere until you answer me about dinner."

Suzanne stopped picking and looked down at him. "Why are you so stuck on dinner?" she asked.

Tom shrugged. "'Cause I'm hungry, I guess."

Suzanne tossed him another apple. "Here," she said. "Eat this."

Tom did and left, but not before he'd asked the orchard foreman what time the pickers were off. At four o'clock he was waiting for her at the side of the road. Without too much resistance she got in his car, and the two of them went to the Kentville diner for supper. From then on Tom drove up to Kentville whenever he could, though he never told anyone where he was going. I was busy with exams that spring. I'd failed Grade Seven math the year before and was determined to pass this year. My failing was no surprise to my teachers, who thought that since both Tom and Billy had flunked out before me I would be next. I was determined to prove them wrong. Every night I sat with the overhead light on at the kitchen table, struggling with mathematical figures that made little sense to me, while my mother rocked quietly in her chair, mending socks and refashioning her house dresses to last another season.

It was on one of these long summer evenings that Tom brought Suzanne home to meet us. When we heard his Charger coming up the Cape road and pulling into the driveway, neither of us stirred. Even when he came in, we didn't look up from our work.

"Hi everybody," he called out cheerfully. We didn't notice that behind him, in the shadow of the porch, stood the figure of a girl.

"Hey, Tom," I said. "I'm beginning to understand why you and Billy dropped out of school."

"Mom?" Tom said.

"What?" My mother looked up, irritated at being interrupted at her work. I looked up too, just as Tom brought the girl forward.

"This is Suzanne Carey," he said. "Suzanne, this is my mother."

"Hello, Mrs. Conrad," said Suzanne softly.

"Hello," Mom said. I could see she was surprised.

"This is my brother Luke," Tom said, waving in my direction.

"Hello, Luke."

My mother and I just sat there, uncertain of what to do. One of Tom's wool socks dangled from her darning needle. The figures written on the page before me blurred into insignificance. Suzanne stood before us, a petite, slim girl in a blue dress tied with a sash, worn especially for the occasion, and gazed curiously around at the interior of our kitchen. It wasn't just that we had a girl in our house — that in itself was rare enough — but Suzanne was, by any estimation, a very pretty girl. Her hair was long and deep auburn, her skin pale and lightly freckled. None of the girls in the Cape looked like Suzanne. They were all dark haired, buxom, with heavy breasts and wide faces. Suzanne seemed to me incredibly neat and worldly. I wondered where in the world Tom had found her. I was sure she wasn't from here. I surely would have noticed her before. As it was, she looked so out of place in our house in the bright blue dress and long hair that I imagined the only place to do her justice would have been the yellow mat I was born on, when it had been new.

In other words, Suzanne added a splash of colour and vitality to our house that I was unused to seeing.

Tom seemed if anything more awed by her presence than any of us. "Do you want some tea?" he asked her nervously. "I can make some."

"You sit down, Tom," my mother said, quickly recovering from the shock of having a stranger in her house unannounced. "I'll get the tea." She set aside Tom's sock and the needles, and got up to go to the pantry while Tom directed Suzanne to a seat. He gave her my father's rocker and pulled up a kitchen chair beside her.

"What are you doing?" she asked me.

"Math," I told her, too seriously.

"What grade are you in?"

"Eight."

Tom said, "Luke is gonna be the scholar in the family. Billy and I never made it past Grade Eleven."

"Do you like school?" asked Suzanne.

"No," I said. "I'm failing. My math teacher thinks I'd be better at English, and my English teacher thinks I'd be good at math."

Suzanne laughed, a clear, light sound that surprised me. Our house had known very little laughter over the years, even when my father was alive. Tom watched her, unable even to smile he was so overcome. It was as if she belonged to a different species entirely and Tom was only just discovering her.

"You must be good at some subject," Suzanne said.

"Yes," I said. "I like to draw."

"Luke will be a great artist someday," Tom said. He appeared to be desperately trying to impress her with whatever he could. I'd never seen Tom so unsure of himself. He couldn't sit still. He squirmed in his chair and was up every time Suzanne

moved, asking her if she wanted anything. When my mother
came back with the tea cups and put the kettle on the stove to
boil he became, if anything, more nervous. He kept looking
from Suzanne to my mother and back again, as if waiting for
them to either kiss or attack each other. My mother, for her
part, directed all of her questions at Tom, although Suzanne
was the one to answer them.

"So where's your friend from, Tom?" she said.

"Kentville," answered Suzanne promptly. "My father owns a
store there."

"It's a dry goods shop," Tom added.

"Kentville," my mother said thoughtfully. "When did you
meet her, Tom?"

"I went hunting," Tom said. "Suzanne was picking apples in
the orchard."

"But the second time we met," Suzanne said. "I was in
Oldsport."

"She has a cousin here," Tom added.

"Oh? And what's her cousin's name?"

It went on like this while my mother got the tea ready and
distributed the cups among us. It seemed my mother knew
vaguely of Suzanne's cousin's mother, which seemed suddenly to
make her more herself around this stranger. My mother was like
that. She hardly had anything to do with anyone in the Cape or
Oldsport, except Etta. But she knew of everyone. If a name was
mentioned she didn't know, by one of us or by Etta, my mother
would need to trace that person through their cousins or sisters
or parents or grandparents and wouldn't be satisfied until she
found a name she at least recognized. Then, in her way, she made
a judgement on that person's character by what she knew of
the family. Suzanne's cousin in town wasn't a Carey but a
Whynot. My mother, as tactless as ever, said, "Oh, those

Whynots. Didn't James Whynot get in trouble here a few years ago? Lost his boat, or something?"

"Yes. Well, that James is my uncle," said Suzanne uncomfortably.

"Why did he lose his boat?" I asked without thinking.

Suzanne looked at me and said frankly, "He got caught hauling lobster out of season. Twice."

My mother looked extremely pleased with this, like a detective who's just solved a case based on one small clue. She sat down to drink her tea, looking at Suzanne with undisguised satisfaction. Suzanne and Tom continued to talk about the more honest members of her family until the conversation, no longer contributed to by my mother, simply dried up. There was a long uncomfortable hiatus where the only sounds were the clicking of cups against saucers. My mother broke it finally by saying, "Well, Tom. Don't you have something to tell us tonight?"

Tom didn't know what to do. He looked at Suzanne, then over at my mother, then at me, then down at the floor, then back up at my mother again.

"Yes," he said finally. "I guess I do."

Suzanne, with a boldness that shocked me, took Tom's hand in hers and squeezed it. Her expression was mild, but defiant. My mother glanced at their clasped hands and without betraying any emotion looked back at Tom.

"Well, come on," she said. "Get out with it. I got work to do tonight."

Tom stumbled uncharacteristically over his words. "Well. I thought, you know, that tonight might be a good night to tell you, that, uh, Suzanne and I might be getting married."

Neither of us were surprised. We couldn't imagine any other reason for bringing the girl home to meet us. What was surprising was the way Suzanne spoke right up, directing her words unflinchingly at my mother. "We thought we'd do it this summer if it's alright with you."

"Me?" my mother said. "What's it got to do with me?"

"Well," Suzanne said. "I know Tom does a lot around here, and I just thought it might be hard for you to get along without him."

Tom flinched and tried to pull his hand away from his girl, but she wouldn't let him. He knew this was the wrong thing to say to my mother, who didn't like to be reminded that she was in any way dependent upon his income from the mill. I thought that would be it. Mom would send this girl out of her house on the toe of her shoe. We were flabbergasted when my mother laughed. It was not bright laughter, and next to Suzanne's silver-throated voice it sounded harsh, brutal, and there was more than a little sarcasm in it. But it was laughter just the same, and hearing my mother laugh wasn't something Tom and I were used to.

"Don't worry about me," my mother said. "You two just do whatever it is you want."

"But Mom," said Tom, so surprised by my mother's answer that he himself grew bolder. "What about money? Your pension isn't enough to keep the house going and Luke in school too, is it?"

"Just you never mind about that," my mother said harshly. "I've been keeping this house going on what I make since your father died, and before that. I guess I can manage it if one of my boys decides to get married."

I thought that was the end of the conversation. My mother picked up the sock she'd been darning and went to work on it again. It seemed expected that Tom and Suzanne would leave.

But they didn't. They only sat watching my mother until she finally put the needle and sock down into her lap and said, "Well, what is it?"

"Well," Tom began. "It's just that, if Suzanne and I are gonna get married, we're gonna need a place to live."

"And what is that supposed to do with me?" asked my mother. "If you get married, Tom, you're the one who is gonna have to worry about those details, not me."

"I know that," Tom said, lifting his shoulders in indignation at the suggestion that he couldn't provide for his wife. My mother ignored this, and went back to work on the sock.

"I just thought," said Tom suddenly, "that maybe we could live in Grandfather's house, since no one is using it."

My mother didn't even look up from her darning. "Absolutely not," she said.

Suzanne spoke up so quickly that I thought perhaps her part had been rehearsed. "I thought part of that house belonged to Tom," she said quietly. "Didn't he leave it to all of you?"

"Suzanne," Tom pleaded, "let me deal with this." If Suzanne had rehearsed her part, Tom had obviously not been let in on her plan. Suzanne waved him away. My mother stopped her darning again and looked at this strange, bold girl sitting in her kitchen with what, for her, might have amounted to some kind of respect. At least she didn't look angry, though with my mother it was hard to tell until she opened her mouth.

"Yes," she said. "The old bastard left it to all of us, but I won't be letting anyone move into it while I'm still drawing breath."

"Why not?" Suzanne asked, and Tom seemed almost to draw away from her the way you would from someone about to be shot.

"Because," said my mother slowly, "that's the way I want it.

And I would advise you, little girl, not to go poking your nose into business that don't concern you. If I say no one's moving into that house, then no one's moving into it, and that's all there is to it."

Suzanne looked as if she was about to say something else, but before she could Tom was out of his chair. His temper, in its way as volatile as my mother's, had kicked in.

"For chrissakes," he said. "It's only a house. Suzanne's right. It does belong to all of us. And I'm not gonna sit around and watch it rot to the ground because you're too stubborn to take something someone gave you."

"You don't know what you're talking about," my mother shot back. "I've got my reasons, and I ain't gonna let some nineteen-year-old tell me they ain't no good."

"Where in the hell are we supposed to live then," Tom shouted. "Here?"

My mother shrugged. "I guess you'll have to wait until you can afford a place."

"We can't wait," Suzanne said. "I'm pregnant."

Tom turned to her. "I thought you was gonna wait until you were sure," he said.

"I'm sure, Tom. Or mostly sure anyway."

"Well, why in the hell didn't you tell me!"

Suzanne looked at my mother while she answered. "I was going to tell you later tonight, but I guess everyone else might as well know."

"I figured as much," my mother said. She set aside the sock and got out of her chair. "I'm going to bed," she said. "Luke, you turn out the lights in an hour, as soon as you're finished that work you're doing." She started toward the stairs.

"But what about us?" Tom shouted after her. "What are we gonna do?"

My mother turned back to Tom in the doorway of the parlour. "Boy," she said, "you're the one's got yourself into this trouble. I guess you're the one's gonna have to get yourself out."

"It's not trouble," Tom said angrily. "It's good news. And I just want to know why in the hell you won't let us move into that house. You're not using it, and it belongs to us."

"It belongs to no one," she said, "but your father's father. And no one will live in it as long as I'm alive." Tom stood there listening to her climb the stairs until the sound of her footsteps could no longer be heard.

"So what are you gonna do, Tom?" I asked.

"I don't know," he said, scratching his head and looking earnestly at his wife-to-be.

"Don't worry," she said to him. "We'll figure something out."

"But I want that house," Tom said. "I just don't understand what she has against it."

"Sounds like she's got something against your grandfather," said Suzanne. She had seemingly recovered from the confrontation, if she'd ever been bothered by it at all, and her voice once again had become light and controlled. I looked at her with respect. No one, not even Etta, had ever spoken to my mother the way she had and gotten away with it. At first I assumed it was because she wasn't from the Cape and didn't know my mother. Maybe she thought she was dealing with a reasonable woman. But I now think Suzanne knew who she was dealing with from the start. Tom wouldn't have brought her home without warning her. It was just that Suzanne lacked that one essential element my mother expected in all people: fear. She wasn't afraid of my mother. I could never figure out exactly why this was. All people, even those who didn't know my mother, were instinctively afraid of her. Even Tom at nineteen, a young, burly, good-looking man, couldn't hide his fear of her. Nor could he hide his respect for this young, unassuming woman he'd brought to our house.

"You wanna go home?" he asked her now.

Suzanne shrugged. "Might as well. We can go and tell my parents."

The two of them left. Suzanne wished me goodbye as if nothing unpleasant had happened. I listened to the car pull away from the house until my mother called for me to turn out the lights and come to bed. I did as she asked, and I lay alone in the room, thinking of the girl my brother had brought home. I liked her, and even though she wasn't yet a member of our family, I felt as proud of her as if she was my own sister. It was as if, in our battle against our mother, we had suddenly gained a new ally.

⁓

Over the next few days my mother never stopped running Suzanne down. She called her the usual. Slut. Wharf whore. Baggage. Even a few new ones I had never heard her use before.

"That girl is the goddamndest nosy parker I ever saw in my life. Imagine," she moaned to Etta, who dropped over the next day for a visit, "telling me who owns that house on Gaston Road. As if she lived here all her life. As if she owned the damned thing herself, for chrissakes." My mother stood near the sink, her sleeves rolled up to her elbows, furiously kneading a lump of bread dough that lay before her on the counter. Her words were given more force each time she lifted the dough, slammed it back on the counter, and threw her shoulders back into the kneading.

"I thought she was a sweet thing," Etta said characteristically. My mother stopped her kneading.

"When did you meet her, I'd like to know?"

"Last week," said Etta. "Tom brought her over for tea."

"Oh," my mother said, driving her fingers back into the dough. "Well, she might look sweet to you, but I'm telling you that girl is trouble. I knew it the minute she opened her mouth. I'd be surprised if that baby was even Tom's."

If my mother was surprised, or hurt, that Tom had introduced Etta to his fiancée before his own mother, she didn't show it. Etta apparently assumed my mother had already met her, for she didn't mention it either.

"What did you think of her, Luke?" I was just home from school, and had burst in on the conversation. Etta asked me this as I was taking off my boots, and I paused to look back and forth between the two of them. My mother continued her kneading, her back to me, and didn't turn around, so I concluded my input was welcome.

"I thought she was nice," I ventured.

"There you go," announced Etta loudly. "Everyone likes her except you, Dora."

"There ain't no liking involved," my mother said. "I know a wharf whore when I see one. And I'm telling you if Tom marries that girl he'll regret it to the end of his days."

"Go on now," said Etta laughing. "There isn't no mother-in-law likes the girl her son's going to marry. Why I remember at home when I was a girl . . ." I went upstairs to change into my play clothes. By the time I got back downstairs they had changed the subject. But knowing my mother, it wouldn't be long before she got back on it and Etta tired and went home. She misunderstood, I think, my mother's vendetta against Suzanne. It wasn't the usual dislike of a mother for a daughter-in-law. I believe my mother saw what I did. Where we had found an ally, my mother had found an enemy. Not only was she losing Tom's income, she was losing Tom himself. If it was arguable my mother had ever mastered Billy, gained control of him like she had Tom and me, at least she was not used to having her authority challenged. That is what Suzanne had done.

Outside the house that day, splitting wood for the stove, I saw my mother's arguments as ridiculous, but inside the house my fear of her made whatever she said hold a strange logic. Even Etta couldn't hold out against that kind of intimidation for long, and yet Suzanne, at least in the short glimpse we'd had of her, seemed oblivious to it. She allowed us to see, if only for a moment, that my mother's authority was not all-encompassing. Here at last was someone my mother couldn't control. Already I loved Suzanne for it, and could barely stand to hear her being bad-mouthed so unfairly. I began to pray, though I didn't then believe in God despite my father's many attempts to make me, that Tom would bring Suzanne home again, even if only for a few minutes. For awhile I believed that I was actually in love with her, and those abnormal longings for boys that gnawed at me day and night seemed to slip away. But alas, when Tom came home now it was only to sleep, and he never brought Suzanne with him. My mother didn't mention her or ask about her, and neither did Tom bring up her name in conversation. Tom seemed to feel what I felt. It was as if Suzanne was rescuing him by degrees. He became less responsive to my mother's demands. He talked back sharply to her, though he never shouted at her as he had that night. He was home less and less. At the end of the month he paid his board and still gave his extra to keep the household going. But then he'd be gone and we would not see him for days at a time.

My mother, for her part, seemed to demand less of him. She no longer asked him where he'd been. She accepted his money wordlessly, and only asked that he tell her when he was coming home for supper so she could prepare enough for three. We ate silently as tension increased. Though I think that both Tom and my mother were stubborn enough to let it go on forever, it was broken the day Tom came home from work and announced the date of the wedding.

"It's in Kentville," he told us. "Next month. Suzanne's Dad will stand up for us, and I want Luke to be my best man."

"Me?" I said, surprised and delighted. "What about Mike McNeill?" Mike McNeill was the boy Tom worked and hunted with. Though Tom didn't speak of him often, I thought for sure Tom would ask him to be his best man.

"No," Tom said. "I want it to be you, Luke."

"Don't expect me to be there," my mother said.

"I'm not gonna force you. You can come if you want. I only want to know if Luke can go."

I waited breathlessly for my mother, who sat in my father's rocker looking out the window at the ocean, to answer. She didn't for a long while. It didn't occur to me to defy her if she said no, like Tom and Billy had both done in the past. I was only thirteen, and couldn't imagine being on my own. I suppose had she refused, I could have gone to live with Tom and Suzanne. How differently things might have turned out then. But as of yet they had no clear idea of where they would live. Finally my mother ended the suspense and answered.

"I suppose he can go. But you'll have to pay for it. I don't have the money to give Luke for that foolishness." That 'foolishness,' my brother's wedding, would not, Tom assured her, cost her anything. I could come up with him two days before the wedding and Etta and Roland, who were driving up on the day, could bring me back.

"He'll have to miss a day of school," Tom warned.

"It's his school," she answered. We left her there, staring out the window. I was deliriously excited at the prospect of Tom's wedding. Not only because I would be my brother's best man, but also because I would get a chance to leave Queen's County, something I had never done before. I began counting the days to the wedding, but was careful not to speak of it too much around my mother.

Etta was naturally incensed when she found out our mother wouldn't attend Tom's wedding. She stormed into our kitchen the afternoon she found out with me sharp on her heels. My mother was upstairs working. Etta didn't even wait for her to come down.

"Dora!" she shouted. "Dora!"

"What?" my mother called irritably from an upstairs bedroom. "I'm busy."

"Drop what you're doing and come down here a moment." My mother obeyed, but she took her time. She must have known what Etta wanted, for when she appeared her expression was passive but set. "What do you want?" she asked Etta, who stood just inside our kitchen door, barely able to contain her agitation.

"I can't believe you," she began. "Luke just told me you're not going to Tom's wedding."

"I'm not," my mother said, and without asking moved the tea kettle to the hottest part of the stovetop to boil. She fitted two cups with bags and filled them with hot water. Etta watched without speaking, as if she needed to prepare what she wanted to say. When she took a cup of tea from my mother she seemed to calm herself somewhat, and seated herself in one of the rocking chairs. My mother seated herself in the other and I sat down at the table to see how Etta would approach this. She did so promptly, after one sip of hot tea.

"It's shameful, Dora," she said. "Not going to your own

son's wedding. What in the world would Harold say if he was alive to see it?"

My mother shook her head. "It's not as if I care what anyone would think," she said. "Not even Harold. I'm not going."

"Why in the world not?" Etta asked. "What has that girl ever done to you?"

"I don't like her," my mother said. "That's reason enough."

"What about Tom, then? Even if you don't like Suzanne, Tom's your son for God's sake."

"I told him not to marry her. She'll only ruin his life." But my mother hadn't said this to Tom. She hadn't dared. She'd said it to me, and Etta, and anyone else who would listen. But she never made it clear exactly *how* Suzanne would ruin Tom's life, and Etta took the opportunity to ask her.

"How am I suppose to know how a woman like that works?' my mother said. "If Tom wants to get some woman knocked up, that's one thing. But letting her rope him into marrying her is another. She's a gold digger. All she wants is that house of Harold's father, and I'll be damned if she's getting it."

Neither Etta nor I saw the logic of this. Etta pointed out that Tom didn't seem to be getting 'roped' into anything. In fact, according to Etta, it was Tom who'd talked Suzanne into marriage, not the other way around. But my mother was adamant, though both of us could see she had no clear reason for not going to the wedding.

"You'll regret this, Dora," Etta told her. "You'll regret this till the end of your days."

"Maybe," my mother answered. "I'll have to regret it then."

"And what about the child?" Etta asked her. "You'll probably never get to see it if Tom don't bring it around."

My mother shrugged. "They can do what they want."

Etta finished her tea and went home shaking her head. I

followed her back to her house. "Now why on earth is your mother acting this way?" she asked me as we crossed the field. "I don't know," I said. "I guess she just don't like Suzanne." Etta scowled. "That isn't a reason for not going to the wedding. Lots of mothers don't like their daughters-in-law, but there's such things as common human decency to go by too." I agreed. I could see no reason why my mother shouldn't attend the wedding. In the Cape it became a sort of scandal when it became generally known my mother wasn't going to the wedding. Not that many people from there would travel all the way to Kentville to go either. But the mother of the groom not attending? There were rules to be followed, and once again my mother had broken them. In the month before the wedding the townsfolk seemed to take a personal interest in the mini-drama unfolding up at our house. Whenever I went in for mail at the post office, Eileen the postmistress asked me, "Your mother changed her mind about the wedding yet?"

"No ma'am."

"Tsskk," the old woman said between clenched teeth. "It's a shame. An awful shame. You tell your brother not to worry though. A wedding without a mother around is a lot more fun. I know. My mother-in-law didn't come to mine either. Of course, she was living in England at the time. Not like she had to travel only a few short miles as Dora Conrad would have to."

I was asked similar questions by Robichaud, and by Carson whenever I saw him on the street (I never again went into the pool hall after that night with Billy), and by Uncle Joe. Uncle Joe was going. Etta and Roland had agreed to drive him up. When my uncle heard that my mother wouldn't be going he only shook his head.

"I ain't surprised," he said, though he explained no further.

177

"I ain't surprised at all."

If my mother ever regretted her decision, as Etta said she would, I never knew of it. But on the day that Tom and I were to leave for Kentville, on a Thursday night, my mother helped me pack a few clothes into a suitcase. We had only one suitcase in our house, that was never used for its intended purpose. My mother kept her sewing things in it, but she unceremoniously dumped its contents — half-knitted socks, spools of thread, and balls of wool — onto her bed and brought it into my room.

"Here," she said, tossing the open suitcase onto my bed. "Don't pack any more than you need. I don't want to be doing laundry for a month after you get back."

"Thanks Mom." I placed the few T-shirts and pairs of pants I had into the open case. She watched me, leaning up against the door jam as she always did, never stepping inside our room unless to clean it.

"And don't be taking anything to drink at the reception," she said. "I don't know what kind of boozehounds that girl has for a family, but I don't want any son of mine getting drunk." I didn't say that she had one son, whom we had not seen for close to two years, who used to get drunk all the time.

"Don't worry," I said. "I won't touch a drop."

She watched me for a few minutes longer while I nervously packed my clothes. I was still afraid that at the last minute she'd decide I couldn't go. I wouldn't be completely relieved until I was in the car and on my way to Kentville with Tom. Eventually she left me alone to work in peace. As I struggled with the large suitcase on the stairs, she called out to me from the silence of her room. "There's an envelope on the table downstairs. I want you to give it to Tom."

This surprised me. I assumed at first it was money, but when I got to the kitchen, I saw the manila envelope was too large to be just a few dollars for a wedding present. I took it and put it in my suitcase so I wouldn't forget it, and sat down in a chair to listen for the sound of my brother's car. It was completely silent and dark except for the overhead light in the kitchen and the ticking of my mother's alarm clock from somewhere deep inside the house. I waited without moving from my chair, straining to hear the sound of Tom's car, nearly sick to my stomach with excitement. When I finally heard him pull into the back lot I stood up.

"He's here!" There was no answer, only the incessant ticking of the clock. "I'm going now. Goodbye. I'll see you on Monday!" But my mother didn't answer me, and I left her and carried my suitcase to Tom's car.

Tom never mentioned my mother the entire three-hour drive to Kentville, though after I put my suitcase in the car, I saw he too had been worried she might change her mind at the last minute. He smiled at me and said, "So you got away okay?"

"Yup," I told him. "I'm real excited, Tom."

Tom nodded. "So am I."

"Where are you going on your honeymoon?"

Tom told me that he and Suzanne had booked a three-night stay at the Old Orchard Inn right in Kentville. It was an old hotel, he said, with whole apartments for rooms and a swimming pool and real room service. Tom had never stayed in a hotel before, and this one, he told me, had to be better than the Sea Cottage Inn in the Cape. That 'hotel' was only a handful of barely furnished cottages strung along the shore off Main Street, reserved for the occasional tourist who happened to drive through our little town wanting to spend the night. The owner, Holland Wilson, the husband of Freeda Wilson of the now defunct Cape Heritage Society, also owned the fish plant, and was always threatening to tear down the Inn or use it for something else.

The few guests who stayed there during the summer months complained that the smell from the cod plant next door kept them awake at nights. But Tom assured me that the Old Orchard Inn was a class act.

"How can you afford such a fancy place?" He didn't make a lot of money, and a place like that was bound to be expensive.

He smiled. "That's the best part. I don't have to pay for anything. Suzanne's father's covering the whole thing. It's our wedding present."

Hearing of wedding presents made me think of the envelope my mother had given me. I had locked it away in the suitcase, which I'd put in the trunk, and I promised Tom I would retrieve it at the next stop. Tom only grunted when I told him about it. When, after driving for close to an hour, we stopped for gas and sodas, I ran back and opened the trunk to get at the suitcase. When I brought the large envelope to Tom, he took it and threw it on the seat between us.

"Aren't you gonna open it?" I asked him.

"Later," he said, and pulled out of the station. On the way to Kentville, we talked about everything. He pinpointed the moment when we left Queen's County and drove into Annapolis. I felt at that moment like a real man of the world. Because it was dark I couldn't see much of anything. Tom assured me there wasn't anything along that stretch of road but trees and hills. But being away from home for the first time in my life was a great thrill, and being with Tom, two days before his wedding, was a greater one. We discussed my duties as best man, although I was nervous having to get up in front of all those people I didn't know. Tom assured me I would be fine.

"All you have to do is give me the rings when the preacher asks for them."

"Who do I get the rings from?"

Tom laughed. "Don't worry about it, Luke. It'll all be taken care of."

So I didn't worry about it. We talked of Billy. Tom wished he could be here. But we didn't know where he was. The last letter had not been answered, and Tom said he didn't have time to hold off on his wedding until Billy made up his mind to call or write. Tom was actually worried about him, and expressed this to me on the way up.

"I hope that fool hasn't got himself killed or anything," he said. Having also worried about Billy over the past year, I confessed I had the same thoughts. We both missed him like crazy. I think we were both hurt that he hadn't kept in touch, though we wouldn't admit it. Tom said that if he ever did come home, he was going to put a beating on him like he'd never had before.

Interlaced throughout all our conversation was nearly constant mention of Suzanne. I listened as Tom listed off her good points, which were apparently endless. He told me of her family, her friends, her childhood, what she did in the morning, in the afternoon, and at night. At several points I grew so bored hearing about her that I tried to change the subject. But somehow he always got back to it. Everything Tom said was filtered through a 'Suzanne says.' By listening to him you'd think the girl had an opinion on everything in the world. I wanted to ask what Suzanne thought about Mom not coming to the wedding but I didn't dare. Tom hadn't mentioned our mother, and I got the feeling anything I said about the subject would be quickly passed over.

We stopped at the second gas station because I needed to use the bathroom. We had less than an hour left on our journey, and when I got back in the car, I saw that Tom had opened the envelope my mother had given him. It lay again between us, not referred to. I wanted to ask what was in it, but hoped Tom would volunteer the information. When he didn't, after driving for ten minutes in silence, I could no longer help myself. I asked him about it.

"See for yourself," he said. I took the envelope and Tom turned on the dome light for me. I forced open the top of the envelope and withdrew its contents. Upon looking at the first page of the thick document I knew what it was, though I had never before laid eyes on a deed.

"She's giving it to you?" I asked in amazement.

Tom shrugged and said quietly, "I guess so."

I slipped the deed back into the envelope and laid it once again between us. If Tom was happy my mother had relented and given him the deed to our grandfather's house he wasn't showing it. We drove the rest of the way into Kentville barely speaking to each other. Tom was lost in thought.

"Well," I said. "At least now you have a place to live. Suzanne will be happy."

"I suppose so," he said.

"Where do you think she had it hid all these years?" I was remembering Billy's frantic search. I didn't expect Tom to know, but he surprised me with an answer.

"It was under his mattress, along with the keys to the Thunderbird."

"What?"

Tom nodded. "I found them about a month after he left. I was looking for a shell from my gun that rolled under yours and Billy's bed. I saw the keys and deed then, duct taped to the underside of the bed spring. I guess Mom figured it was the only place he wouldn't look for them."

I laughed aloud at this. Tom didn't crack a smile. In fact, he seemed troubled, but when I asked him what was wrong he wouldn't answer. Perhaps he was wondering what could have caused in my mother this sudden change of heart.

⌒

Even on the weekend of his wedding Tom was spoiling for a hunt. He'd taken my father's gun with him, stored away under an old blanket in the trunk of his car. The morning after we arrived in Kentville we woke up early in the house of Tom's in-laws and took the car to the edge of town, to go hunting for pheasant in an orchard of apple trees. I had barely slept the night before, partly due to the strange bed, but mostly because Tom was in the same room with me and we spent a good portion of the night talking like we used to. Only now the conversation centred almost entirely on Suzanne. Tom's new in-laws had strong superstitions when it came to weddings, and Tom wasn't allowed to see the bride before the big day. So she stayed with a cousin on the other side of town and Tom and I stayed at her parents' place. Tom was complaining to me the next morning, as we left the car parked along the edge of a dirt road and climbed down into a ditch and up the other side into the orchard, that he couldn't even call Suzanne on the phone.

"I thought it was bad luck to see her," Tom said. "I didn't know it was bad luck to talk to her too."

"Maybe things are different up here," I suggested. "Maybe up here it's bad luck to have contact with a bride in general."

Tom was dismissive of that. "Isn't no different here than anywhere. The rule has always been the same. Bad luck seeing, not talking to."

I didn't argue, but I was of the opinion that Kentville was as different from the Cape as it possibly could be. I knew this when I got up that morning in the Carey house and looked out the kitchen window at the splendour I'd been unable to see the night before. Kentville sat at the head of the Annapolis Valley. From the Carey house you could look out onto the North Mountain. By Rockies standards, North Mountain in the Annapolis Valley is little more than a colossal hill, but to me it was exactly what it said it was. I looked up at its green flanks, shrouded in early morning fog, stretching across to form the north rim of the valley, and wondered if I could get Tom to take me up there over the next few days. The town, flanked by these high hills, its outskirts crowded with apple orchards in full bloom, reminded me of a fairy kingdom. I had heard of the valley, but had not realized it was so beautiful.

As the sun burned away the ground fog and dried the grass in the orchard, Tom and I got a chance to see the blossoms up close. Each tree was heavy with them. They nodded and conferred with each other in the morning breeze, so many you would almost think it had snowed. Even Tom, hunting through this tiny paradise for a pheasant to shoot, didn't spoil the mood for me. He shot three before he called it enough. Two he caught sleeping in the trees and shot unceremoniously off their flower-laden branches. The other we flushed as we walked. We gathered the dead birds, tied their feet together with twine brought for that purpose, threw them in the trunk of the Charger, and drove back to the Carey house.

Tom and I couldn't imagine living in a family like Suzanne's. First of all, it was so much bigger than ours. She had four brothers and six sisters — so many that Tom couldn't keep track of them all. There was Mariah, Bonny, Sharon, Dorothy, Candice, and Melanie, Ted, Ronald, Brian, and Archibald. I'm not even sure where Suzanne fit age-wise among this group — somewhere in the middle, I think. Some of the clan lived at home at the time of Tom and Suzanne's wedding, but most did not. None, however, lived very far away. The Carey house, though bigger than ours, was crowded and always noisy. Someone always seemed to be coming or going. There was always an event among one of the children, something that had to be prepared for. Always two or three different conversations going on and food being cooked. It was always somebody's birthday. The weekend of Tom's wedding was apparently more chaotic than usual. Everyone was home preparing for the celebration. Tom and I were accepted into the fray without reservation. Tom knew most of them and they treated him like a brother. Everyone asked his advice about everything. Even the father, David Carey, took time with Tom, offering him drinks that he never took himself, and asking questions about hunting and Tom's work.

Mr. Carey was a small man who, in the entire time I was there, never removed the white apron he wore all day in the dry goods shop. Balding, with glasses, he revealed an overly white set of false teeth every time he smiled, which was often. He removed his teeth to drink his tea, setting them temporarily aside on his saucer. Looking at such a small, unassuming man, you were surprised he had it in him to create all those children. The family alone could have populated a small town, with all the grandchildren running around.

For two days these kids, most of them younger than me, though one or two my age, led me around town. We played in orchards and on hay wagons, in barns and in a neighbour's cider house, though we were warned to stay away from the actual presses, which Suzanne's mother considered somehow dangerous.

Much of our time was spent travelling to and from the store to gather things mother and daughters needed for the wedding. We travelled in packs, and for the life of me I couldn't tell you the names of the children I played with over those days. I was unused to children of any age. The few friends I had in school I didn't play with once classes were over. I was shy around other children in general. But these kids didn't seem to mind. They included me in everything, and one or two of them, the eldest, immediately befriended me.

Those few days were a whirlwind of activity, and after that first morning I saw Tom rarely and Suzanne not at all. I understood why she stayed at her cousin's. Had she been at home, she would never have gotten a thing done! At night some of the family went to their respective houses, though many more stayed. There was some drinking, though not much. Laughter and conversation abounded.

The Careys, I discovered, were a musical family and on the second night, the Friday, out came guitars and fiddles and harmonicas. Impromptu performance arose from this, with the men playing and the girls singing. The Carey girls had sweet voices, and three of them, Dorothy (Dot for short), Bonnie, and Melanie, had made quite a name around town singing at local variety concerts. They billed themselves as the Carey Sisters, and it was the opinion of the family and town in general that these three would be as famous as the Andrew Sisters some day. At one point in the evening they got up and sang, "The Streets of Laredo" in exquisite three-part harmony. For once the rest of the large family quieted, and by the time they finished to riotous applause I too was convinced, by the hurtful aching feeling inside, that someday these three would be stars.

I went to bed that night exhausted, my ears still ringing with conversations and songs from the evening. More than once I caught myself wishing I'd never have to leave the valley. I hoped that this family would adopt me, and I felt extremely jealous of Tom that he would now be a part of it. I swore to myself that despite the secret desire I had for men, I would grow up and marry one of these girls, perhaps one of the grandchildren, so that I too could be a member of this wonderful family.

⌒

During our entire stay no one mentioned our mother. Even Dot and Mrs. Carey didn't ask about her when they helped me get ready for the wedding on Saturday. Instead they asked questions about the Cape itself, and my school, and what Tom had been like when he was younger.

"I think it's sweet," said Mrs. Carey, while she was ironing the pants of my suit (one of Ron's lent to me for the day), "that you're standing up for your brother, Luke. Archibald stood up for Ron when he got married, and Melanie was the maid of honour at Bonnie's wedding."

"Yeah, well," I said. "Billy might have done it, but he's in Toronto now."

"Really?" said Dot, who sat with me at the kitchen table and was busy polishing a pair of shoes, also lent to me from Mrs. Carey's collection of clothes outgrown by her sons. I sat between Dorothy and her mother, unused to such attention and nervously squirming in my seat. I wanted to help but I honestly didn't know what to do. It was one of those rare moments in the Carey house when no one was around but us three. Everyone was either upstairs resting or already gone to the reception hall to lay out the food and put up the last-minute decorations. Mrs. Carey and Dot told me to just sit and relax. I'd have plenty to do at the wedding when I got up in front of all those people, they said.

At the wedding rehearsal that morning I found what I had to do was relatively easy — just pass the rings to the Reverend when he asked for them. Tom kept the rings in his pocket, afraid I'd lose them, and said he'd give them to me just before we started. I was nervous about this, but not terribly so. More of a concern to me was the fact that I had only one more night before I had to go home. Etta, Roland, and Uncle Joe had driven up that morning as promised. They called from their motel, and Mrs. Carey assured them that everything was ready. The day was bright and not too warm. So far everything was going well, and I had only to get dressed in my suit in order to be ready.

"What does your brother do in Toronto?" Dot asked me, finishing one shoe and moving on to the other.

"He's a writer," I said, thinking of nothing else to say, though I had no clear idea whether Billy had written a word after he left home or not.

"Really?" said Mrs. Carey. "What does he write, Luke?"

"Well," I said evasively, "he just writes stories, I guess." The thing was, I didn't know what Billy wrote. He'd never let Tom or me read anything. I'd only said 'writer' because I knew of nothing else to say. I couldn't very well tell Mrs. Carey and Dot that Billy was a pool player.

"Well," said Dot, sensing my reluctance, "I'm sure he's very good at it, whatever he does. It's just too bad he couldn't be at the wedding."

I thought for sure they would ask me about my mother then. Surely they must have thought it strange, or had Tom already explained the situation? He must have, or they guessed the problem, for they didn't say a word about it. I couldn't imagine a member of this family missing anyone's wedding. If there was a toenail cutting in the family, I thought, they would all be present. It seemed to me that these people had perfect lives. There were some problems, of course. Archibald, for example, drank a little too much, and had come downstairs that morning with a bruised cheek from a fight at the tavern the night before that he couldn't remember. There had been some fuss over it, and a stern warning from David Carey to his son about drinking. But it could hardly be taken seriously by anyone, since the old man had made it while drinking his tea and so was toothless at the time. But even a perfect family has to have one black sheep, and Archibald was the youngest boy, only eighteen, a year younger than Tom. Secretly I was of the opinion that he'd got into the fight over his name. With a name like Archibald he probably got into a lot of scuffles, I thought.

But even Archie was an attendant at the wedding, bruises and all. None of the Carey boys were especially handsome. Tom and Billy were far better looking. Of the girls Suzanne was the prettiest, though Bonnie came a close second, being the only other member of the family with the red hair that gave Suzanne some of her glow.

All of them gathered together at the church were quite a sight. The children, and their children, plus the other relatives from town took up practically one whole side of the church. On the groom's side sat Etta, Roland, Uncle Joe, and Mike MacNeil, Tom's friend, who had driven up alone for the event. So the difference wouldn't be so noticeable, Mrs. Carey had reserved only one row on the groom's side for family, and filled the rest of the pews with guests from town. The church was crammed full, and the wooden overhead fans toiled ceaselessly to send cool air down on our heads. But the sun pouring in through the tall stained glass windows, with all those bodies packed in so tightly together, made it unbearably hot despite the relative April cool of the day outside. Even before the service began, many men had loosened their ties and opened the collars of their shirts. Standing up in front of the crowd I couldn't do so, and sweat poured in rivulets down the back of my neck, soaking my own collar.

Standing before the congregation, next to a garrison of

bridesmaids in peach-coloured flounced dresses, I was struck with a paralyzing nervousness. I became painfully aware that of the crowd of strangers sitting behind me in the pews, staring at my back, I knew only a handful. Once, when I turned to scan the crowd, Etta gave me a wave and a smile, and so did Uncle Joe, who looked like he was just coming off a drunk or beginning one. But this didn't help. I thought the organist, playing softly while the guests were directed to their seats by Suzanne's male cousins, standing as Tom's groomsmen, would never launch into the wedding march. When she finally did, holding heavily onto those first notes while her feet wildly pumped the foot pedals, I heard a sudden concert of creaking pews and the rustle of clothing as the entire congregation stood up behind me. Tom turned around, and I followed his lead. Suzanne swept into the church trailed by more bridesmaids in peach dresses. She wore the traditional white gown, though everyone already knew she was pregnant.

"Here she is," Tom said breathlessly, and I knew he was capable of speaking no more. Suzanne was beautiful, all white lace and delicate veil, and I wondered at that moment if my mother had looked like this on her wedding day. I could not imagine it.

As Suzanne passed, the congregation made the usual whispered comments to each other about how beautiful she looked, and I supposed had cameras been allowed in the church there would have been a fusillade of flashbulbs firing. But Mrs. Carey hadn't wanted cameras in church. She was afraid the flashes of light would blind her daughter and cause her to trip in her gown. Suzanne told me later that, even without cameras, she felt exactly like a movie star.

"Can you imagine?" she said to me. "Feeling that way every time you go out of your house?" She laughed. "I think I'd spend all my time throwing up."

By the time the bride reached the altar the congregation had seated themselves again, with more noise than they'd made in standing up. The Reverend launched into his sermon. It was a short wedding. Any longer and I think some of us would have fainted in the heat. I performed my part flawlessly, producing the rings when asked for them and managing to place them in Tom's outstretched hand without mishap. A few tears were shed on Suzanne's side of the family, and before I knew it the whole thing was over. Tom and Suzanne walked out of the church, under fire from the usual mini-projectiles, rice and confetti, and the crowd headed across the church common to the hall rented for the evening. Etta, Joe, and Roland found me just outside the church and rescued me from a crowd of strangers.

"Luke," called Etta, forcing herself through a crowd of guests to kneel down and give me a great hug. "You looked good up there, young buck."

"Thanks," I said. "Where's Roland and Uncle Joe?"

"Right here," Etta said. They came up behind her. Uncle Joe was drinking something out of a paper cup, probably whiskey, and Roland was imbibing with him.

"It was a damn good wedding!" Joe shouted, and I realized at last he was just beginning his drunk instead of ending it. His face was flushed red, though for once he was clean-shaven, and the suit he wore wasn't too creased. It was the same threadbare suit that he'd worn to my father's funeral.

"Congratulations, Luke," said Roland shyly.

"What are you congratulating him for?" said Etta. "He isn't the one who tied the knot, you old fool!"

Embarrassed, Roland took a quick sip of whatever was in his cup and looked away. Etta turned back to me.

"So your mother didn't come after all, did she?" she said.

"No Etta," I answered her.

She took my hand. "Come on," she said. "Let's go to the reception. I feel like tying one on tonight."

"Good stuff!" hollered Uncle Joe, and turned away so fast we lost him in the crowd. Etta, Roland, and I followed, though before long Roland got separated from us as well.

"Don't worry," Etta said. "We'll catch up."

"Etta?"

"Hmmmm?" Etta was on her tiptoes looking over the tops of heads, trying to see her husband as everyone crowded through the open doors of the reception hall. "What?" she said absently.

"Did you have a big family when you lived in Scotland?"

Etta looked down at me, wondering what I was getting at, but couldn't answer before the crowd surged forward behind us and we were carried along in the crush. When we got inside, she pulled me to one corner of the already crowded room. "We'll wait for Roland here. Now what was it you said to me?"

"Did you have a big family in Scotland?" I repeated.

"Not that big," she said. "There was six of us. Now why do you ask?"

"Did you ever have fun together? All of you?"

"Why sure we did," Etta said with a puzzled smile. "Why wouldn't we?"

I only shrugged and said no more. Etta tried to get more out of me, but couldn't. I looked around at the crowd. Some of the Carey girls had already gotten out on the centre of the floor, had kicked off their shoes and were dancing in their sock feet, though the band hadn't yet set up on the stage. The boys were gathered together in one corner, drinking punch and laughing with the guests. David Carey was chief among them, his false teeth already out of his head while he sipped on his paper cup of spiked punch and talked with his grown sons. Etta and I stood to one side, she still holding my hand, and waited for Roland. We were out of the way, and no one spoke to us. We watched Uncle Joe work the room. Occasionally we'd see him in the midst of a crowd of people laughing at the stories he told. Even drunk, my Uncle Joe was a passable storyteller.

Of all the nights of my childhood I remember that one best. Yet there is so little to say of it. Uncle Joe got roaring drunk, and halfway through the night got up on stage and danced the Oldsport Jig, and though I was embarrassed and Etta called him a "drunk old fool," no one seemed to mind. They even applauded politely when he was done. Tom and Suzanne stayed only part of the evening. Early on Suzanne changed out of her wedding dress, and Tom out of his suit, and at one point they danced a plainclothed waltz for us. But halfway through, the impatient crowd surged onto the dance floor. Somehow I ended up dancing with the bride, she taller than me by a foot.

"Are you having fun?" she asked me. Her breath smelled of spearmint and whiskey, a strange combination, but lovely to me.

"Yes," I shouted over the band. "It's great."

"It is, isn't it?" said Suzanne, and before I could say more, someone broke in and danced her away. Before midnight the bride and groom left in their getaway car. The Carey boys had plastered it with Just Married signs and flowers fashioned from Kleenex, and had tied tin cans to the rear bumper with string. We all gathered outside to watch, though the couple had to drive only twelve miles in the car to get to the Old Orchard Inn. They drove away amidst a crowd of people wishing them farewell and shouting as if they were taking a journey to the far side of the earth. After they'd driven off, we drifted back inside and the band struck up again, and we danced and drank and laughed with each other into the wee hours of the morning. I didn't drink, as my mother had asked. Etta kept a close eye on my glass to make sure I kept to the unspiked punch. Eventually, when everyone was drunk, or exhausted, or both, the hall began to empty. I wasn't staying at the Careys that night. Etta and Roland and Joe had asked that I sleep with them in their motel room so we could get an early start in the morning, but everyone managed to say goodbye to me when we left. Mrs. Carey kissed me on both cheeks, and gave me a hug, though I barely knew her.

"You make sure Tom brings you back up around here soon," she told me. "You tell your mother you can stay with us any time you like."

"Alright," I said. "I'd like that."

She kissed me again and we parted. The five-minute drive back to the motel was quiet. Etta was tired, she said, and Roland as usual said nothing. Uncle Joe had passed out in the back seat beside me. I suddenly became depressed. Tomorrow I would be going home again, and this new part of my life would be over as quickly as it had started. I didn't doubt I'd get to see the Careys again. I planned on begging Tom to take me back and I was pretty sure he would. But the change I'd felt that afternoon was still with me. It was the first time I'd seen how other families behaved, how perhaps families were supposed to behave. I was struck then by the beginnings of what was to become a familiar resentment and anger, a deep and bitter envy that life could be like this for others and not for me.

SACRED PRINCIPLES

~

$\mathcal{I}$ remember the years after Tom's marriage and his move to the house on Gaston Road as a time of short, barely sustained conversations — long nights spent in the kitchen with only the whisper of my pen on paper, the clink of my mother's tea cup against her saucer, and no other sounds. Tom, aware of the boredom I was suffering, tried to convince my mother to get a television.

"Everyone has them," he told her. "Suzanne and I bought one almost as soon as we were married. Why don't you get one too?"

"Where am I gonna get the money for that foolishness?" my mother answered. But money wasn't the issue. Tom offered to buy her one. She didn't want it.

"I don't believe in them," she said, but would elaborate no further. I believed in them. I spent nights with Etta and Roland

195

watching *The Twilight Zone, Bonanza, The Rowan and Martin Show,* and *Don Messer's Jubilee.* These nights I looked forward to eagerly, not simply for the shows themselves but for the chance to get out from under the oppressive umbrella of my mother's moods. I was never much for making friends in school. There were only twelve students in my class in Grade Eleven, most of whom I had spent my entire school career with. We got along and some of them, I suppose, were my friends, at least on school grounds. But my mother always demanded my presence after school, to help her with chores, and I never dared invite any of them home. Saturdays and Sundays I could have spent with kids from town, but I almost always chose to spend the weekend with Tom and Suzanne at my grandfather's house. At first my mother didn't want me to go there. Tom and Suzanne were newlyweds, and she assured me they wouldn't want me around. But Tom insisted it was alright. It became routine for him to pick me up after supper every Friday night with a promise to return me in plenty of time on Sunday so I could help bring in the wood for the following week.

In the fall Tom and I hunted together. With age I got over my fear of shooting deer, but he preferred to hunt for those himself anyway. We hunted partridge, and rabbit when the snow was down. There were no pheasant in our part of the province — they were plentiful, as far as we knew, only in the Annapolis Valley. But Tom struck on an idea. He arranged with Suzanne's brothers to snare a large clutch of pheasants and carry them down to our part of the province in the back of David Carey's truck, with a tarpaulin thrown over the cage to fool the birds into thinking it was night. Everyone, even Suzanne, thought it was a stupid idea.

"Don't you have enough innocent creatures down here to kill?" she asked.

My mother, when she heard of it, was her usual dismissive self. "I've never seen anyone as fool for a gun as that boy."

Even Suzanne's father, when he heard of Tom's plan, removed his hat and scratched his bald head thoughtfully. "Well, I dunno Tom," he said. "There might even be a law against it." But there was no law, and Tom was convinced that he could make the South Shore pheasant country.

"Have you ever thought," I asked him, "that there aren't any pheasant here for a reason? Maybe they can't live down here."

"Why not?" Tom asked. "There isn't nothing different about here than there."

I couldn't agree with my brother. As far as I was concerned the Annapolis Valley was as different from the Cape and the South Shore as could be. Yet Tom brought them down, and released them, nine hens and three cocks, in the woods behind his house. He made a promise to his wife that he wouldn't shoot them until the population had grown enough to make it worthwhile. He travelled a circumference of twenty miles to his few neighbours to elicit the same promise. Everyone agreed to wait two years before they started shooting. But what Tom hadn't thought of was that with no men to hunt them, and no natural predators in that part of the province, the birds, which weren't known for their intelligence, would become tame. In two years the pheasant population had grown so much that Tom's field was overrun with them. In the spring brown hens with orderly lines of chicks marshalled behind them filed to and fro past the front door. The cocks, regal and resplendent in brilliant tail feathers and iridescent green breasts, strutted their stuff on the front lawn. Tom cursed and wanted to shoot them anyway, but his wife wouldn't hear of it.

"They're tame!" she cried. "If you start shooting there'll be none left after a week." Tom knew she was right, though some of his neighbours shot them anyway. But at Tom's house the pheasants lived in no danger. Ironically, the home of my brother, the hunter, became a safe haven for these birds and his yard something of a pheasant reserve. He satisfied his resentment by kicking at them as he walked through his driveway, though they, knowing there was no real threat, only clucked lightly and moved jauntily away.

My brother's home became a sort of safe haven for me as well. It was as if I belonged to another family entirely, and though Suzanne was only six years my senior I sometimes pretended she was my mother. The three of us would eat lively dinners, take walks, play with the birds in the front yard, and spend nights in front of the TV. At some point during the weekend Tom and Suzanne would become amorous, their playful caressing on the living room sofa during Ed Sullivan turning heated. They would excuse themselves, wish me goodnight, and go upstairs to bed. I turned the volume on the TV up louder so I couldn't hear them, and it might be hours before I followed them up the stairs to sleep in my own room. How I wished that I lived with my brother at those times!

In the mornings I slept late. When I awoke breakfast was on the table, though Tom and Suzanne often had already eaten. I noticed that Tom did all the cooking and the cleaning. Suzanne talked to me or read books while he worked. In my ignorance I carried this fact to my mother, who used it as leverage against the girl she already disliked.

Only two short months after the marriage, Suzanne miscarried. The doctors didn't know why, and for several months I didn't see either of them while they recovered from the shock, made even worse for being so undramatic. Suzanne started bleeding heavily one afternoon. In the hospital that night they told her she would not have the child. They gave no reason, nothing that she and Tom could blame or hold on to. Incredibly, my mother blamed Suzanne for the miscarriage.

"She didn't act like a pregnant woman should. Running around, doing this or that. No wonder she lost it!"

She broached the subject only once with Tom, who exploded at her. "Don't you ever speak those words again!" he shouted. "If you ever say anything like that around Suzanne, we'll leave and we won't ever come around here again, you hear me?" He stalked out of the house and we didn't see him for two weeks. When he finally came back for a visit, my mother gave him tea and they talked of other things. Tom unthinkingly told Suzanne what my mother had said. She resolved never to lay eyes on our mother again. She never inquired after her and avoided any conversation that contained her name.

In the spring I landed a job as a packing boy in Robichaud's grocery. Robichaud always hired boys under the age of eighteen so he could pay them below minimum wage. I liked the job. It got me out of the house afternoons and Robichaud's store was air conditioned, so in the hottest part of the summer I actually looked forward to spending the day in the cool, quiet aisles of the supermarket. Robichaud himself put on a grim exterior. He never smiled, and bustled about the store as if we were always on the edge of some catastrophe. He shouted a lot, in French and in English, saying we were lazy and he should fire us all. But because his cashiers paid no attention to him whatsoever, I learned to do the same. Sometimes we wouldn't even stop our conversations when he came storming out of the office, shouting that something that needed to be done. Often you could call his bluff. He'd be in the midst of bellowing out orders, and seeing no one was listening would stop and shake his head.

"You're no good," he'd say. "A bunch of lazy workers."

Then he'd go quietly back to his office until the next time.

Because I worked on Saturdays I didn't spend as much time at Tom and Suzanne's that summer. When winter came I stayed on at Robichaud's after school and on weekends and saw even less of them. When not working I was drawing. I'd always been a doodler. Even when my father was alive and I was barely able to walk, he'd tear off a piece of mill paper from the roll in our front porch and hand me a pencil. Teachers had been noticing and encouraging my ability since Grade Five, and pictures I had drawn with school markers, crayons, and pencils were left hanging on the walls of every classroom long after I'd moved on to another grade.

The two things I liked to draw most were landscapes and people. I obsessed for hours over both, but never combined them. My drawings of the ocean and beach in front of my house were devoid of life, and my people — sketches of my family, my classmates, even portraits of Robichaud and his daughters drawn from memory after work — hung suspended on white backgrounds without place or time to ground them.

Tom bought me my first easel and paints and gave them to me on Christmas Day at Etta's. Suzanne hadn't come because her own family was visiting. My mother hadn't come over either. She'd said she had work to do. I had no idea any of it was coming, and I didn't know what to make of the gift — a white board wrapped in plastic, and a few cans of primary colour oil paints and an easel built out of unfinished strips of pine. I'd never seen an easel before. All my drawing had been done with pencil on mill paper.

"What is it?" I asked them, after I'd opened it and they all stood around beaming at me.

Tom laughed. "It's what you wanted, isn't it? It's a paint set."

I couldn't say anything for a while, and everyone grew very quiet. "What's the matter?" Tom said. "Don't you like it?"

"I like it," I said. I was unable to say more. The easel set, cheaply made, would have been scoffed at by a real artist. The paints were cheap as well. There was no canvas. Etta had thought to tear off a piece of mill paper from a roll kept in the sunporch to start me off. But it was, and remains, the greatest Christmas present I ever received.

"I want to go use it," I said, jumping up and tucking the easel under one arm and the white board under the other.

"Now?" said Etta. "You'll catch your death of cold, boy. It's twenty below out there."

"Doesn't matter," I said. "I want to start."

I carried my easel and paints outside. Etta, Tom, and Roland followed me and I set up at the head of Etta's cape. Etta was right. It *was* cold. I fumbled with gloved hands to place the board properly on the easel. We fastened the flimsy mill paper to the easel with clothespins fetched from a bucket in Etta's sunporch. Then they all stood back and let me go. I didn't mix the paints. I didn't know how, never having worked with them before, but that would come. Yet I knew as soon as I started that this was what I was meant to do. From the first tentative brush stroke across the blank paper, that first nervous slash of blue, I was home. A peace settled over me, and I no longer felt the cold, the wind or even the presence of those behind me. I didn't rush. I laid my three colours on carefully, layering them, gently creating before me a world of colour where none had existed before. Time stopped. Etta, Roland, and Tom slipped away out of the wind, leaving me to create my first real work of art. Two hours later I sheepishly returned, the easel and the still drying work under my arm. The sunlight was leaking out of the sky, and Tom was ready to go home and be with Suzanne and her family. They were all anxious to see the finished product.

"Well, it's about time," said Etta. "You must be freezing your privates off."

"No," I mumbled. "Not really."

"Well," said Tom excitedly. "Let's see it!"

They all waited while I set up the easel again. I was cautious — nervous, but thrilled too. I wanted them to see it and I did not want them to see it. I would grow accustomed to that feeling of ambivalence around showing my work — every artist does, I suppose. Back then I knew only that my work was not done. This baring of it, the search for approval, was part of it as well. Finally I positioned my painting the way I wanted it and stepped back. Their praise came immediately.

"I like it," said Tom. "I really do."

"Yes," agreed Etta. "It's very good. Roland, what do you think?"

"Good job, Luke," Roland said heartily.

And even though they talked about it some more, comparing it to other paintings they didn't know the titles of and barely remembered seeing, I felt a growing disappointment in their response. I wished they could feel when they looked at it what I felt when I painted it. It was a simple work, my first, though hardly my last, painting of the ocean. But in that simple work was everything I knew. My love of the ocean. My fear of it. My inability to articulate either except through this means. There was every emotion I knew at that young age, expressed in colour and form, and it became apparent to me after hearing only a few of their comments that I had failed. I hadn't transferred the passion I'd felt to the paper. I became uncomfortable having the painting exposed to them and put it away.

"Don't worry," Etta said when I expressed my feelings in confidence later. "It's your first try. You'll get it right one day."

I nodded, and made the resolution that I would do it over and over again until I finally did get it. I didn't know then that it was at that moment, and not at the moment I applied brush to paper, that I became an artist. I also didn't know that in becoming one, I would discover years later what all artists know. We get better, but we never really get it right.

I got drunk for the first time at the end of that winter. Friends from school planned it weeks before, and Uncle Joe bought us the booze. We gave him enough to get us two pints of lemon gin and himself a pint of rye. He even offered to drink with us. "I can show ya how," he said, laughing at our inexperience. We told him we preferred to do it by ourselves. After work that Friday night we picked up the bottles, hidden under cast-off boxes behind the grocery, and headed for the seclusion of Stone Mountain Bluff. From the top of the bluff you could see the entire town, set out below us like on a map. But on the lee side of the hill we were completely hidden from view. The only way anyone could see us was from the sea, and we were too high up to be made out clearly by the boats coming back from a day's fishing.

I remember little of our times up there. We were laughing one minute, and trying to have a serious discussion the next. Everything we said took on an earth-shattering importance. I finally staggered home after twelve — drunk-sick and unsteady, but sober enough to know my mother would be waiting for me. She was out of her chair before I even got in the door.

"Where in the hell have you been? It's after twelve o'clock."

"Out," I said.

"What were you doing out at this hour?"

"Nothing," I said gruffly. "Just out." I didn't feel like arguing with my mother. I felt so bad I wanted only to crawl into bed and sleep. But she walked over, stood in front of me, and sniffed at my clothes like some kind of trained animal while I was removing my shoes on the mat.

"You've been drinking. I can smell it on you."

"So?" I said. I kicked my last shoe off and started through the kitchen for the stairs.

"Where do you think you're going?" she said to me.

"To bed. Where else?"

"Who else was drinking with you?"

"Goodnight."

"Hold on right there, Luke," she commanded. Tiredly, I stopped and turned around to hear another one of her lectures.

"That's it for you and those kids from town," she said. "You're not hanging around them any more. No son of mine is going to run around this town drunk all the time. Do you want to turn out like your Uncle Joe?"

"It's not anyone's fault," I said calmly. "No one forced anything down my throat."

"Just the same," she said. "You're not hanging around them any more."

"Yes I am," I said quietly. "I'll do whatever it is I damn well please." The lingering effects of the alcohol were giving me courage perhaps, or I was too exhausted to feel fear. My mother, I could tell, was surprised by my statement. I had never before spoken up to her. From Billy she'd been used to it, even from Tom, but I think my sudden rebellion confused her, though she shook it off in a second.

"I mean it," she said. "You won't be living here if you don't live by my rules."

I shrugged, so tired and sick now I could have just lain on the floor and slept. I had heard this a million times when Tom and Billy were home. "Then I guess I won't be living here," I said.

Before I could register what she was about to do and move to protect myself, she brought up her hand and slapped me hard across the face. The blow sobered me entirely.

"That's for talking back," she said calmly, as if her sudden action had won the argument. "Now get upstairs to bed. I'll deal with you in the morning."

I had begun to turn automatically away and do as I was told. So often this was the way arguments ended with her. Her hands and not her tongue gave the final word. I might even have let it go, if she hadn't said to me, "What would your father think if he saw you now?"

I whirled on her, hardly aware of what I was about to do. "What would he think!" I shouted. "And what do you care! You act like you never liked him anyway. All you ever do is run him down, say he was no good at this or that, and how you're so much better at it! What would he think if he saw you hitting me all the time?" I screamed. "What would he think about you not even going to Tom's wedding!"

My mother was so shocked her face drained of colour. She took one step backward before forcing herself to stop. But one step was all I needed. It was more than I'd ever achieved before. "You're drunk," she said. "You be quiet right now."

"I won't!" I took one lurching step towards her. I *was* drunk. My mother was right. But I also felt it was freeing me. I felt my whole angry history roar up inside of me.

"I don't have to listen to you," I shouted. "Why should I? You don't care about me. You don't care about any of us. You drove Billy out, and you drove Tom out. Suzanne won't even come and visit us. And now you're trying to drive me out too!"

"Get out," my mother hissed, as if she hadn't heard anything I'd said. "Get out of this house and don't you ever come back!"

"I hate you!" I bent over and scooped up my shoes. "I hate

you and I'll be glad to get away from here! You fucking bitch!"

"Get out!" she screamed again, and reached for the broom leaning against the wall. She swung it wildly at me, though because I was bending over putting on my shoes it whistled over my head. I jumped up and ran out into the night in my sock feet, a shoe dangling from each hand. My mother followed me to the front stoop.

"Don't you come back," she screamed, her voice shattering the silence of the Cape. "You ungrateful little bastard!"

I didn't stop running until I was halfway down the Cape road, past Etta's place, and into the long stretch of field before you hit the secondary road that leads into town. It was far enough for me. I could no longer hear her screaming. I sat down on the side of the road, and went to put on my shoes over torn and dirty socks. I realized suddenly that I'd lost one. It must have slipped out of my hand while I was running. I put one shoe on and stood up, took a few steps along the road. Walking with only one shoe was uncomfortable, and I sat down and took it off again. Then I peeled off my socks, stuffed them into the remaining shoe, turned around, and threw the shoe blindly into the field. I stood there, looking after it, wondering where it had landed and if I would ever find it, or the other one, again. Already my feet were getting cold. It occurred to me they were the only shoes I owned. The thought that I'd thrown my last shoe into the field where it might never be found struck me as funny. I only started chuckling at first, but pretty soon I was laughing so hard I had to sit down again in the grass to keep from falling over. When the laughter and the sudden, unexplained elation wore off, I felt the wind and shivered. I'd left without my jacket. There was no chance I was going back to get it. I had no clothes, no money, and no place left to go. I could have walked back to Etta's. She would have understood and taken me in for the night, but I didn't want to wake her. Instead I crept back to the house, making sure all the lights were out and my mother had gone to bed. Covering myself with an old piece of tarpaulin, I curled up like a dog in a corner of the barn and tried to sleep.

We hate her, I heard Billy say from somewhere in my past. *We'll never leave you alone Luke.* But they had left me alone with her. Billy. Tom. Even my father.

I awoke in the morning with dew on my face — cold, hungry and miserable. I judged from the quality of light and the fog not yet burned off in the sun that it was still early, perhaps only shortly after sunrise. I got up from where I lay on an old piece of cardboard. My legs were stiff. As soon as I stood, the muscles in one of them cramped painfully. I reached for the spot with both arms, crying aloud and hobbling around until the pain passed. When I could walk normally again I crept out of the barn. I didn't even look at my mother's house. I went straight across the Cape to Etta's front door. I pounded on it for several minutes until Roland came out, in his underwear and half asleep. He registered no surprise when he saw me.

"Luke," he said. "You're up early."

"Is Etta home?" I asked.

Roland scratched his head and yawned. "Sure she is. But she's in bed."

"Can I come in?" I asked him.

Roland stepped aside to let me in. He offered me a chair and said he'd wake Etta up.

"I guess the old woman has slept long enough anyway." The clock above the stove said it was twenty after six. I wondered if my mother was up already, and if she'd seen me come over to Etta's house. I didn't care. I waited quietly until I heard Etta's footsteps on the stairs.

"Luke!" she said, coming into the kitchen still wearing her housecoat, her hair done up in curlers. I'd never seen Etta in curlers before. I didn't even know she used them. Her hair had never looked curly to me. It had always looked as straight as a board. "What in the world are you doing here this time in the morning?"

"Where's Roland?" I asked shyly.

"He went back to bed," she said. "You woke us up."

"I'm sorry."

"So, what are you doing out of bed at this hour?"

"Mom kicked me out."

"This morning?"

"No, last night."

"You mean you've been outside all night?" Etta was shocked. "Where did you sleep?"

"In the barn."

Etta looked at me, shook her head, and said, "That woman!"

"Etta? Can you make me something to eat?"

She fried me two eggs, and made toast and tea. She didn't eat anything herself, but sat watching me. She didn't press me to tell her what had happened, and while I ate I didn't volunteer the information. I hadn't realized how hungry I was. I cleaned the plate in no time at all. When I finished she took the plate from me and poured me some more tea from the pot on the stove. This time she took a cup herself, and when the two cups sat steaming on the table she looked straight at me. "So? Are you gonna tell me what all this is about?"

"I guess so," I said, and preceded to tell her how my mother got mad because I didn't come home after work, and the things

I said to her, and the fight. When I finished Etta shook her said and repeated, "That woman."

"I don't wanna go back there," I told Etta.

Etta looked at me frankly. "Where will you go?"

I shrugged, then quietly, while looking at the floor, said, "I thought maybe I could live with you and Roland."

She didn't answer right away, and I didn't dare look up at her. I realized when I told Etta the story of what happened the night before that I didn't want to live with my mother any longer. I could no longer stand those quiet nights, the silent accusation. Without Tom and Billy I was no match for her. If Etta didn't let me stay, I decided, I would leave. I had no idea where I wanted to go, but I knew I wanted to get away, and that was enough.

"Luke," Etta said to me finally, "you know you'll have to go back. You're only sixteen, for God's sake."

"So what?" I muttered. "I'm sick of her trying to tell me what to do."

"That's her job, Luke," said Etta softly. "She's your mother."

"How come she had to drive Billy and Tom away? Is that her job too?"

Etta shook her head. "She didn't drive them away. Tom got married, and Billy always wanted to go to a city."

"Oh yeah?" I said, my voice rising. "How come Billy never writes then? And Suzanne won't even come down to visit. It's because of her! It's all her fault!"

"It may be some of her fault. But Billy was always a wild one. You know that. And Suzanne and your mother just don't get along."

"How would you like to live with her?" I shouted. "How would you like to live there? She don't even talk to me, and when she does she just runs me down. I'm tired of it, I tell you. I don't want to live there anymore!"

Etta sighed, and got up for more tea.

"I promise," I said, "if you let me stay here, I'll pay my way. I got a job. I won't be any trouble."

"Your mother would never allow it, Luke."

"You could tell her Etta," I said eagerly. "You could tell her you're gonna keep me."

Etta silently poured tea into our cups, and replaced the pot on the stove. We drank in silence. Etta asked me if I was tired.

"God yes," I said. "I hardly got any sleep outside."

"You go on up to the guest room then," she said. "We'll figure something out when you come down."

I did as she said. Etta came behind me to prepare the bed. It was a double, and I was unused to sleeping in such luxury. As I crawled under the covers, Etta helped pull them up over me, to my chin, then suddenly bent down and kissed me on the forehead.

"Sleep tight, Luke," she said. I stayed awake, listening to Etta downstairs in the kitchen preparing Roland's breakfast. When Roland went down I sat up and strained to hear them.

"I can't believe that woman," Etta was saying. "What trouble is Luke, now I ask you? The boy never gave anyone any problems that I could see. Now Billy I could understand her fighting with. Even Tom. But Luke? A sweeter kid you'd never find. That woman couldn't get along with Jesus Christ himself."

"What are you gonna do?" I heard Roland ask.

Etta didn't hesitate. "I'm going over and try to talk some sense into her, that's what I'm gonna do."

"Now don't you go getting Dora riled," said Roland. "It ain't none of our business, really."

"What ain't none of our business?" cried Etta. "I've been taking care of those kids since they were babies. For God's sake, I even helped birth Luke. And there she is, treating them like they were dirt again. Hitting Luke. He's right, you know. All that woman knows how to do is hit."

"It ain't none of our business," repeated Roland stubbornly.

"Maybe it ain't," Etta said. "But I'm damn well gonna make it my business."

There was a long silence between them, and I thought they had given up discussing, when I heard Roland ask, "What are you gonna do if she don't take him back?"

"He can live here," Etta said. "He can live here as long as he likes."

When I woke up and came downstairs, Etta was waiting for me at the kitchen table. Roland wasn't anywhere to be seen.

"He's gone to town for a little while," Etta told me.

"Did you go see Mom?" I asked her.

"Sit down," she said.

I sat, and she served me lunch. She asked me if I was going to work that afternoon.

"I have to, I guess."

"Good. Roland said he'd be home in time to give you a drive. Your mother said you work at three."

"Good."

I ate quietly, not daring to ask what had gone on between her and my mother. I could tell by her mood things had not gone well. Finally she said to me, "Your mother says you can stay here for awhile."

I nodded. "She doesn't want me back?"

"Not right now she doesn't."

"Is she still mad?"

"She's upset for you saying she drove Billy and Tom out."

"Why? It's true, you know."

Etta shrugged. "I don't know what's going through her mind.

All I know is she says she won't be supporting you. She says you'll have to make your own way."

"I got a job," I said. "I can pay my own way."

"What about school?"

I thought about it a long time. "I guess I'll quit, and go to work at Robichaud's full time. He's always saying he needs someone."

"You'll do no such thing," said Etta firmly. "If you're going to live under my roof, you'll get all the education you can handle, or you won't be living here at all."

I nodded, and kept eating. Etta's words, though reminiscent of my mother, gave me the verbal permission I already knew I had. I was going to live at Etta's, at least for awhile. After I finished eating, I helped with the dishes, and at two o'clock she chased me upstairs to get ready for work. Roland came home as promised, and waited while I changed into my work clothes. As I was leaving, Etta said to me at the door, "What time do you get finished?"

"Seven," I said.

"Roland will be waiting for you outside the store."

"That's okay," I said. "I can walk."

"I want to tell you, Luke: the same rules apply here as they did at your mother's. Right home from work, and right home from school. Roland will be waiting for you."

"Alright," I said, and left. When Roland and I walked out to the car, I looked over at my mother's house. I had never seen our house looking so small and rundown. It huddled on the bare Cape like a rabbit without shelter from the wind. I thought I caught my mother's shadow at the screen door, but I couldn't tell for sure. I felt no guilt. I felt no shame. I felt only relieved. At long last my dream had come true. I had another home.

I think neither Etta, Roland, nor my mother ever expected that I'd stay away so long. I believed I would stay there until my mother ordered me home one day, and Etta believed it would only be a few days until my mother cooled down. But winter ambled on into spring. A few days after I moved in, Etta retrieved for me my clothes, my toothbrush, and other necessities, and I didn't see my mother for months. Etta visited her, perhaps to talk about me, but she always came home without revealing a word of what had been said. Tom called the first night I was away, obviously informed of the situation by my mother. Etta called me to the phone.

"What happened?" he said, as soon as I got on the line.

"We had a fight."

"About what?"

"Nothing much," I said. "I didn't come home after work right away."

"That's all?"

"I guess I said some things I shouldn't have."

"Like what?"

"Things," was all I would say.

"You can stay out here," Tom said to me. "You shouldn't be bothering Etta and Roland with all of this."

"They don't seem to mind."

"Still," Tom said. "You can come out here if you want, is all I'm saying."

I thought about it. I would have liked to, but I couldn't see how I'd manage to get to school and work from there. I told Tom this.

"I guess you're right," he said. "Anyway, you won't be out long. She'll calm down some, and then you can go back."

"I don't want to go back."

"Why?"

"I hate her."

"Luke," said Tom quietly. "You shouldn't say those things."

I didn't say I learned to hate her because of Tom and Billy — that day we all lay in bed together after Mom beat us. If it hadn't been for Billy and Tom telling me they hated her, I never would have known it was allowed. But all I said was, "I know I shouldn't say it. But I'm saying it anyway."

"Yes, well," said Tom, obviously uncomfortable with my opinions. "Give me a call if you need anything. Do you want to come out next weekend?"

"I can't. I have to work."

"Oh. Okay. 'Bye Luke."

Tom began to split his visits between Etta's house and my mother's. He also never said what he talked about with my mother, though once I asked him if she ever asked about me.

"No," he said. "She doesn't."

"Not at all?"

"You know Mom, Luke."

I knew her, and the longer I stayed away the more determined I became not to go back even if she asked me to. Of course, it was becoming apparent that she wasn't going to ask me. Etta said she believed that if I were to ask I would be allowed, though my mother hadn't said as much. But I had, at least in part, inherited my mother's stubbornness. I wouldn't be the one to ask. Besides, I was having a great time at Etta and Roland's. I could watch television as long as I had my homework done. And meals between us were fun. At my mother's we ate in silence, and I always ate too fast (a habit I carry with me to this day) so I could simply get away from the table and out from under her critical eye. But at Etta's it was different. Etta, Roland, and I talked of anything and everything that came to mind, and we often stayed at the table and drank tea long after the meal was over. Sometimes Roland pulled out the cribbage board and we played three-handed for hours. Best of all, I could have people over. I invited a few friends from school, and we sat with Etta and Roland watching TV.

One Friday night Tom and Suzanne came down. Roland opened a quart of whiskey and poured drinks for everyone. Even Etta, who drank little, took one with hot water and honey. Roland wanted to pour me a fifth of a tumbler, but Etta wouldn't hear of it.

"You don't give a sixteen-year-old his first taste of liquor, Roland," she said. "You wanna be the one responsible for him liking it and ending up drunk every Saturday night?" I smiled secretly to myself, undisturbed by the denial. I'd sworn off alcohol. I didn't have Billy's taste for booze.

We ended up playing bid whist. Etta and Roland were partners against me and Tom. Suzanne, who was down on a rare visit, sat and watched and then traded off with me as Tom's partner. I went in to watch television while they played. Suzanne, taking a break, wandered in to see me.

"How are you making out?" she said to me from the doorway of the living room.

"Fine, I guess. Nothing much on."

"I mean with not living at home."

I shrugged again. "I like living here."

Suzanne smiled at me coyly. I'm sure, of all of them, she understood my position best. "Tom said you could stay with us if you want to."

"Yes," I said. "But I got school and stuff."

"I know," she said. "But school's almost over. Keep us in mind if this lasts."

"If I have my say," I told her, "it will last forever."

As I knew she wouldn't, Suzanne didn't say what everyone

else did — that my mother was bound to cool down eventually. Though she now occasionally went to my mother's with Tom for visits, they were typically short. Her tolerance for my mother and her ways had not increased at all over the years she and Tom had been married. Perhaps because of her own large family she had no need to try with my mother. Suzanne had all the family she would ever need. Though I'd talked many times of going back to Kentville to visit the Careys, I had never managed it. Suzanne went regularly, often for a week or more at a time. Sometimes Tom met her there on weekends, but I was always working and couldn't go. A couple of times Suzanne had me out when her parents or one or the other of her sisters or brothers were down. I asked Suzanne now if the next time she went, if I was free, I could go with her.

"Sure. Anytime, Luke. You know that."

"Suzanne!" Tom bawled from the kitchen. "Come back out here! We wanna play again!"

"You too Luke," shouted Etta. "No need for that noise box to be blaring! You can watch to your heart's content some other day."

The two of us trailed back out into the kitchen and took our places at the card table.

Amidst all the laughter and good natured bitching over the incompetence with which our partners played their cards, the phone rang. Roland went into the living room to answer it. Etta stopped playing only long enough to say, "I wonder who that could be at this hour?"

When Roland returned he said, "It's Dora. She wants to talk to Luke." The table grew abruptly silent, and everyone looked at me.

"Well," said Etta, when I didn't move from my chair. "Are you gonna answer it?"

"Why should I?" I said sullenly. "She probably figured out I was having fun and wants to put a stop to it." Everyone, even Etta, hid their smiles behind their hands and their cards.

"Go on now," Etta said. "Don't keep her waiting." Reluctantly I got up from the table and went into the living room. I picked up the receiver where Roland had set it down beside the phone, and lifted it to my ear. I could sense that everyone in the kitchen was straining to hear what was about to be said.

"Hello," I said softly.

"Luke," was my mother's quick reply. "What's going on over there?"

"Tom and Suzanne are here. We're playing cards."

"Oh," she said. "Well, I just got a call from Robichaud and he asked if you could come in early tomorrow."

"Okay," I said. "I'll call him tomorrow morning and tell him."

"Make sure you do. And don't be taking anything to drink over there, not that Etta would let you have any."

"I won't," I said, and before she could say anything else I hung up. When I went back into the kitchen they had resumed card playing, but the atmosphere wasn't as boisterous as before. I could tell they were all dying to know what my mother had wanted.

"So," said Tom, when I took my seat without volunteering the information. "What happened?"

"Robichaud called," I said glumly. "I have to work early tomorrow."

"Is that all?" said Etta laughing. "By the look on your face I thought she told you your house had just burned down." Everyone smiled at this, and Tom threw another card on the table and urged everyone to follow suit. I sat and watched. They didn't seem to understand what I did. In the past my mother had relayed all messages of this kind through Etta, so talking to me directly must have meant she would soon be wanting me to come home. There was also the way she warned me about not drinking, as if it had been two hours instead of five months since we'd last talked. I stayed quiet for the rest of the evening. I was even glad when Tom and Suzanne left. Etta knew something was going on, for as soon as Roland shuffled off to bed, she said to me as she was throwing away empty chip bags and washing up glasses: "It was strange for your mother to call, don't you think?"

"She wants me back," I said. "I know it."

"Probably," Etta answered. "It couldn't last, Luke. You knew that."

"I don't see why it couldn't," I said. "I don't see how we're not both better off with me here and her over there."

"I would imagine," Etta said, "that she needs you."

"She seems to get along okay," I said resentfully. "I see her splitting her own wood and doing the chores by herself."

"She might be lonely too. Your mother's not used to living by herself in that house. She's always had someone in it with her."

"It's her own fault," I said stubbornly. "And if she makes me go back I'm getting out of that house as soon as I can."

Etta stopped what she was doing and looked at me. "Do you hate her that much?"

"Yes."

Etta shook her head, and sighed. "I don't understand you," she said finally. "But if she wants you back, neither you nor I can stop her. You'll just have to live with it until you can see your way to going somewhere else." With that Etta, tired from the long evening, went to bed, drawing a promise from me that I wouldn't stay up too late. I sat in the kitchen with all the lights off thinking of what Etta had said. She didn't understand my mother either. Etta, like many before her, thought that beneath my mother's tough exterior lay another woman — kinder and softer of heart. We all want to believe that about the people who confuse us. Yet, though I hadn't said it aloud, I hadn't seen evidence of this in all the years I lived with her. Never once did my mother say a kind word to me that I could remember. The most you could hope for from her was indifference. And I'd finally grown tired of it, the way Tom and Billy had tired of it before me. My mother might get me back in her house, but it wouldn't be long before I went to live somewhere else. As soon as I finished school I would leave the Cape with the intention never to return. Heartened by my own resolve, I went to bed. I wasn't surprised when I returned from school on Monday to find my mother sitting at Etta's kitchen table.

My mother was never given to displays of emotion. If she felt anything after not seeing me for months she didn't show it. As soon as I was in the door she turned to me, and as I was taking my boots off on the mat, she said, "Hello, Luke."

"Hello, Mom."

"Is school going alright?"

"Yes. Alright."

"Luke," Etta said, "why don't you sit down here for a minute and have a cup of tea with us?"

But I didn't want to sit down with them. I didn't know what to say to my mother. We hadn't spoken except that once since the night she kicked me out, and I still felt the old resentments burning inside. "I've got some homework to do."

"Never mind the homework," said Etta. "You can do it later."

Reluctantly I pulled up a chair from the corner. Etta got up and poured me a cup of tea. My mother refused to look at me.

Through Etta's kitchen window she watched the clouds move over the water.

Etta set the teacup down in front of me. "Your mother and I have been talking." Etta retook her seat and wrapped her fingers lightly around her own cup. "We think it's time you made a decision about what you're gonna do for the summer."

"I already made it," I said quietly. "I got a job. I'm paying my own way."

"That's not what we meant," my mother answered.

"Your mother wants to know where you're gonna live," said Etta.

I hesitated only a moment before making my announcement, although I suppose they already knew what I would say. "I'm staying here. I've made up my mind."

No one said anything for a long while, then Etta spoke up. "Dora thinks it's time for you to come home, Luke."

"You been here too long," my mother said. "Enough of this foolishness."

"It's not foolishness. I want to stay here. I like it."

"It doesn't matter where you like it and where you don't," she said. "The fact is you ain't Etta's boy. You're mine, and I'm the one responsible for taking care of you."

"I take care of myself," I repeated stubbornly. "I pay my own way."

My mother laughed. "You think that pittance you get from Claude Robichaud is paying your way around here? I got news for you, Mr. Man. It doesn't cover a quarter of what you cost."

It was true, I knew. And I also knew that Etta was taking the money I gave her and putting away for me for next year when school was finished. I overheard her tell Roland this one night when they thought I wasn't listening.

"I told you, Dora, that it has nothing to do with money,"

Etta said. "I'm just concerned that the boy isn't living with his own mother."

"It might not have anything to do with money for you, but I won't have someone else paying his way."

Is that all that matters to you? I wanted to ask. But the voice I had found that night I left our house wouldn't come back to me. I could only sit there and listen with bowed head to the two of them discuss me like I wasn't in the room.

"I don't mind having him here," Etta said. "And Rolly don't either. But he should be with you."

"He'll only come back if he behaves," stated my mother. "I'm not putting up with any of his sass anymore, or it will be right back out with him." I loved how she could change tacks so suddenly. First she was asking me back and then she was acting like I was the one begging to be let in the front door. In the end, though, it was Etta who wanted it. Not that she didn't want me, like she said, but, I believe, she wanted me too much. She felt guilty about taking me away from my mother. She was also concerned about what my mother and the town thought. It was a hot topic of conversation in the post office that summer, the fact that I no longer lived at home.

"It's settled then," my mother said. "Luke, you'll come home with me."

There was no use arguing. If it came right down to it, Etta, and not my mother, would be the one to force me home. "Alright," I said quietly, "But I want to stay for dinner with Etta and Roland first."

My mother, now that she had me back under her control, wouldn't have allowed this, but Etta insisted. She went home with a warning for me to be in right after dinner. Once she was gone I sat in the chair and, fighting my depression, waited with Etta for Roland to come home.

"I got some apple pie for desert," Etta said, as soon as my mother left, and got up to begin preparing dinner.

"Good," I answered without enthusiasm.

After dinner, I gathered my things and left.

If anything my mother and I became more cautious around each other from then on. We rarely spoke, and when we did it was only for necessary communications — "Bring in the wood," and "Where are my socks?" or, "What time will you be in?" I was rarely at home anymore, and though I always stuck to the curfew my mother imposed and gave her what money I could, we both understood that I'd be there only until I finished school. It was my few months at Etta's house, under her instruction, that taught me school was my ticket out of the Cape.

"With an education," Etta said, "you can do anything. Go anywhere. If you finish high school you could even go on to college."

Of this I was doubtful. Billy had wanted to go to college, but when the time came there was no money for it. I thought it would be the same with me. Etta had reserved the few hundred dollars I'd given her for my college fund, but we both knew it was only a drop in the bucket. My mother wouldn't contribute. College for her was not even a consideration.

"I have never fathomed," she said once, "why Billy was so intent on going to another school when he could barely get through the first one." To my mother even the higher grades of high school were unnecessary — an evasion, she thought, of the more important aspects of life such as job and family. My mother had left school in Grade Seven.

"I learned how to read," she said. "I learned how to write. And even that has done me little damn good, I can tell you."

Yet she didn't oppose my plans. She couldn't, for I was getting older and more independent. At the same time she probably thought they would never come to fruition. And perhaps they wouldn't have, if Etta, in my final year of high school, hadn't brought home a form she'd picked up at the Oldsport post office. It was an application for a Canada Student Loan.

"It's a new program," Etta told me excitedly. "All you have to do is fill this out."

"And they'll just give me this money?"

"Loan it to you," Etta corrected. "As much as you need to go."

I sat staring at the papers she handed me. It seemed too good to be true and I told Etta this.

"Don't worry," she said. "I checked it out. I called the number there at the bottom of the form. All you have to do is fill it out, prove that you don't have the money to go, send it away, and they'll loan you the money."

"How do I prove I'm poor?"

Etta cleared her throat. "Your mother has to fill out this financial form."

"Mom? What does Mom have to do with it? I thought they were loaning me the money?"

"They are," said Etta, "but if you're under the age of twenty-one, they need to know how much money your family makes in order to justify lending it to you."

"Well, I guess I can forget this. She'll never fill it out."

"Don't you give up!" said Etta, with such fierceness it surprised me. "If you give up so easily you'll never get anywhere in this world!"

"I told you before. I don't want to ask her for anything."

Etta just looked at me. "Suit yourself." She sat down heavily in the chair across from me. Roland was away as usual, and the house was quiet. We listened to the wind — the beginning of a storm that was supposed to last for the next three days. For now it was but a brisk wind and a little blowing snow.

"You know why I hate it so much here sometimes?" Etta said to me finally. "You know why I get down sometimes?"

"No," I said. "I don't."

"Ever since I was a child all I've ever wanted in life was opportunity. I'm like your mother in one respect, I suppose. I never wanted anything handed to me, except opportunity. I look around here, at the Cape, at your mother, at this town, and I think that this is the life I've chosen for myself. When Roland first brought me here I said to myself, 'Here is the new world.' Here things will be different. But they weren't. Somehow I managed to change my country without changing a damned thing. And all the while I said to myself, if the opportunity ever comes along, I will take it. I will change. And now I'm going on fifty and nothing has changed. Roland and I don't have any kids. The opportunity was there, but we always thought there would be time. And by the time we seriously considered having 'em, the opportunity was lost. I'm here to tell you, Luke, that nothing happens unless you make it happen. I've had my opportunities. Sometimes I couldn't see 'em as such, and sometimes I saw them and chose not to take 'em. But you," she said, looking at me with a sadness I never knew she possessed, "you have an opportunity that isn't hiding, Luke. It's staring you right in the face. And if you waste it, you'll regret it — I warn you!"

Etta sighed. "I've lived here longer than you. I'm older than you. I can tell when someone will be happy and when they will not. I can tell you that if you stay in this town and don't do anything with your life you'll live to hate it. There are people who can spend their whole life in a town like this and it'll never bother them. And some can't. There are some who, if they stay, it'll kill them. You'll be killed by this town, Luke. Mark my words."

She got up, took a damp cloth and wiped down the top of her wood stove. The metal hissed and steamed.

"Which one of those people are you, Etta? The kind that can live here, or the kind that can't?"

"Oh, I'm the kind that can live here all right," said Etta. "It ain't killed me yet, and I don't suppose it will. Take this opportunity, Luke. Take it and don't look back. If you waste the chances you got there isn't any greater shame on God's green earth."

Suddenly I saw Etta as a woman, not a neighbour, or a mother figure, or even someone I loved. I saw a person, someone independent of me, and what hurt was that as much as I loved Etta, I couldn't help but see her as a kind of failure.

"I'll ask her," I said. "I'll go and ask her right now."

"You do that, Luke." But there was no triumph in her voice. I think she had talked herself, with that little speech, into one of those realizations we all have at times; that if we don't actively participate in our lives then we are carried with them, like driftwood to the shore, tossed up any old place and left to rot in our regrets.

Perhaps I would have thought more about this, but the endearing thing about teenagers is that they are largely self-involved. They can think of no one but themselves for very long. I left Etta and began to think how to approach my mother with the news that I needed her to tell the government how much money she made in a year.

My mother distrusted all government on principle. She had gone from a time in the early thirties and forties when its participation in the lives of its citizens had been minimal, to the late sixties when the state stepped up its involvement. My mother received a census once in the mail. It was the short version, asking her how many people were in her family, how much money she made, and, the kicker for my mother, how she got to work.

"What goddamn business is it of theirs how I get to work, or whether I work at all? Next they'll be wanting to know what colour my bloomers are and whether or not you kids got the measles last year." And with that she tore the census into pieces and threw it in the stove, though we all saw the typewritten disclaimer on the envelope: YOU ARE REQUIRED BY CANADIAN LAW TO FILL OUT THE ENCLOSED FORM.

"I'll admit," said Billy later, "that I don't see how it's any of their business either, but if three hundred guys dressed in blue suits come up to our door with handguns, I'll tell 'em anything they want to know."

My mother, however, wasn't afraid the government would take action. She was afraid of very little. We waited for government officials to come and arrest us for not filling out the census, but none did. When it was apparent there would be no retribution she took it as a sign of the basic cowardice and ineffectiveness of government institutions.

"They won't even follow up on their own threats," she said in disgust. I think she was looking forward to the day they'd come and challenge her over the destroyed census.

My mother did pay taxes, though as a widow on a pension she was entitled to a small refund each year. Usually it was only enough to pay the taxes on the house.

"The government giveth with one hand," she often said, "and the government taketh away with the other."

I knew, of course, how she'd react to the news that she had to fill out the financial form that came with my student loan application. But I chose not to try and trick her into it. Instead, one night when we were sitting in the kitchen I simply pulled the papers out of my school bag and handed them to her.

"What are these?" she said, shuffling through them.

"It's an assistance program form. They'll pay my way to school if I fill these out and send them in."

"When did you get this fancy idea in your head?" my mother said. "Haven't you got enough of school already?"

"No, I haven't. I want to continue on in university. I want to make something of my life," I added, thinking of Etta.

My mother silently scanned each official document, and handed them all back to me without a word.

"So?" I said to her.

"So what? Go ahead. Send them off if that's what you want to do. What does it have to do with me? You won't listen to anything I say anyway. You boys never did."

"You need to fill one of them out," I said boldly.

My mother held her hand out to me again. "Which one?"

I handed her the form. She read it over slowly, twice, and said finally, "You know I don't give anyone this kind of information."

"I know."

She set the paper aside, and got up out of her chair. She did it slowly, and I saw that right before my eyes my mother was getting old. She smoothed down the skirt of her dress with her palms and started into the living room. "You'll just have to figure out some other way," she said. "Maybe they'll let you in this thing without that form."

"Maybe they will," I answered calmly. I felt no surprise, no disappointment. I had expected her to act exactly as she did. Only it hadn't occurred to me that my mother was refusing to fill out the form for a reason other than the one she'd given. Eventually, I put the papers away and followed her upstairs to bed. The next day I went over to Etta's. She immediately asked me about the form.

"She said no," I said. "I told you so."

"Where's that paper?" Etta asked me.

"Right here." I gave all the forms to Etta and was surprised when she put on her coat.

"Come on," she said. "Let's go."

The two of us walked across the Cape and found my mother on her hands and knees scrubbing the kitchen floor, a cedar bucket full of hot water beside her. Before we could step into the kitchen she shouted at us. "Keep off it! It's not dry."

Etta stood in the doorway and held the papers up for my mother to see. I stood behind her, leaning against the wall of the porch and waiting. "What's this," Etta said, "about you not filling out this form for Luke?"

"I already told him," my mother said, still scrubbing. "I don't give out information like that."

"You do realize," Etta said, "that if you don't fill this out, Luke won't be able to go to school."

"He'll have to find another way," answered my mother, and placing one hand on the floor, and the other around to the small of her back for support, struggled to her feet. She then lifted the bucket, carried it across the room, and poured the dirty soapy water down the sink drain. "I don't care if he goes to school or not," she said. "But I won't have some office hound knowing what it is I'm spending every day at the grocery store."

"For God's sake, Dora," Etta said. "You are the most frustrating woman I've come across in two continents and thirty years!"

"Forget it, Etta," I said from the porch. "I'll find another way."

"That's right," answered my mother, setting the bucket underneath the sink and starting right in on the dishes. "He'll have to."

"What's the big deal," said Etta, "about filling out this little form so your youngest can have a chance in this world?"

"I didn't say I don't want him to have a chance. I just won't be filling out some form so all and sundry can know what I make for a living."

"Listen Dora!" Etta stepped into the kitchen with her boots still on, ignoring my mother's former warning about wet floors. "If you don't fill this in, I'll fill it in for him, with your name."

"You'll do no such thing," challenged my mother. "You know you won't."

"Maybe I won't," said Etta, her bluff called. "But I'll give him the money myself to go then."

"Go ahead," said my mother. "Give it to him."

This was an attempt by Etta to stir up my mother's feelings about charity, but it didn't work. All of us knew that Etta did not have the money to give me, even if she had been serious.

Etta turned away from my mother. "Luke? Go outside a minute, will you?"

"What for?" I said.

"Never mind," answered Etta. "Just do it."

I shrugged, and threw a final glance at my mother before I left. She hadn't even stirred from her dishes. I wondered what Etta had up her sleeve.

"Go on now," Etta said. "You can come back when I tell you."

I nodded, and went outside. It was January, and the wind off the ocean was gusting hard. I pulled my jacket around me, and thought to take a walk down the side of the Cape to the beach, then thought better of it. I snuck around the side of the house to the kitchen window, where the two of them standing at the sink couldn't see me. My mother left the windows open during the day, even in winter, because of the heat from the constantly burning stove. The yellow curtains she had tacked on the inside fluttered and twisted in the wind. The conversation had already started, and I came in at the middle. Etta had just finished saying something about me, and I heard my mother answer her.

"What does he need to go to school for anyway? Why waste all that money on such silliness?"

"Because." I heard Etta say. "He wants to."

"We all have wants," my mother answered, "and we don't always get them."

"If you don't let that boy go," said Etta, "you'll regret it to the end of your days, Dora."

"Why would I regret anything?" my mother said. "He's old enough now to not be my responsibility."

"He is your responsibility," said Etta. "You owe him."

"I don't owe him a goddamned thing!" my mother shouted. The word 'owe' was always enough to get her going. "I've given these boys everything I could give them."

"No, you damn well haven't!" Etta shouted back. I held my breath and waited for my mother's response. It was her endless theme that she had provided for us. No one until now ever dared challenge it.

"What is it you think I owe them?" said my mother.

"You owe them whatever it is you can give them. You owe him the chance to be happy."

My mother scoffed bitterly. "Happiness? Whoever heard of that as a reason for anything? Do you think I'm happy? Do you think I even had the chances God gave my boys? At least they had a mother. At least they had a place to sleep and eat in that they didn't have to look after. That's more than I ever had."

"Why don't you want him to go?" Etta asked quietly.

"He can go. He's just not getting any help from me."

"I think you don't want him to go."

"Stop with such foolishness!"

"I think you're afraid to be alone in this house," Etta said.

"I said stop with this!" hollered my mother. I heard her pound her foot once, hard, on the kitchen linoleum floor. But Etta wasn't giving up. "Let him go, Dora," she said quietly. "He can't stay here forever."

"Who said I wanted him to?"

"I know it's been hard for you. First your mother, then Harold. Living in this town where nobody's business is their own. But you can't take it out on Luke, Dora. He deserves a chance to get the hell out of here."

"He's got the chance. But he'll have to do it himself. Now I would appreciate it if you, woman, would keep your damn nose out my business."

When Etta came outside I was waiting for her at the front door. "What did she say?" I asked innocently.

"Forget it," Etta said, and then added her constant refrain when it came to my mother, "I just don't understand that woman. I don't understand her at all."

Etta went home, still grumbling, and I went in. I didn't say anything to my mother, and she said nothing to me. But I felt some power over her then, knowing that what Etta said might have been true, even thought she hadn't admitted it. My mother did not want me to leave. She was afraid of being alone. But I would leave. I would not stay with her. Being alone, I thought, is exactly what she deserved to be. I left the form my mother wouldn't fill out on the table where Etta had laid it and the other papers. That dream, I thought, was dead. Perhaps there was another way, but I couldn't think of what it might be.

"Are you going to Tom's this weekend?" my mother asked me when I came downstairs with a knapsack over my shoulder.

"Yes," I said, and said no more. I waited around that Friday evening for Tom to finish work and come pick me up. My mother worked around me, and I became suddenly talkative. I felt no resentment that she wouldn't perform the nearly painless act of signing the form. I told her of all the things I'd do anyway. Move to the city. Leave town the day I finished school.

"I'll work in a gas station if I have to. It doesn't matter that I can't go to school. Maybe you're right, I've had enough school already."

I asked my mother if she'd ever been to Halifax. She told me no.

"Don't you want to see it?" I asked. "Just once?"

"No," she said. "I got all I want to see right here."

It baffled me how someone could live one hundred miles from a city all their life and not go there. What restraint that required! I had never seen the city, but as soon as I got a chance I would go, Canada Student Loan or no Canada Student Loan. It wasn't school or opportunity that called me, as much as the city itself. The ache for anonymity. I knew what I was. I was different, and there, I believed, I could finally be myself. Perhaps my mother never felt the need to go anywhere but her own house in order to be herself.

"Tom's here," she told me pointlessly, for we'd both heard the sound of his car. I got up, shifted the knapsack up further on my back, and went to the door.

"Luke," she said, and I turned back.

"What?"

"I know you were at the window listening."

I shrugged. "So?"

She said slowly, "I just want you to know that Etta's wrong. I'm not afraid to be alone in this house."

I shrugged again. "Then why not fill out the form?"

"Because it's against my principles."

"It's just a stupid form, Mom. There aren't any principles involved."

"Yes there are. You want me to tell the government how I haven't got anything so they'll give you money. That's too much like asking for something that you ain't got. I've lived forty-seven years on this earth without asking anyone for anything, and I ain't about to start now just because you want me to."

"It's a loan," I said. "It isn't charity."

"Charity is charity, whether there's a promise of payback or not. What if you can't pay it back when the time comes? Where will I be then, with my signature on that dotted line?"

I could have said a thousand things. That I would pay it back. That they were loaning the money to me and not to her. I'd been living with my mother all my life and hearing the same old arguments about self-sufficiency. I could even have told her my blossoming theory about how refusing to take anything from anyone was as selfish and extreme as taking anything you could get. But it would have accomplished nothing and I knew it.

I nodded instead. "Goodbye, Mom."

"You come home early on Sunday. There's chores to be done."

I went out the door to Tom's waiting car, whistling.

"What are you so happy about?" Tom asked as soon as I got in. "Did she fill out the form?"

"No," I said, and smiled. "She ain't going to either."

Tom looked at me strangely. "Then it's an odd time to be whistling Dixie."

"Never mind," I answered. I couldn't explain what had just happened. How I'd discovered my mother's fears and by extension her weakness. And how I was more sure than ever I would get out of the Cape, whether I went to college or not.

"Are you still gonna go to the art school?" Tom asked me finally.

"I doubt it," I said. "Unless the money falls out of the air."

"Maybe you could get a scholarship?" he said. "Or maybe you could work a few years and save the money? Suzanne and I could even lend you a little bit."

"Maybe," was all I answered.

Suzanne had a cousin staying with her for a few weeks over the summer. His name was Jamie — a short muscular boy a few months older than me. He had fine blond hair, which fascinated me. Like Suzanne's, it was an unusual hair colour for our part of the world. Almost right away I fell a little in love with him. There were three bedrooms in my grandfather's house. Tom and Suzanne shared one, the guest bedroom where I slept was another and a second guest bedroom sat at the end of the upstairs hall. It happened that on the first night we were there Suzanne was washing the sheets and giving the second guest bedroom a good cleaning. The room was littered with buckets, sponges, and bottled cleansers. The bed was stripped.

"I'll finish it tomorrow," she said. "You don't mind sleeping in the same room with Jamie for tonight, do you?"

Jamie and I looked at each other over the supper table. "No," I said. "I don't mind." Jamie said he didn't mind either. But when Tom and Suzanne climbed the stairs Jamie and I made no move to follow them. We stayed where we were, watching television, though I was certain and still am that there was a rising anticipation in both of us. Finally after many hours Jamie got up and shut off the TV.

"I guess it's time," he said.

I nodded and followed him up the stairs. In the room we gravitated to opposite sides of the bed and started to undress.

We did so shyly, turning slightly away from each other. We stripped to our underwear and quickly jumped in bed to hide under the covers. We talked for a little while, inanities mostly. I think we both knew what was coming. Jamie turned out the light, and we lay there, totally aware of each other's bodies and of our own. I felt just a whisper of feeling across my thigh, so light it could have been my imagination. As his leg finally rested against mine neither of us moved. I became focused on that single contact, my heart beating faster. I felt almost sick with sexual excitement. I was the one to make the bravest move. I laid my hand on his arm, and in return he placed his on my chest. It was then that whatever was hiding in both of us was unleashed — the need for contact and the sexual passion of boys, both powerful enough on their own but together unstoppable. We fought for control of each other. At some point I let Jamie win, and when I finally came it was the sweetest, strongest thing I've ever felt, building in a secret place down inside me and erupting with such force I had to clamp my teeth together to keep from crying out. Jamie came at about the same time. Then we slept, as far away from each other as we could with a strip of mattress between us, a kind of guilt-laden no man's land.

In the morning at breakfast we couldn't even look each other in the eye, so burdened were we with guilt. It seemed the world would never be quite the same, that I would never recover from such remorse. I judged that Jamie, by his uneasiness, must have felt the same way. I swore that I'd never do any such thing again. Even Tom and Suzanne noticed there was something between us.

"Don't you like him?" Suzanne asked when we were alone. "Did you two have a fight?"

"No," I said. "We didn't."

"It sure looks like you did."

I made an effort to be more talkative that afternoon with Jamie, so Tom and Suzanne wouldn't think anything further was wrong. But we spoke awkwardly and of nothing important, certainly not of what had happened, and couldn't look at each other directly without feeling ashamed. That evening Suzanne prepared the second guest bedroom. I hadn't been in my own bed a half hour with the lights out before I heard someone coming down the hall. A shadow appeared in my doorway.

"Jamie?" I whispered.

"Yes," he said, and climbed into the bed. Once might have been enough to dismiss what we'd done, to pretend that it had been a moment of weakness and could be avoided in the future. But twice, never. When dawn came I was still lying awake, feeling that already familiar onslaught of guilt. I didn't speak the entire drive home with Tom. Jamie and I had said goodbye at the house. It had been awkward and brief, much like our love-making had been the night before. I couldn't have cared less if I ever saw him again. I later wondered, though, what became of him. Suzanne mentioned once that he'd got married and had children. Was the memory of those two nights for him a secret shame or a secret pleasure?

When I returned home that Sunday I found the form I'd left behind lying completed on the kitchen table. My mother had altered a sacred principle for the second time. The first was when she'd given the house to Tom. And now she had altered one for me. It didn't occur to me that she'd done it out of love. I was too anxious to leave and be the person I now knew I was to worry about her motives.

THE BOY AND THE WELL
～

*M*y mother rarely if ever spoke about her own childhood or the family she grew up with. The most she would say if we complained about something was that we were lucky — she'd had to take care of herself, her brother and her father from the time she was fourteen years old.

"You should be thankful you have a mother at all," she would sometimes say to us.

My Uncle Joe was less close-mouthed. Occasionally when we were children he regaled us with stories of our maternal grandparents and his and my mother's childhood in the small fishing village of Port Shine near Yarmouth, Nova Scotia. Their mother had died of pneumonia when they were both young. According to Uncle Joe it was sudden and quick. One week she was fine, the next she caught a cold, and it worsened one afternoon after she insisted on bringing clothes in off the line in an afternoon squall. The next day she had trouble breathing and couldn't get out of bed. Two days after that she was dead. My uncle admitted he didn't remember much of her, except that she had long, dark hair and was very beautiful. Our own mother inherited the hair if not the looks. All through our childhood, and later when her hair had turned grey, she wore it pinned up. The only time we ever saw her with her hair down was when we caught a glimpse of her in her room just before bed, or when she washed it in the bathroom sink. Of her mother, our mother would say only this: that she married a fool for a man, had fools for children, and picked a foolish time to do her laundry. This was as close as my mother ever got to examining the past.

⌒

My Uncle Joe knew his sister disapproved of his lifestyle — his drinking, the shack he lived in, his bachelorhood. As children we knew exactly how much she disliked him. He was rarely in our house. A couple of times a year he might drop by to say hello, always clean shaven and smelling of cheap cologne. "To cover up the smell of cheap booze," my mother would say after he left. He'd take a chair by the door as if planning a quick escape. She offered him one cup of tea for which he thanked her several times before she even had it poured. Then she sat in her rocker and fired the same questions at him she always did.

"So," she'd say, "how you getting along?"

"Fine, fine," he'd answer. "Might have me a job coming up soon."

"Oh yeah?" she would ask. "Where?"

Joe never gave a straight response. "Just around town," he said, or, "A little extra work on the boats." Both knew there was no job — there never was for my uncle. Yet it was his job to lie, and my mother's job to pretend to be interested, though she never did hers very well. Before his tea was half finished she was out of her chair saying she had some chore to do. Joe would quickly drain his cup and stand to go.

"Well, Dora," he'd say, "it's been mighty nice seeing ya." And with that he'd be off. We never knew how long it would be before he'd drop by again, though it was a sure bet he could be found drunk around town on Friday or Saturday night.

For a few years, in his teens, my uncle lived in Halifax. No one knew what became of him there, or if he ever found a job, but before any of us were born he came staggering into the Cape from the city without a place to stay. With my father's help Uncle Joe built a small shack on the far side of the wharves, just off Main Street and on the outskirts of town, and settled into it, presumably for good. That was Crown land, and he had been fortunate enough never to be asked to move off it, and so became after twenty years or so a legitimate squatter and landowner in town. He lived on what work he could get on the boats or by acting as a kind of stevedore on the wharves, helping the men carry their catch into the plants. Most of the time, as soon as he got money, he drank it up at Carson's tavern. "Blessed are the poor in spirit," my father had often said of him, "for theirs is the kingdom of heaven."

Once Tom was married and out on his own he became my Uncle Joe's sometimes provider, bringing him vegetables from the garden when it was the season and clothes that his wife picked out especially for him at second-hand shops. Tom lent him money occasionally, though he made it a point never to expect the money back. His expectations were never once, to my knowledge, disappointed.

"I only give him what I can afford," Tom told me when I

asked him about it. "Blessed are the poor in spirit, remember?"

"You'll be poor in everything," my mother said to him once, "if you keep giving to that old man." But as much as my mother disapproved of Tom's giving and my uncle's taking, she could do nothing except complain. Even I, after I'd finished school in Halifax and started working at the graphic design firm, would make short visits to Joe's, always parting with five or ten dollars from my wallet before I left. Once I suggested to Tom we should stop 'lending' him money to buy booze.

"He's just killing himself," I said, "and we're just helping him along."

Tom thought about what I said, then answered thoughtfully. "I think it's too late for Uncle Joe," he said.

"What do you mean, too late? If he stops now his body might repair itself."

"Not likely," Tom said. "The man's sixty years old."

"The least we could do is get him help. I don't mind lending him the money, but I hate to see him drink it away like that."

"Listen, Luke," my older brother said, "if we didn't give it to him, he'd just get it somewhere else. He might even go and drink cleaning fluids, or aftershave or something, and that would really kill him."

The thought was truly abhorrent to me that my uncle could sink so low. But once Tom had mentioned it, I knew he was right. So we continued to take care of him. Once in a while Tom bought the liquor for him when no one else would and he couldn't get out himself. A few times even I went, though mostly I would give him the money but didn't buy the rum. It was too much like giving a suicidal man a loaded gun. At sixty years of age, Uncle Joe had already suffered a series of gross indignities at the hands of the bottle. He carried a cane. He walked leaning over to one side, even when he was sober, so that sometimes he just lost his balance and fell. He was thin, red-faced, and sniffled and coughed with a perpetual cold. One eye had begun to cloud over with a cataract. He wore a patch under his glasses, and his one good eye stared out at you in bloodshot glory. No one could deny that my uncle was an alcoholic, though my mother claimed there was something wrong with him before he ever took a drink.

"He was always lazy," she said. "No one could ever get that man to do anything." In her one concession to virtue in her brother she added, "It ain't like he hasn't a got a head on his shoulders." It wasn't so much a head for knowing, she sometimes said, as a head for doing. He could fix anything. If the motor on someone's boat conked out my uncle could tell at a glance what was wrong. Sometimes he knew just by being told about it. He could do the same with a car or a tractor. Once the conveyor belt in the cod plant jammed, and Joe was called in to see what was the matter. Although he'd never worked on a conveyor engine before it took him only a few minutes to figure out what the problem was. He was a natural mechanic and could have had a thriving career even in a town as small as the Cape. But he was unreliable. It was easier to take your car to a mechanic in Oldsport or try to fix it yourself than wait for my Uncle Joe to show up on a Saturday morning. If he did show up, he would be drunk. Drunk, he was useless. Drunk, my mother always said, Joseph Cameron Smith couldn't tell a drive shaft from a clothespin.

⌒

In the two months I was home caring for my mother and her broken hip, Tom and I saw more of each other than we had in years. Every spare minute when he wasn't managing his carpentry business was spent with me. We didn't do much except talk and go for long walks on the beach. I talked to Tom about my life in the city, about our childhood, and about how, since leaving home almost twenty years ago, I felt as if I'd never gotten or gone anywhere.

"I think I have wasted my life," I told him. The two of us were walking along the coast in the early evening, away from our house and along the beach down towards the tip of Tyler's Woods. That little bit of beachfront property had never been what you would call prime. You had to constantly make your way around boulders sunk halfway in the sand and step over pieces of driftwood tangled in seaweed and tossed up by the tide. Tom wasn't surprised at what I said. I'd been telling him the same thing since I'd come home.

"And how exactly have you wasted it?"

I made some noises about no longer being an artist, if I'd ever been one.

"But you could be one," Tom said. "All you have to do is pick up a paint brush, don't you?"

I shrugged. "It isn't that easy."

Tom sighed. "Maybe not. But I really don't see what you have to complain about. Seems to me Billy's the one who really wasted his life."

"I miss him," I said.

"Me too."

"Do you think he'll ever come home?"

"He said he wouldn't."

Billy had finally picked up the phone and called us just the year before, after all those years of silence. It had been so long I rarely thought about him anymore. Yet he was always there, just below the surface. His sudden return to our lives was as shocking and heartbreaking as if my dead father had managed to pick up a phone and call us from that heaven he always talked about.

"He won't come," I said finally. "How could he? Isn't even allowed to leave that silly centre he's at."

Billy, now forty-three, was in a rehabilitation centre for drug and alcohol addiction. He had been there for nearly a year before he called. Tom and I weren't surprised when we found out, though Billy made us swear not to tell our mother. When he finally picked up the phone and called her, shortly after talking to Tom and me, he told her that he'd been busy.

"For twenty years!" my mother cried. "How can anyone be busy for twenty bloody years!"

Tom laughed when she told him of the call. "Leave it to Billy," he said, shaking his head. "He never did like explaining anything to Mom."

My mother didn't let the hurt she felt, if any, show. She talked about Billy no more now that he kept in touch than she had when we never heard from him. She did not, as Tom and I did, ask him to come home, though it had been years since we had seen him. Tom and I endlessly speculated on what he would look like now.

"Balding likely," Tom said, "and running to fat." This was no great guess. Tom had done both, and though I kept myself trim with workouts and long walks, my hairline had also begun to recede. We brothers were more alike than just in looks. None of us had succeeded in the things we had set out to do. I had failed as an artist. Billy had not become a writer. Even Tom admitted he and Suzanne had problems.

"She says I'm locked up too tight," he told me. "She says she can't get anything out of me." Then there was the fact that none of us had children. Tom and Suzanne no longer even talked about having any. Although there had been some discussion after the first miscarriage, there had been two miscarriages since, and Suzanne was now forty-one and Tom forty-three. They'd stopped trying.

Billy, for all his excesses, was childless as well. "At least," he told me, laughing, "there aren't any I know about."

It bothered me that there would be no one to carry on our name. My father would have wanted it. I brought the subject up with my mother.

"Doesn't it ever bother you," I said to her, "that none of us has any kids?"

She shrugged. "Why should it? It's your choice."

"I know, but it's too late now. Dad didn't even have any brothers and sisters to carry his name on for him. Doesn't that bug you?"

"It's not too late," she said. "You're only thirty-seven. It's not unheard of to meet a woman and have kids at that age, you know."

As usual when my mother brought up the subject of marriage, I shut up. But after supper while we were doing the dishes she said to me, as if there hadn't been a half-hour break in the conversation, "So, when *are* you going to find someone and settle down?"

I started to say something, bit my tongue, and continued to dry the dishes she placed in the rack. She washed the last dish, drained the sink, and hobbled without the aid of her walker into the living room. I dried the rest of the dishes, wondering how much to tell her. Before I had put the last dish away in the pantry, I'd made up my mind. With the dishrag still in my hand, as a sort of comfort prop, I marched into the living room and stood at the door.

"Mom," I said, "about me marrying and having kids, and all that . . ."

"What about it?" She didn't even look up from the screen where some talk-show starlet was turning letters on a giant 'hangman' board.

"You are aware," I said, "that I'm a homosexual."

She waved me away with her hand without looking up from the TV. "That's pure foolishness," she said. "You're no such thing."

I smiled. I knew she would react this way. The couple of times before that I'd tried to broach this subject — out of some compulsion, or perhaps merely to shock her — she had acted similarly. She refused to believe it, though I knew she and Tom discussed it often.

"It's true," I said. "I like men, not women."

My mother shook her head in irritation, as if that could make me go away. She tried to concentrate on her televison program. "It's a phase. You'll get over it."

I laughed. "I've been doing it for half a lifetime now. That's a pretty long time for a phase."

"It's a long phase then. Now get out. I want to watch this show."

"Don't you care?" I pressed. "Doesn't it mean anything to you?"

"Why should it? Why should I care what you boys do with your life?"

"It's not that bad," I said. "I'm perfectly happy being the way I am." It was a lie, and I think she knew it.

"I don't care what way you are," she said, turning to me for the first time. "Just stop talking about it, will you?"

"I just thought," I said, "that you might want to know."

DARREN GREER

"Don't you think I know!" she shouted suddenly. "Tom and I talk about it! I know what you do. Now get out, I said, and leave me alone!" I saw that there were actual tears in my mother's eyes. I could scarcely believe I was the cause of them. God help me, it felt good to get such a strong reaction from her.

"Sorry," I said.

"Get out!" she shouted again. I turned and left, leaving her to the television. I drove out to my brother's on Gaston Road, to tell him I had figured out why none of us had any children.

"Why?" he asked, as we sat sipping tea at his kitchen table.

"Because," I said, "we didn't want to subject them to the kind of childhood we had. I think we all unconsciously knew that abuse is cyclical, and we left our children unborn to save them from it."

Tom sighed. "Luke," he said finally, "you think about things way more than is good for you."

Suzanne laughed. "It's true, Luke. You do."

I only shook my head and finished my tea.

The night I announced the Sunbeam was restored was a Friday, and once again Tom was coming down. Friday used to be his and Suzanne's night out for dinner in Trenton, but when I asked him about it he said they'd stopped doing that quite a while back. I just assumed they'd grown bored with their little rituals — they would be celebrating their twenty-fifth anniversary the next year. I was too self-involved to notice the hurried, dismissive way Tom skipped over the subject.

I hadn't let Tom help much with the Sunbeam, especially as the job started to come together and I began to feel no small sense of accomplishment in what I'd done. I did allow him to pick me some of the parts I needed from his auto-mechanic buddies in Trenton, and I showed it to him in its various stages of completion.

246

In the barn I took off my shirt and gave the bike one last lookover. A peace settled over me, the same way it used to when I painted. I hadn't painted seriously, as I'd told Tom, for nearly sixteen years. It felt good to be doing something as meticulous, if not quite as creative, as painting again. I had run an extension cord from the house to the barn, over my mother's protests of power wastage, and in the gathering gloom I switched on a caged mechanic's light, hung it from a nail in one of the overhead beams, and kept working.

Tom still hadn't arrived when I wheeled the Sunbeam out into the front yard, straddled it, and coasted to the edge of the Cape. I had no idea what I would do with it, but I had found one of Tom's yellow hard hats in the barn, from his days at the mill, and wore that for safety purposes, for lack of anything resembling a motorcycle helmet. Billy had never bothered to buy one.

As I sat on the bike wondering what I should do with it now that I had it fixed, a disturbing thought crept into my head. I could picture myself starting the Sunbeam and racing forward over the edge of the Cape into the ocean. It was high enough, and the shore rocky enough, to make sure I wouldn't be coming back up. I sat there toying with the thought. The sun was setting behind me. The future looked as flat and featureless as the ocean before me. The life I had built for myself in the city was no great shakes — endless solitary dinners taken in a small apartment, few friends, even fewer lovers. Whatever life I had once had here, in Tyler's Cape, was gone. The only thing that was clear to me was my past, the cherished memories of me and my brothers. It occurred to me that I did have a kind of second sight, Etta's vision, after all. I was always looking backwards.

"What ya doing?"

Tom's voice startled me. I hadn't heard his truck pull into the yard. He walked up beside me and stood there, instinctively reaching out and placing a hand on the handlebar nearest him. It was almost as if he had read my mind but when I turned to him, he too was staring out over the water.

"You never get used to it, do you?"

"What?"

"The ocean. Remember what Dad used to call it?"

I nodded. "The most mysterious of God's miracles."

He laughed and stood back, surveying my handiwork. "It looks great," he said. "You did a fine job."

I had at that. The Sunbeam's chrome handlebars and spoked wheels glittered in the dying sunlight. I had repainted the gas tank fire-engine red, and I felt some secret pride in how smart and new the whole thing looked.

"Can I try it?"

I leaned the bike on its kickstand, climbed off and passed the yellow hard hat to Tom. He looked at it strangely but put it on, threw one long leg over the Sunbeam, gripped the handlebars and pulled it upright. He rolled it back from the edge and turned the front wheel sharply to the left, but before he could kick-start the engine to life, I said to him, "I'm going home tomorrow."

Tom looked at me. "Mom think it's okay?"

"She'll be glad for me to go."

"Alright," he said. "I guess you put up with her long enough."

"I'm not coming back," I said softly.

Tom stood with his legs spread, the bike balanced between them. "What do you mean?" he said. "Not coming back?"

"I'll come see you and Suzanne but I'm finished with her. I don't understand her. I don't get along with her. I feel nothing for her. Why should I pretend anymore? I'm tired of it, Tom."

Tom laid the bike back on its kickstand and got off. He stood beside me, lightly brushing his hand over the Sunbeam's new black leather seat. Tom had found an old motorcycle seat in a junkyard, had cut the leather off the seat down to size, and I had glued it on the old metal seat of the Sunbeam.

"You sure did a good job. Too bad Billy can't see it. It looks better than when he bought it."

"Did you hear me Tom? I said I'm finished with her. Name one thing that woman's done for us since we've grown up. She never has a civil word. She runs your wife down like she wasn't any good for anything, and she runs you down too when you're not here."

"I know," said Tom quietly.

"I don't understand why you keep coming back, after all the things she said about Suzanne."

"Because," he said slowly, "she's my mother."

"What in the hell does that matter?" I was nearly shouting at him. "She drove all of us out of this house, one by one. There is not an ounce of motherly love in that woman's fucking body. What kind of mother is that?"

Tom shrugged, but still wouldn't look at me. "She's all we got."

"She abused us, Tom," I said heavily. "You might not know that because you've never had any other parents to compare her to. Neither have I, but I've spent some time talking to people who know, and I'm here to tell you she abused the hell out of us. The kindling sticks, the beatings, the yelling, the name calling. My friends all think I should have stopped talking to her years ago."

Finally Tom did look up at me. "I know what you're saying, Luke. But it doesn't make any difference. You do what you have to, but I'm still coming down here whenever I have the time."

"But why?" I said angrily. "Don't you see? She doesn't

deserve us. Etta knew that. She as much as told us."

"Doesn't matter," Tom said, shaking his head stubbornly. "She's our mother."

"Oh for fuck's sake," I said. "If Jack the Ripper were our father, would you still talk to him?"

But I could get no other answer out of Tom. If there was anything I could say about Tom it was that he was bulldog loyal. When anyone in school would even begin to say anything about our mother, Tom would be on them, beating them until they took it back. Tom was a fatalist, and as I watched him get on the Sunbeam, start it up and drive it out of the yard, I thought that if Jack the Ripper were our father he still would have talked to him. Tom was a resigned man. He could handle anything that came along only by accepting it, something Billy and I could never do.

We took turns racing the motorcycle up and down the dirt road in the back field. Tom took the last ride, and when he got off and shut it down, the sun had set and the light was almost entirely gone from the Cape. He sat on the porch beside me, handed me the old helmet and said, "Suzanne's leaving me."

"What?"

"She's going to live with someone else."

"Who?"

"Some fella who works at our bank. She's been seeing him for awhile now. I just found out."

I couldn't believe it. The two of us sat there on the porch stoop and tried to fathom it, though Tom didn't say much. All he said was that she came home last week with the news. He had kept it locked up inside himself until now. It was getting late but we sat side by side, listening to the ocean and the faint voices from my mother's TV carried out from inside.

"Won't you fight for her?" I asked him finally.

"Fight what, Luke? How can I fight someone I love?"

"Can't you contest the divorce or something?"

"Why? If she's gonna go, she's gonna go. Isn't anything I can do about it." That was Tom all over. But I felt some sense of shock and loss myself. I loved Suzanne dearly. If she divorced my brother, she divorced all of us.

"What if Mom had made her feel at home?" I said. "Maybe this wouldn't be happening."

"It's not Mom," Tom said. "It's me."

"You? You've never done anything but good for her, Tom!"

"Have I?"

"Yes. You love her, for God's sake."

"Apparently that's not enough."

"Well, it should be. If it isn't enough for her, than maybe she's got the problem, and not you."

"Oh, Goddamn it, Luke! When are you gonna grow up? Haven't you learned yet that you can't go around all the time blaming everyone else for your problems."

"I'm just saying . . ."

Tom stood up, and I could see that I'd gotten him angry. "I know what you're saying. You're saying it's Suzanne's fault our marriage isn't working. Well, I tell you, it's no one's fault."

"But if only she would give you a second chance."

"There are no second chances," Tom said bitterly. "We've had all we're gonna get. Your problem, Luke, is you haven't learned that at some point in life you have to shake off the things everyone has done to you and take some responsibility for yourself. You blame Mom for everything. You even blame her for the fact you're a faggot, for chrissake."

I had confessed this to Tom in a moment of brutal honesty. I now regretted it.

"You're responsible for yourself, Luke. Your life is your life.

Suzanne's is hers, mine is mine, and Billy's is Billy's. You can drink it away, screw it away, do whatever you want, but it's yours. You're responsible." With that, Tom turned and stalked away. I listened to the crunch of his shoes on the chipped rock in the drive. I waited for the sound of his truck's engine, but it didn't come. I heard him walking back in the darkness towards me.

"I'm sorry I called you a faggot," he said.

"It's alright. I call myself that sometimes."

"Maybe," he said, "it's not your fault you're unhappy. Maybe you're not responsible for anything bad that happens in your life, but it's your responsibility to fix it. Do you get what I'm saying?"

I did not, could not, answer.

"Suzanne and I will be okay. We might not be together but we'll be okay. You I don't know about. You don't have to come back here. You don't ever have to leave Halifax if you don't want to. But before things can get better, Luke, you have to find out what the problem is and fix it. Even if the problem isn't your fault."

We let these words stand between us for awhile, saying nothing. I had heard them before. Then Tom said "I love you, Luke."

I couldn't answer. I was paralyzed. I always had been. What's happened to us? I cried to myself. What in the world has happened?

Tom left me sitting in the darkness on the front porch. I heard his truck start this time, heard it pull away and the sound of its engine fade. Eventually my mother came out to see where I had gone.

"Are you coming in?"

"Later."

"Suit yourself." She closed the porch door again. I sat there for God knows how long, a man with a question, and now an answer. What happened to us? Doesn't matter, as long as we fix it. How do we fix it? Tom didn't tell me that. I didn't know. It didn't occur to me then that my father had given me the answer long before he died. It was a secret my father knew that wasn't a secret. He knew that the only way to fix things was with glory. "There is," he used to say, "glory all over the world, Luke. It is God's gift to us. All we need to do to find it is to look for it."

But at that young age I didn't know what glory was. In fact, I thought it was a flower, as in morning glory. In a sense it was a flower, according to my father. "Glory is beauty. God's beauty, God's glory. There is beauty in everything, and it is the salvation of us all." I didn't know what he meant by salvation either. But glory intrigued me. I saw it as something tangible, something I could hold — like tiny clouds of white cotton batten lying hidden somewhere in the fields.

"Is there glory on the Cape?" I had asked my father.

"Oh yes," I remembered him saying as he swung me up into his arms. "Glory on the Cape. Glory everywhere."

We gave up the idea of forcing my mother out of her house. She wouldn't go. Yet there was no more frantic housecleaning from her, even without the walker, and I had the feeling there would be little of it even if she healed fully. The two months I was home practically every night was spent with her in front of the television. She watched every televised Toronto Blue Jays baseball game. Where this sudden interest in sports came from, when there had been none before, I couldn't tell.

That evening after Tom left I got into my car without telling my mother where I was going and drove to my uncle's. I wanted to say goodbye. I had been visiting him regularly since I'd been home, though I'd had to force myself. The shack was small, big enough only for a bed, the stove, a scarred chest of drawers with a small black and white television on top of it, and a kitchen table crowded with bread, opened packages of fig new-tons, and jars of preserves and peanut butter. My uncle was too old to clean himself or his home. Both reeked of sweat and stale cigarette smoke.

I parked my Toyota along Main Street, and before making my way down the path to his shack picked a handful of lilacs from a bush flowering in the field. When I carried them in, he was sitting in his faded, overstuffed armchair next to his little wood stove. He was awake, and sober.

"Hello Luke!" he said happily. "What you doing here so late?"

"I'm leaving tomorrow," I told him. "I just wanted to come over and say goodbye."

My uncle laughed. "Had enough of Dora, eh?"

I nodded. "I brought some flowers to spruce the place up a bit. You mind?"

Joe said he didn't, and I pulled a dusty glass off the counter, filled it with water from the bucket beside the sink, and arranged the lilacs in it. I set them down beside him on the kitchen table after pushing a few jars and opened bread bags out of the way. My uncle stared at them a long time. Anxious to leave but not wanting to hurt the old man's feelings, I chose the only other seat in sight, a hard-backed wooden chair next to the door.

"Did I ever tell you kids," he said finally, "that I hate lilacs?"

"No," I answered quietly. "I'm sorry. I thought you might like them." In fact, I thought that the smell of the lilacs might over-power the stench in my uncle's cabin. He waved my apology away. And then said something strange. "She never told you anything, your mother. Did she?"

"No," I answered. "She never did."

Uncle Joe nodded. "She never liked to talk about it at all. Whenever I would try and bring it up she would just tell me to hush. But I ain't hushing now. Just don't seem to be any good reason to hush anymore."

"Hush about what, Joe?" Lately my uncle talked a lot about his past. I listened to him when I could, but most of the time he was drunk and it didn't make any sense. Tonight, however, I was in no mood to listen to him, drunk or sober. I wanted only to go home, pack my things and be ready to leave the Cape early the next morning. Yet my uncle fixed me with his one good eye, as if he knew exactly what I was thinking, and it became apparent to me why people still referred to him as smart. After all the damage he had done to himself there was still a sharpness in that gaze of his.

"Now we might as well start at the beginning," he said, leaning back into his chair and tossing his cane on the bed. "Except that I'm feeling pretty dry right now."

I knew what he was after, but I didn't have the time to make the twenty-minute drive to the bootlegger's in Oldsport to buy him a bottle. I got up and fetched him a glass of water instead. When I handed it to him he made a face, but said nothing. He drank it all down in one gulp and set the glass aside.

"You know," he began, "that our mother died when we were just little."

I nodded.

"I was eight," he said. "That would make your mother about fourteen, I guess. She's sixty-six now?"

"Right," I said.

"You know," he said after a pause, "I got an awful lot I could tell you, Luke, that you don't know. I told you some, but there's a lot more."

"I know, Joe," I said. "But maybe we could do this some other time. I really have to get up early tomorrow."

"Stay, Luke." He wasn't asking. I wasn't used to hearing the ring of authority or command in my uncle's voice. My mother seemed to get all of that between them, but I was hearing it now. I stared at him, surprised. He smiled, but there was no real pleasure in it. He looked old and tired, beaten. I felt more pity for my uncle in that moment than I ever had in all the times before combined.

"I've got a story to tell you," he said.

My mother was born Madora Agnes Smith in July of 1927 in Port Shine, the first and only daughter of Cameron Smith and Cordelia Whynot Smith. My Uncle Joseph was born seven years later, and, like myself, was born at home. Their father had fought in the First World War, with a Canadian regiment at Ypres Salient, and had lost a leg to a German bullet at Passchendaele. He rarely discussed the war. He was present in 1916 when the world's first tanks came rolling over Flanders Fields, destroying everything in their path. He had seen ground level flak blow holes the size of a fist through the body of his best friend and the only other boy from Port Shine of fighting age. He spent a year and a half in rehabilitation in London, was fitted with a wooden leg and learned how to walk on it, and then came home to Nova Scotia, married my grandmother and, despite the disability, took work on the boats. When my grandmother died, my grandfather, according to Uncle Joe, was away at sea fishing, and there was no way to get hold of him. When he finally walked into the kitchen four days later, his oilskins on, a duffel bag slung over one shoulder, bringing his wooden leg round in a short arc with every step he to took, nearly everyone from town was in my mother's house.

Cordelia died in August, the height of summer. Because the body was laid out according to custom in the home of the deceased for days after the death, she had already begun to decay. A neighbor who'd been looking after my mother and uncle tried to counteract the smell by going to a bush in the yard and bringing in armful after armful of lilacs, which she carefully arranged in the coffin with my grandmother. Far from overpowering the stench of decaying flesh, the strong, sweet fragrance of the flower only mingled with it. My grandfather took one look at the body, turned back to the silent, expectant group of people in his parlour and said, "She stinks. It's time to bury her." My grandfather then left the house of his wife and children, got drunk at the tavern, passed out at home on the kitchen floor, and didn't even make it to his own wife's funeral the next afternoon.

"You know," my uncle told me, "people said it was shock, but I always wondered about that myself. How much shock can a man be in so he can't go to his own wife's funeral? Dora and I were there, sitting right up in front, and no one mentioned our father. They talked about him enough behind his back, but that didn't bother him. He was never one to mix with people much, or care what was said about him."

I didn't have to think for long who such a description reminded me of.

"Your mother burned that lilac bush," said my Uncle Joe. "Did I tell you that? I came home from school one day and there weren't nothing left but some ashes and a blackened stump in the front yard. Dumped gasoline over it, lit a match and watched it burn. And nobody was allowed to bring a lilac into the house after that, not that I ever wanted to. I don't much like the smell of them myself." He lapsed into silence. I thought, for a moment, that it was the end of his story. He reached over and fingered the stem of one of the lilacs in the glass.

"Uncle Joe? You okay?"

He nodded, without looking at me. "Uh-huh," he said. "I'm alright."

"You want me to go?" I asked. "It's getting late."

"No," he answered. "Just need some more water." I poured him some, and took my seat again by the door.

"I don't like talking about this next part," he said. "I ain't ever told a living soul about what went on over those next few years. Don't like to think about it, but I suppose it's got to come out sometime." My uncle sighed, and pinned me again with his one good eye.

"We didn't ever get along with him, Dora and me, but then again we rarely saw him. He'd be gone long weeks at sea fishing, and Dora would do for us what needed to be done. Mom used to say he was the only one could ever get Dora to listen. Even when she was a baby, she said, all he had to do was look at her crossways and she'd quiet up.

"Less than a week after the funeral he went back out fishing, but before he went he made Dora quit school. She didn't want to, I remember. She fought him, and when he asked her who she thought would keep the house while she was off with her nose stuck in a book somewhere, she said Mrs. Vivian from next door didn't mind helping out. But he wouldn't hear of it.

"'I ain't havin' one of those old biddies from the village poking around in this house when I'm gone. She'll have the size of every pair of drawers I own advertised in the Port Shine *Advocate* by Sunday.'

"So Dora quit school, though she was doing pretty well that year, and that's when I came home, right after Dad went back out fishing, and found the lilac bush burnt. When I asked

Dora about it she just shrugged. 'I hate the smell of 'em now,' she said.

"Mrs. Vivian came over when she saw it to give us three shades of holy hell for burning down one of God's living things, but when Dora said why she did it, she softened up a bit. Mrs. Vivian was good to us those years. She showed Dora how to cook a meal, though it was a few years fore she caught on to that good, and how to sew and boil jam to get rid of the scum. I helped out when I could. After school the two of us would do whatever chore she had picked for me that day, like wash down the windows or split wood. We went to church every Sunday, like our mother always told us to do, and Dora took care of me. It wasn't like it was with Mom, 'cause Dora really didn't know what she was doing, not for those first few months anyways, but it was alright. At night the two of us would play cribbage in the kitchen or listen to *Country Jubilee* on the radio, and Mrs. Vivian would always stop in before she went to bed to make sure we was okay. We talked about our mother a lot, and sometimes the two of us would get to crying. Once Mrs. Vivian came in and found us both letting loose and she stayed with us most of the night and put us to bed.

"'It's hard to understand,' she said to us, 'why two children should have to lose their mother and make their own way in the world, but that's just the way it is.'

"She never mentioned our father. Both Dora and I knew that the village was scandalized that he would just up and out so close after his wife died, and leave his children all alone like that. But we never thought much about it. To tell the truth, it was harder on Dora than me. The housework was getting her down. And she missed her friends from school, she said. A few of them would come over, and Dora would serve 'em tea and they would sit and talk like they'd seen their mothers do a thousand times. But when it came time for those girls to go, Dora couldn't go with them. They was all interested in boys, but not one of 'em was interested in getting their little brother's supper on the table and mending what socks Dad had left behind, like Dora had to do. Still, we did okay, except for the times he was home.

"We always knew when he was coming. News of the boats came in now and then, and he would send Dora a note by one of the men on an earlier trawler to have the house ready. He also sent a list of things to be done, and the nights before he came back Dora and I didn't play cards or listen to any radio. We were too busy scrubbing floors, cleaning out the root cellar, anything else he could think of. By the time the old man limped in the door on a Friday night we had that place spotless, I can tell you. Not that it usually wasn't anyway. People were already starting to say Dora kept a better house than our own mother had when she was alive.

"It was always the same — the two of us sitting at the kitchen table waiting for him. He usually stopped off at the tavern first, so most times he had a skin full of beer and a hate on for someone or other on the boats when he finally came into the kitchen. Dora would jump up right then and get supper ready and my father would sit down at the table without even taking his oilskins off and wait for Dora to serve him. He didn't ever ask what we'd been up to while he was gone, but he had his spies. If Dora and me did something not to his liking we'd hear about it, and more than likely get a whipping with a kindling stick after dinner. Then he'd go up, change, and come back downstairs to head out to the tavern for the night. That's mostly where he could be found when he was home — at the tavern or hungover at home. The first time he came home after our mother died, Dora looked at me when he left for the night and said, 'Ain't he a sweet little ol' thing?'

"That got the two of us to laughing, though we was still half-scared of him. For years he hardly had any doings with us at all. It was our mother he talked to, and shouted at, and got angry with when he was drinking. But now it was only us and him. Dora said to me once when he was home that it was like she'd never known who he was before, and she didn't care to get to know him now.

"'Maybe we could run away?' I told her that time. 'Somewhere where he won't ever find us?'"

"'Nowhere to run,' she answered. 'And nothing to run with.'"

For the next five years my mother took care of my uncle and her father. She washed, cooked, cleaned, bought whatever groceries were needed at the dry goods store. She even dressed my uncle in the mornings. Gradually, Joe said, he began to lose his sister, and gain another mother. Her cooking skills improved, though my uncle confessed he never did enjoy much of what my mother made. I could understand that. Even after so many years of cooking for her brother and father, and then her own husband and children, my mother had never really become an accomplished cook. Her meats were always dry or slightly burnt, and the vegetables soggy or underdone. She continued to go to church and be involved in the community although, Joe said, she began after awhile to adopt her father's views on God rather than her pious dead mother's.

"If God is so powerful," she said to my uncle once, "and he cares so much about people, why doesn't he come down and clean this house in the morning, 'cause I'm getting damn tired of doing it!"

For my mother this had always been the standard argument

against the existence of God. A truly loving one would have made life as easy as possible and eliminated all suffering. She saw God as some kind of traitor or coward, whereas Billy, Tom, and I had always seen Him as a kind of giant Chargex account in the sky to which you prayed for the things you wanted. But she continued to go to church because it was what was expected of her, and, when my grandfather was home from the boats, it gave her a place to go on Sunday mornings to talk with other women and get some peace, even if the peace she was looking for was the secular kind. In church she met my father.

Though I never gave it much thought when I was growing up, I now see my father and mother as one of the world's most unlikely couples. There is a picture in my mother's parlor of my father as a young man. It is in black and white, but even across the expanse of years there is something about my father, in his black Sunday suit, his blond wavy hair not yet beginning to recede, that reflects an intense, irrepressible optimism. He looks like a man full of the word and aware of his glory. How my mother ever contained or satisfied a man with such a look I will never know. But somehow she ended up marrying him. I'm inclined to think contentment or satisfaction was never a component of their coupling.

Though my mother never described to us children the first time she met my father, he told us before he died that he'd met her because he was in the choir. I don't remember him having an especially good singing voice, but his father the Reverend made him sing in the church choir anyway. The choir apparently never suffered from my father's lack of training or natural ability, for they were considered good and were often invited to other Baptist churches in the province to perform. It happened that somehow my father's choir was brought to my mother's tiny village. I don't know from my father or mother if it was love at first sight, but knowing my mother, I doubt it was love at first anything. I suppose it was possible their eyes met, my mother sitting quietly in the pews, probably bored out of her mind, and my father standing robed and solemn before her with the other choir members, singing loudly for the Lord. My uncle told me that they first spoke to each other after the service, when the church auxiliary, of which my mother was a infrequent member, held a pot luck dinner in the church basement on behalf of the singing guests. My mother was serving grape punch and rolls. My father stopped in the line to talk to her across the serving table. There are no records of what was said. Only my father and mother were there to report it and they chose not to. But my uncle knew that something had happened for it wasn't long before my father came to my mother's little village again. This time he wasn't with the choir but alone and driving his father's green Thunderbird. The car would have been brand new then and must have impressed my mother in spite of herself. Not one member of their town owned a car. My uncle reported that my father took my mother for a drive around town in it that first Saturday. When my mother came home my uncle, then thirteen, was waiting.

"So how was it?" he asked her excitedly. "Did you go fast?"

"Silly machine," my mother reported. "What good is it if you can't travel a cow path? We could only stay on the main street!" Then my mother, inadvertently anticipating the invention of the four-wheel drive, added, "Until they make cars so you can drive all over hell's half acre, they're not worth the metal they put into them."

But even my uncle could tell his sister was taken with my father. He knew because she never spoke about him. A sure sign my mother was considering you for something was if she didn't include you in her endless list of those who weren't worth the 'breath God gave 'em.' My uncle only watched in amusement as my father came down every Saturday in the green Ford and took my mother out driving. At the end of each day, she would come home full of contempt for automobiles but without one bad word for Harold Conrad. Even her father began to notice that something was up. One Saturday evening after the drive, in my uncle's presence, he sat her down to talk about it. My mother, of course, was fearful he wouldn't approve.

"Not that he gave a crap what we did," my uncle said. "As long as it didn't interfere with his plans."

"How," I asked, "would Mom marrying Dad interfere with his plans?"

My uncle only shrugged. "Your mother was afraid he wouldn't want to let her go."

"Because of the housework?"

"Yes. She was nineteen, but she was still scared of him. If my father decided she couldn't marry, she wouldn't."

I was surprised that at this point my mother had already decided she would marry my father. I asked my Uncle Joe if they were engaged or something.

"No," my uncle said. "They never talked of it. But I think from the first Dora knew your father would marry her. I think for each of them the other was the first person they'd ever been interested in." I nodded and let my uncle continue with the story. He told how he was helping my mother with the dishes shortly after she'd arrived back from an automobile drive with young Harold. Their father was upstairs taking a nap. He came down, poured himself a cup of tea, and sat down in a rocker. My mother and uncle had been carrying on a conversation about Harold, but stopped when their father came into the room. All conversations had a way of being halted when my grandfather was around.

"Dora," he said after a few minutes of watching his children at the kitchen sink together. "Put down that rag and come over here and talk to me."

My mother did, throwing an unreadable glance at my uncle. Uncle Joe stayed at the sink doing the dishes but kept a sharp ear to the conversation taking place behind him.

"Who is this Harold fella you've been going out with?" my grandfather asked as soon as my mother sat down across from him. "And why is he up here every Saturday squiring you about in that fancy car of his?"

"I guess it's 'cause he likes me," my mother answered. "I don't know why he comes up."

"He likes you huh?" asked my grandfather. "He like you enough to do things to you in that car of his, Dora?"

"What things?" my mother asked boldly. My uncle, who knew 'what things,' though he was only thirteen and had never done them, and knew his sister knew as well, smiled to himself and kept washing dishes.

"You know what things I'm talking about," my grandfather said. "Don't play little Miss Innocent with me, Dora. I want to know if you've given yourself over to him."

"No," said my mother firmly. "I have not."

"Well," my grandfather began, "I don't care if you do, one way or another, but I'm telling you if he gets you knocked up, he better be prepared to marry you, 'cause I ain't feeding another mouth around here, you got that?"

"Yes, Dad," my mother said.

"So," my grandfather said, after a pause. "You gonna or what?"

"Gonna what?" my mother asked.

"Marry him, dummy!"

"He ain't asked me yet."

"What's this fella do for a living?"

"Well," my mother began slowly, "he don't do anything right now, except sing in the choir. His father's a minister."

"Sing in the choir?" my grandfather said. "You sure you want to marry a man who sings in a choir, Dora, and don't do anything for a living?"

"Oh, he'll get a job," said my mother. "I don't plan on marrying anyone who won't work for a living."

"What kind of job?"

"I don't know," said my mother uncertainly. "He's been talking about going to lineman's school in Halifax and working for the power company. They say that's pretty good work, and steady."

"What about preaching?" asked my grandfather. "I hear that's the steadiest job they got. There's always some poor sucker out there will buy into it."

"He doesn't want to preach," said my mother. "He told me that. I really think he's going to lineman's school."

"Well, when you two are ready, you just send him over to me to ask for your hand."

"I will, Dad."

My uncle and my mother thought that was the end of it. My grandfather never spoke about it again. My father went off to Halifax for a six-month course in lineman's school and when he came back still there was no talk of marriage. People around my mother's village began to say my father was only toying with her, and that eventually he'd marry another girl from that inland town he belonged to. People in those parts distrusted anyone who didn't fish for a living. They couldn't imagine what other work a man could do and be satisfied with. But the day came when my mother and my father, who had never before stepped foot inside her house, came in together. My grandfather, as usual, was sleeping off a few pints of ale from the tavern. My uncle, who happened to be hungover from his first, but not last, night of secret drinking, ran upstairs to wake him. When my grandfather came down, my mother and father were waiting in the kitchen, and my father, wasting no time, stood up to greet his prospective father-in-law.

"Mr. Smith," he said. "I'm here to ask for your daughter's hand in marriage."

"I guess I knew you were," he said, sitting down after shaking my father's hand. "Dora," he said, "fetch me a cup of tea."

My mother got up and poured some off the stove, while my father continued with what must have been a prepared speech. Perhaps he and my mother had cooked it up in the car before coming in.

"I know it's hard for you to lose your daughter," my father began. "But I want you to know that I'll take very good care of her. I got my lineman's ticket now and I'll be starting work in my hometown in less than a month. I was hoping, with your permission, Dora and I could be married by then."

"In your hometown?" my grandfather asked, and without a word of thanks took the teacup my mother held out to him. My mother cast a glance back and forth between the two men, then turned and went back to her seat. She looked over at my uncle, who stood in the doorway to the living room, watching, and shooed him away with her hand. But my uncle didn't move.

"You planning on taking Dora away?" my grandfather asked.

"Only to my father's house on Gaston Road near Trenton," my father answered. "It's not a long drive. An hour at most. We'll be back often enough."

"Then who is supposed to take care of this place when Dora's gone?"

"Pardon?" My father wasn't sure that he'd heard my mother's

father right, but my uncle knew he had. It was the question they feared he would ask.

"I said," repeated my grandfather, "who is supposed to do all of the cooking and cleaning and washing up around here without Dora to do it?"

"Well, I dunno," my father said, obviously not prepared for such a question. But if he wasn't, my mother sure was. She stood and said to her father, "You can't expect me to hang around here and take care of you all my life, can you?"

"Not all your life. But a few more years of it anyway. I'll tell you what, Harold, you go and find me a young woman to take care of this place and you can have Dora."

"But Mr. Smith . . ." my father said. He was unable to say more before my mother pushed him aside and stood before her father's chair. "Don't be ridiculous, Dad. I've been here long enough, and Harold and I are getting married. You'll have to do the cooking and cleaning yourself."

"I can do it," my Uncle Joe said. He'd stepped into the room to get a better view of the action. But my grandfather looked at him contemptuously. "You? What do you know about cleaning? You're out all night drinking with those kids you call friends. I heard you come in this morning, don't you worry, and I smelled the booze on you still this afternoon." My uncle, having been so exposed, slunk away like a fox out of the kitchen, and sat down in the unlit parlor. From there he heard these words from my mother.

"I know you want me to wait, Dad," she said. "But I can't. Harold and I are going to have a baby."

A silence filled the house. Uncle Joe waited breathlessly in the dark to hear what his father would say. Finally the words came. "So you got knocked up, did you?"

"We were gonna tell you," stammered my father. "We were gonna get married anyway."

"And I suppose," said my grandfather, "that you know for sure this baby belongs to young Harold here?"

My mother told her father to be quiet. Uncle Joe listened quietly from the living room. He knew, as did my mother, what their father was referring to. His sister had taken the place of their mother in more ways than one with his father, though until the night he told me about it he'd never said such a thing aloud. There had been a few nights when his father had come home drunk from the tavern, and he heard him go into Dora's room, and afterwards listened to his sister cry, and curse, and swear that she'd cut it off if the old man ever came near her again. There was no one for my mother to tell. These were things you didn't talk about in that place, or in that time. It was a secret my mother was intent on keeping from her future husband. It was a secret she felt she had to keep.

"You miserable old son of a bitch," she said to her father. "I hate you, do you know that? I can't wait to get out of here, away from you, away from this Goddamned house!"

My uncle heard his father get up from the chair, heard him slap my mother. "I'll be telling you when you can get married and when you can't. And where you can go and where you can't. And we'll be examining any babies that come out around here for looks and eye colour, I can tell you that!" My grandfather was still shouting at her to stay when my mother, shouting back, pulled my bewildered father out the front door. My Uncle Joe, with his father still cursing in the kitchen, ran away upstairs and hid in a closet, knowing that the anger could turn on him as easily as it did his sister. After about an hour, when he heard nothing but silence, he crept out again. He tiptoed down the stairs, through the parlor and into the lighted kitchen. His father was gone, probably to the tavern to drink. Joe went back upstairs, and crawled into his bed, but not before wedging a chair under the inside knob of his bedroom door, in case his father came home with a few in him, wanting to take out more of his frustration. He went to sleep knowing that he wouldn't see his sister inside the house again.

"Did she come back?" I asked him. He'd been talking for nearly two hours by then, and it was nearing eleven o'clock. My uncle was sober, and looked tired. But he answered me. "No. 'Course she didn't."

"And when did you leave?"

"About six years later. I'll tell you, those years alone in that house with the old man were hell. Pure hell."

"I bet they were," I said to him.

Although I'd heard some of my uncle's stories before, about him and my mother, though never in such honest and disturbing detail, the woman Uncle Joe was describing wasn't the woman I knew. I resisted this version of my mother as happy-go-lucky turned by life and circumstance into the bitter woman my brothers and I had grown up with. A few sob stories and the realization, which I'd had before, that she'd had no easy life wasn't going to make me forgive her. This, however, my uncle already knew.

"But," he said, "these things you should know just the same. These things your mother ain't ever told anyone."

"And the baby," I said. "Who did it belong to?"

"It was Harold's. A couple of times the old man might have been at her, but for a long while she wouldn't she let him near her. The old man made her hard, like him, he did. And then, when he saw he was losing her, he tried to keep her there with that terrible secret. But she wasn't having it."

Uncle Joe looked down at his hands on his lap — rough, red-veined, and crippled with arthritis in the fingers. "I always felt sorry for your mother, that she had to live with that. She was a nice girl once — pretty and young and funny. The things that happened to her made her hard. The things that happen to us make us all hard. I just wanted you to know that."

I waited for my uncle to finish, but it was getting late, and I didn't want to hear any more of this. "Uncle Joe," I whispered finally, "I have to go now. I have things to do."

Yet he, that quickly, had fallen asleep in his chair, his head on his chest. I felt such a surge of love then, for this old man trapped in a failing body. I felt like going over and planting a kiss on his grizzled cheek. I opened my wallet instead, left twenty dollars on the table beside him, and left his little shack. I was nearly back at my mother's when something occurred to me. The realization came so suddenly I almost drove the car off the road into a field. I had to pull over. I thought of calling my uncle when I got home, knowing I could not wait until next week to ask him the question I'd just thought of. But he had no phone, and before I knew what I was doing I'd turned the car around. I broke all speeding limits to make it back to Main Street and my uncle's little house. When I pulled the car off the road and looked down over the bank I saw my uncle's lights were still on. I jumped out of the car, and ran down the hill to his shack. I didn't even knock, just burst in the front door. He was sitting in the same chair, but no longer drifting. He was wide awake.

"Took you long enough," he said.

"I just figured it out."

"I promised your mother I'd never tell."

"But you did tell," I said, fighting for breath from my run. "You told me some of it. How much more can there be?"

"More," said my uncle. "A lot more."

I sat down across from my uncle, as excited as I ever remember being. It was this my uncle had wanted to tell me from the beginning, this he had carried inside him all this time. "Mom and Dad were married in 1947," I said as calmly as I could manage. "That night you were just telling me took place the same year. Tom was born three years after, in 1950."

"That's right," said my uncle. "I thought you was smart, Luke. I thought you would pick up on that right away."

"I didn't," I said simply. "So, when Mom told her father that night she was pregnant, who was she pregnant with?"

My uncle looked at me for a long time before answering. "I told your mother I'd never tell."

"You already did," I repeated. "So who was she pregnant with?"

"As if you didn't know," my uncle responded. "Tom's older brother."

My father and mother married on the 12th of August in the Baptist church in my father's hometown. Few of the guests were for my mother. Most didn't have the means to make the trip to Trenton. My Uncle Joe was there, standing in as ring bearer. My grandfather was not. He said he had to fish that day, though my mother thought that even if he was free he wouldn't have come. My mother didn't talk to him after that. Even when he died four years after of a heart attack, she went up only for the afternoon of the funeral, with my father.

The Reverend Conrad performed the ceremony, with my father's mother looking on. Her appointment with death wasn't to come for another year. The rest of the church was filled with members of my reverend grandfather's congregation. No one gave my mother away; that part of the ceremony was skipped.

A boyhood friend of my father's, already married himself, stood in as best man. The ceremony was typically Baptist — boring, uneventful, and over quickly. There was a reception on the church lawn with no alcohol served. The community my father came from was formed over a temperance pledge and there was no greater proponent of temperance than the Reverend Conrad. Looking back, it's possible that a large part of the attraction my father held for my mother was that she didn't drink. What attraction my mother held for my father I can't say, and I won't try to. There must have been some. My father wasn't especially good-looking, but he was a minister's son, and therefore very eligible. He could have had others if he'd wanted, but for some reason he chose my mother.

My mother stood apart from the other guests at the reception after the receiving line was held, and no amount of effort to draw her into conversation worked. Eventually my uncle, who was no better at socializing with the children of the wedding guests than my mother was with adults, stood beside her. They let the polite celebration take place around them.

"I don't like these people," my mother said. "They're all farmers." As if that was enough of a reason to condemn an entire village, my uncle nodded agreement.

"I'd like to get Harold out of here," my mother said to my Uncle Joe a few minutes later. "But his father won't hear of it."

"Where would you go?" Uncle Joe asked her.

"Somewhere," my mother said. "Anywhere."

"Back home?"

"God no," said my mother. "Another town, where we don't know anyone."

"Good luck," my uncle said. "You already got a house."

They did. My father had rented a small farmhouse near the edge of town, within walking distance of his work with the

South Eastern Division of the Nova Scotia Light and Power Company. Once they had put in a suitable amount of time at the reception, my mother managed to drag my father away. There was no honeymoon. They didn't have the money and he was to start work the following Monday. He and my mother just went home to their newly rented house. None of the wedding guests believed a honeymoon was necessary anyway. They all knew my mother was pregnant, though at the time she still didn't show. My uncle never said whether there was opposition to the wedding from my father's side, though knowing what little I do of my grandfather and how he and my mother never liked each other, I imagine there was some. Suffice it to say that my mother complained to my uncle whenever he saw her, which was rarely, that the Reverend Conrad visited far too much, especially after his wife died. At first, my uncle said, she didn't oppose his visits, but after the first child was born, my mother began to get her sense of worth as a parent and a wife. She took over the little farmhouse at the edge of town, and it became routine for my grandfather to call first before he made the half-hour drive from Gaston Road.

The child, my oldest brother, was born on New Year's Day of 1948. My mother had him at home with a midwife in attendance. He was a big child, my uncle said — 11 pounds and 8 ounces. Soon my parents were consumed with raising the boy.

"They spoiled that child," my uncle told me. "All they talked about was him."

"Spoiled?" I asked, fascinated. "I can't imagine my mother spoiling anybody."

"Yup," said my uncle. "She did."

"So what happened to him?"

My uncle sighed, and repeated, "I told your mother I'd never tell."

"Jesus, Uncle Joe. You're already telling. Just get on with it."

He sighed again and said, "He died, when he was a little over two years old."

I had figured that much out already. "How did he die?"

And so my uncle told how when the boy was two-and-a-half years old my mother was out hanging the wash on the line. She was already four months pregnant with Tom. The boy was playing in the dirt beside her on that July afternoon, and she turned to reach down into her basket. By the time she stood upright again her son had wandered off into the long grasses behind their house. My mother called after him, dropped the clothes basket, and followed him into the field. But the grasses were long and over the boy's head. She couldn't see him, but she could hear him. He was crying for her. Suddenly she heard a child's thin scream, then nothing. My mother knew exactly where to look for him. She ran through the tall grasses to an abandoned well on their property. It had been covered with plywood, but that had rotted through. My mother had discovered it a year and a half before and asked my father to fix it. He said he would. He hadn't. My mother looked down into the well and saw her son lying at the bottom.

"I don't know what she went through," my uncle said. "She never said. Locked it all up inside."

I couldn't imagine how she felt, looking down into the well where her son was lying, motionless. My uncle did know she climbed down into it herself, scraping herself up in the process and tearing her dress, but the boy had hit his head on the side of the well as he fell and was already dead. She picked him up in her arms, but couldn't climb back out again. She held him across her lap at bottom of the well, crying and screaming, until my father came home from work two hours later. He didn't remember the well. He only heard his wife's shouts from somewhere in the field. Eventually he found her, got a rope, and hauled mother and dead child out. My mother laid her first born in the long grasses, and my father, shouting out his grief, fell across the body.

"Oh God!" he cried. "Oh God, why did you do this?"

"Stop praying," my mother shouted. "Go get help."

"He's dead, Dora!"

"No he isn't!" my mother said. "He's just sleeping." She turned away and ran back to the house, leaving my father kneeling and praying over his dead son. When she came back out my father was carrying the boy back to the house, staggering under the awful weight of his grief.

"It's your fault!" my mother screamed at him. "I told you to cover the well!"

But my grandfather, when he came over, blamed my mother. "It's your fault," he said. "You should have been watching him."

"It's God's fault," said my father. "He should have protected him."

"God," said my grandfather, "has a purpose for everything. This is not His fault."

"Get out," my mother said to her father-in-law. "You and your bloody Bible, get out, and don't come back again."

My grandfather went, and to get away from him, my mother convinced my father to move away from his hometown, to Tyler's Cape, where eventually he would die on the power lines. There, they had Tom, Billy, and me.

"Your mother," explained my uncle, "told your father and me never to talk about it. We weren't supposed to tell anyone."

"But why?" I cried. "Why wouldn't she tell us about such a horrible thing?"

"She wanted to forget it ever happened."

I sat, stunned to silence, just allowing the thoughts to come at me. It explained so much about her. She loved her first child. He died. She could never love us as much as she did him. She would not allow herself to. I knew that much about her. But there was one detail my uncle had neglected to tell me.

"What was his name?" I asked. "You never used it."

"Can't you guess? Your father named him after his favorite Gospel."

I nodded, and whispered aloud, "Matthew." But my uncle had another surprise for me.

"No. Matthew was your father's favorite later. He had another before that."

Suddenly I knew. I don't know how I knew, but it came to me with such certainty. It didn't make any sense. Why hadn't Tom gotten his name?

"Your father wanted to name Tom after him right away. Harold thought it would be a good way of forgetting the first child, if they named another after him. But your mother wouldn't hear of it. When Billy came along he tried again, but still your mother picked another name. Then you, and this time she finally gave in, and your father got his way."

"She must have thought of him every time she called out to me," I said. A heavy weight shifted inside me, some great sadness, some grinding rotation of perception. "Every time she looked at me she must have thought of him."

"I suppose she did," my uncle said. "I suppose she must have."

"What a terrible mistake he made. Giving me that name. Why did she let him do it?"

"I told her she should change it," said my Uncle Joe. "But by then it was too late. The name had stuck."

"Luke!" I said aloud, calling not my own name, but that of

the dead brother who I never knew I had. I sat there stunned by the revelation. I could picture perfectly the scene of my dead older brother in the well and my mother with him, as clearly and with as much detail as if I had actually been there. Etta and Billy would have been proud of me. I'd had my first and only vision.

THE RING AND OTHER STORIES
&

My mother finally left her home in the autumn of 1996. Tom took her, and even in the car as they drove into the Cape, he tried to convince her to live with him.

"Arrangements have already been made," she said. "I'll go where we planned."

That was the last autumn my mother was to see in the Cape. As they drove she quietly watched the trees with their coloured leaves slip by her window. Tom took her directly through town on some pretence or other, but what he really wanted was for my mother to have one last look. Of course there wasn't much to see. The grocery store had closed that year and so had the cod plant. The Sea Cottage Inn along Main Street had become rundown and what my mother used to call "paint poor." The post office was still there, but the windows in Milo's second-hand shop had all been broken and boarded over. Even Carson's had closed when the fire inspector condemned the building three years before. Carson was supposed to take some of the money he'd made over all those years and build a new place, but so far he hadn't. If people wanted to drink or buy groceries, or anything else for that matter, they made the half-hour drive to Oldsport. Tyler's Cape was starting to resemble a ghost town. Many people still lived there, but there was little commerce anymore.

My mother sat in front with Tom. She knew very well she would not be back. It had taken Tom twenty minutes to help her into the car. There wasn't anything wrong with her mind. It was her legs that were going. In the spring of the year before, she had broken her hip again in a fall on the icy front steps; that time she'd stayed in hospital until it healed fully, which it never really did. When she walked now, she did so slowly and with much pain, with one hand always on her left hip, almost bent double. She was nearly constantly out of breath from the effort of moving about. She couldn't make it up the stairs alone at first, and then not at all. She had been sleeping on the couch. Since the grocery store had closed, Tom ran her errands in Trenton and drove what she needed to the Cape. But he couldn't be with her at all times. It got so that she could not stand at the stove and cook and was barely able to lift wood from the wood box. There was no question of housecleaning either. Her beloved furniture began to collect dust, and the floors were always dirty. Tom approached her about moving in with him. But my mother wouldn't agree to it, even though Suzanne was no longer there. Suzanne had left Tom as promised. When my mother found out she only nodded.

"I knew it would happen," she said to me. "I knew it from the first." And I wondered if my mother did really know, if that was why she refused to attend Tom and Suzanne's wedding.

My mother, who had sense enough to know she could no longer live at home, told Tom she would rather live in the nursing apartments in Trenton. It wasn't a care facility exactly. Many lived in the apartments independently, but it was cheap, had few stairs, and there were nurses on duty if you needed them. "You come get me when it's time," my mother had said to Tom, "I'll be ready. It won't be for very long," she'd added. Tom had let this go, and packed her up one fall day and drove her down to Trenton, though he tried to convince her the whole way that his house would be better. To the end my mother would not live in my grandfather's house, and since I'd discovered the story of my dead brother and my grandfather's thoughtless accusations, I didn't blame her.

I did not come down the day my mother moved out. Tom thought it would be better if it was just the two of them. But as soon as I decently could, I went to visit my mother in Trenton. A nurse led me into her little ground floor apartment. She was sitting in a rocker beside the window, looking out of it like she did at home. But there was no ocean to see, only a few trees on the lawn of the home and the wide residential streets beyond. I took a seat in the other rocker, my father's. My mother had asked that it be brought with her.

"Hello, Mom."

My mother turned away from the window. "Hello, Luke."

"How are you making out?"

My mother told me stories of the building, without rancour. She spoke with effort of the nurses who pushed her around in her wheelchair when she needed it, whenever her hips were acting up and she couldn't walk. She spoke of other residents, some of whom she talked to, others to whom she didn't.

"There's an old Scot who lives here," my mother told me. "She's about ninety. She reminds me a lot of Etta. We play cribbage once in a while, when she feels up to it."

Eventually, I asked my mother about her childhood. It had become ritual for me, to come and see my mother and ask her questions about all the things my Uncle Joe had told me. My uncle was dead. He'd died the year before, alone, in his shack. Billy came home for the funeral, though he only stayed two days before getting on a plane to Toronto. He had landed a job at one of the newspapers there as an entertainment writer. He sent us his articles sometimes, clipped from the Toronto *Sun*. He was the oldest cub reporter in the history of the paper. Apparently he was quite good at his job, and already starting to get noticed. I'd talked to Billy about the boy in the well, as I'd come to think of him, though for some reason I'd had never mentioned it to Tom.

"What did he look like?" I asked my mother now. Sometimes when I talked of these things she wouldn't answer. At other times she would get angry, but there were times she did answer my questions. Like today. "He was a beautiful little boy," she said. "He had dark hair like you and Billy. I imagine he would have looked a lot like you. You, Billy, and Luke got my looks. Tom got your father's."

"Do you still think about him?"

"Every day," said my mother, and grew silent again.

I stayed for awhile, talking about other things, until I noticed she was looking tired. I kissed her on the cheek before I went, something I had begun to do lately. She didn't pull away. She didn't have the energy. Every time I went to see her I asked her questions about things I wanted to know, and I kissed her before I left. This was how I'd changed.

She was in the home about a year when we got the call. We knew it was coming. She had caught a cold a week or so before, and, like her mother before her, it developed into pneumonia. It moved into her bones and took possession of her lungs. The nurses told us all to come in — that it would be today or tomorrow. I called Billy in Toronto right away.

"Billy," I said. "It's Luke."

"Hi, Luke. How's it going?"

"She's bad," I told him. "They told us all to come in. She won't make it much longer."

"I'll be home tonight," Billy said. I hung up and left my own apartment in Halifax. I had no idea that it would be for one of the last times. I drove into Trenton as quickly as I could. Tom met me just outside the door to my mother's hospital room.

"How is she?" I asked him.

"Bad," he answered. "Go in and see her."

I went in. My mother was lying on her bed, an oxygen tube in her nose, needles in her arms, machines obscure in purpose keeping silent watch around her. Yet she lay peacefully — her hair, now completely white, arranged by some thoughtful nurse in a fan across her pillow. It was the first time I'd seen her up close with her hair down. I couldn't help noticing how beautiful it was. I glanced at her chest under the nightgown. It was still rising and falling. I heard each laboured breath even over the beeps and gyrations of the machines that were helping to keep her alive. I sat down beside her and took one of her hands in my own. She opened her eyes, confused, disoriented. Tom had told me they were giving her morphine. It was the drugs, he said, that would eventually kill her. The doses needed to ease her pain would grow larger and larger until she died of them.

"It's Luke, Mom."

"Luke," she whispered hoarsely.

"How are you doing?"

My mother moved her head slightly on the pillow, but she did not look at me. Instead, she nodded once, and then said, "Is Billy coming?"

"Yes," I answered. "He's coming."

My mother nodded again. "Good. And Joe?"

"Joe's dead, Mom." I said. "Remember?"

She sighed. "Your uncle owes your father and me fifty dollars," she said. "He borrowed it when Tom was little, and he never paid it back. We couldn't afford to lose fifty dollars."

I patted the top of her hand. "That wasn't right," I said.

My mother closed her eyes again. I sat beside her for a long while, monitoring her breathing, waiting for something to happen. But it wouldn't happen yet, for I had something to say to her. I jiggled her hand a little, and her eyes opened again.

"Mom," I said. She only stared up at the ceiling. "Mom. I love you." It was the first time I'd ever said it to her. She didn't move, only continued staring upwards at the ceiling. I didn't expect her to say anything, yet I waited for it. A while longer and she closed her eyes again. I waited around, but she didn't open them again. When I left she was still alive.

Billy came in a rented car from the airport, and Tom and I waited outside my mother's door while he visited with her. Then all three of us went out for a solemn dinner in Trenton. When we came back there had been no change. We went to Tom's house, from which we could all get back quickly in case of any news. Roland, still alive and well in Carleton with his sister, called shortly after we got home.

"She's hanging on," Tom told him. "But it won't be long."

The next morning she died.

Billy stayed for a week. My mother was buried in the Cape next to my father. There weren't many people there. Most of those my mother's age were dead already, and the Cape was a lot smaller than it used to be. The funeral was held at the Baptist church. The new minister conducted the service. He was young, perhaps only twenty-four or twenty-five, and everything he said, even the eulogy, contained the irrepressible optimism of youth. I knew my mother, had she been alive to hear it, would not have approved. Yet the young minister reminded me of my father.

After the funeral the three of us went back to Tom's house. We thought of staying in the old house on the Cape, but no one had been in it for a year or more; it would have been too rundown. So we stayed at my grandfather's house. Tom bought beer and we sat in the living room of his house and Tom and I drank it. Billy drank soda water. It had been seven years since he'd touched a drink. We talked of our lives mostly, and of our mother. Billy and I finally told Tom the story of our older brother Luke. It was as good a time as any. Tom looked as shocked as I'd felt when I heard it.

"You mean she never told anyone?" he said.

"She didn't like to think of it," I told him.

The three of us sat around in paisley-upholstered wing chairs that had belonged to my grandfather. I chose the one nearest to the bronze statue of Tom that I'd made. Once in a while I reached down and touched it. Tom talked a lot about Suzanne, and Billy and I listened. With the help of the beer he cried a little.

"I'm sorry," Billy said when he was done.

"Me too, Tom."

Halfway through the evening, Billy ran out to the car and returned with a briefcase. He sat back down in his chair, put the briefcase in his lap and opened it. Out of it he drew a small volume of stories bearing his name.

"I just published it," he told us. "It won't make me famous or anything, but I thought you should know about it."

Billy passed the book around. The title on the front page read *The Ring and Other Stories.*

Tom handed it back to him, and Billy offered to read us the title story. We agreed. Billy fitted a pair of thick black reading glasses on his face and opened the book. It struck me how much he resembled our father in that moment. He was heavier than our father had been, but his hair had begun to recede, more in fact than our father's had before he died. It occurred to me that Billy was now six years older than my father was at his death. I looked over at Tom. He too looked like Harold Conrad. At forty-six his hair, receding as well, was almost entirely grey, though his face retained the boyishness it had always had. We were all middle-aged men, but now that we were together it was if we were still boys.

When Billy started to read the title story his resemblance to my father deepened. His voice took on a new confidence and cadence, the same way my father's was when he read to us from his beloved Gospels.

"It was a chill, rain-washed afternoon of a late August day," Billy began, "and my brothers and I had taken to the beach below our house to dig up whole sand dollars, and torment unlucky crabs that came crawling in on the beach at low tide. We would carefully lift the crabs and turn them over on their backs to bake them in their shells. If we felt kind we might release them, let them scurry away to the safety of the sea. Or we might kill them, drop a heavy boulder and crush them in their shells. It was our one small cruelty, and it served the purpose of taking our minds off the fact that inside our house, above us on the Cape, our father was dying, and our mother was preparing for a hard life without him."

Billy read to us of three boys who lose their father to cancer and the one son who slips the father's wedding ring off his finger during the funeral. The mother notices the ring gone, but doesn't know who has taken it. The father is buried, and the town expresses outrage against whoever stole the ring. Eventually the boy shows the ring to the other brothers, and all three of them, confused, saddened, and sharing responsibility for the act, attempt to dig the father up again and place the ring back on his finger. They get down to the coffin but no one has the courage to open it. They fill the grave back in again. They go home and sneak back into their bedrooms, and the next morning they get up and throw the ring into the ocean. Billy ended his story this way:

"My father was a fisherman. We only wanted something to keep that was his, something to remember him by, but in the end guilt made us let the ring go. We had our memories, but these, too, were tarnished by guilt. Throwing the ring into the ocean was like a second burial, a burial at sea. It is, I think, what my father would have wanted most. He was, after all, a fisherman."

Billy closed the book. None of us said anything, and he didn't ask our opinion. He didn't need to, and Tom and I knew no words were needed. When you create something from deep down inside of you like Billy had done there is no need to ask what anyone thinks of it. The story was about us. The boys had different names and different personalities. The mother was softer, kinder. Our father had died a different death, at a different age. But it was about us, just the same. I couldn't have complimented Billy on it anyway. I was too moved to speak.

Tom said, "You did it, Billy. You're a real writer." We sat there quietly, thinking about Billy's story, and eventually, we decided to go to bed. Tom surprised us when, after turning out the downstairs light, he led us all to the same room. We looked inside and saw that he had moved an extra bed into it.

"It's silly, I know," he said. "We're grown men, and there's plenty of room, but I just thought . . ."

"It's a good idea," said Billy immediately. "Just like we used to do."

So we all quietly, shyly, undressed — three grown men — and slept together in the same room. Tom lay in one bed and Billy and I in another, just like we had when we were boys. Tom turned out the light, and the three of us talked until the early hours. Just as I was falling asleep I heard Etta speak to me in my head, those words she had spoken so long ago when three little boys travelled across the Cape to see an infant's caul.

"You have the sight, my boy," Etta said. "Don't worry. All who are born with the caul do."

"No," I heard myself say to her. "I could never have foreseen this perfect moment."

I fell down into sleep with Etta's voice calling after me, "You have the sight, Luke. You have the sight!"

CAULS REVISITED — EPILOGUE

I live now in the house I grew up in. I left the city, for I was never happy there, and unless I'm forced to or wish to go visit someone I know, I rarely go back. There was no opposition to me taking possession of my mother's house. Billy is in Toronto for good, he says, and unless it is for a visit he will never come back to the Cape. Tom still lives in the house on Gaston Road. Suzanne and he are officially divorced, but they remain friends. In defiance of her age, Suzanne had a child by her new husband, and she brings the little girl to see Tom once a month, sometimes more. Her new husband doesn't mind. Even if he did, that wouldn't stop her. Suzanne is a woman who can't be contained, as my brother Tom found out the hard way.

Tom helped me fix up our old house to my particular taste. Last summer we ripped off the old shingles and replaced them with white aluminium siding. We fitted green shutters around all the windows and built a new chimney and retarred the roof. We tore down the barn — it was falling down anyway — and in its place Tom built a little shed where we keep Billy's Sunbeam for him to drive on his visits home, and the new gas lawn mower I bought shortly after arriving here. The inside of the house has changed as well. We tore up the old linoleum and exposed the wood floors underneath, now sanded, burnished, and waxed. The parlour was always too dark, so we put in a bay window. We replaced the cupboards in the kitchen, and finally removed the wood stove my mother had used for all those years in favour of a Kemo oil burner to heat the house and an electric range to cook on. I sleep in my parents' old room. We converted our boyhood bedroom into a studio. We replaced its small window with a bigger one so I could have a view of the ocean. The room is always cluttered with easels holding up half-finished works, half-squeezed tubes of paint, brushes soaking in mason jars of turpentine, oily rags, and half empty cans of gesso. I spend most of my mornings here, and in the afternoon I go to the gallery.

There's been something of a revival in the Cape. Etta always told us boys that when something old goes, something new comes along to take its place. That is what has happened here. A man from Ontario bought the Sea Cottage Inn, fixed it up, and started advertising in newspapers in his home city. Suddenly people were coming here, not just driving through. Then some of the man's friends got together and opened a few of the old shops. There's a little corner store now, a gift shop, a tea room, and even one of those fancy restaurants where you're served by young waiters and waitresses dressed to the nines. The restaurant doesn't do very well. None of the people from here can afford to eat there, and the tourists don't flock to the

Cape all year round. But the man who started all this has a lot of money, and he says he loves this little town. Some of the shops do alright, and the Inn is full all summer long.

I myself have benefited from this economic boom. I rent Maude Sanders' diner from her. She doesn't charge me much, and so I'm able to afford to keep a little gallery open. I've even sold a few paintings. Three of them, bought by the man from Ontario, made it to a gallery in Toronto. I heard one of them sold for two thousand dollars up there. I don't mind that I was paid only five hundred dollars for all of them combined. The man — his last name is Jenkins — keeps returning to my gallery. The paintings he most wants I won't sell him. They are a series called "Sketches From Tyler's Cape." One of them shows my mother sitting in her rocking chair, staring out of the window at the sea. Another pictures my father lounging on the tree stump reading his Bible. There is one I painted of Tom and me watching Billy throw his fit. Two of the larger canvasses from this series, each ten feet tall and six feet wide, I have placed in the back room. The stock room is windowless and dark. When I led Tom in to have a look I needed to switch on a light though it was early in the afternoon. The two massive paintings hang on opposite walls in the narrow room. Tom stood before each, straining his neck upwards, then looking down practically at his shoes. He looked back and forth between the two for a half-hour. All he could say at the end was, "Jesus Christ, Luke."

When I brought Billy in he stayed for about as long. His comments were similarly brief. Neither of them ever said if they liked the work. I didn't care. I had painted them, and that was enough. One large painting was of my birth — Etta holding me, my face still wrapped in the caul, with all my family looking on. A streak of blue lightning illuminates the one window painted in the scene. The other painting is a life-size depiction of my father, hanging like a crucified man from a string of wires. I call these two "Connections." It would not have been appropriate to ask my brothers if they liked them. I wasn't entirely sure if I approved of them myself, though I knew they had to be painted.

So I spend my mornings in my old bedroom studio painting and my afternoons in the gallery. In winter the gallery is closed. There are not many year-round residents any more. I get lonely. But Tom spends time with me. I think he's just as lonely in his old house. I can always drive to see a few friends in the city. When things look really black, when I think I'm not going to make it through the day, I call Billy in Toronto. He always says the same thing to me: "I love you, Luke." I know this is true. Billy has met the woman he will eventually marry, and they recently had a child. They named him Thomas Luke Conrad.

Today is a beautiful April afternoon. The gallery doesn't open until next week, and I am getting ready. This afternoon I will spend spring cleaning like my mother used to do. Whenever I clean I think of my mother, though she's been dead three years now. I think of her more and more these days. Of my father too.

There are people living in Etta's house. They use it only as a summer cottage, and this is their first week here this spring. They're from the city. The mother is divorced. This morning I had my easel out in front of the house, painting the ocean again. I caught glimpses of two children playing around Etta's house. I kept my eye on them while I painted, and even though I was too far away to see them clearly, I knew who they were. They were my new neighbour's children, a boy and a girl. I wanted to stop what I was doing and go over to them, but I made myself wait. They will come, eventually. I know children better than I know adults.

At mid-morning the children were called in. A few minutes later I saw the mother in the yard. She started across the cape towards my house. I put down my brush as she walked up to me. She was a pretty woman, younger than me, perhaps thirty-five, with blonde hair and white teeth. She wore an apron with a cartoon rooster on it that said Country Cook. It was starched stiff and immaculately white. It looked like it had never been used.

"Hello," I said, and held out my hand. "My name is Luke."

"I'm Monica," she said, and took my proffered hand and shook it. "We just moved in next door."

"Summer people?" I asked, already knowing the answer.

"Yes," she said. "You?"

"No. I live here all year round. This was the house I was born in."

"Really?" Monica said, appearing surprised. Perhaps she didn't know anyone lived in this town but cottagers. She looked carefully at the house. "Do you live here with your wife, Luke?"

I shook my head. "I'm not married."

Perhaps something about the way I said it made Monica look back at me with interest. She would know in time who I was. It was something I was no longer afraid of telling people.

"How do you like the house?" I asked, gesturing back at Etta and Roland's place. Monica turned back to it and sighed. "It needs a lot of work."

"Well, if you need any help, just let me know."

"I will," said Monica. "I guess you knew the people who lived there before?"

"I did. They're dead now."

"There are still things in the house that belong to them. Do you want them?"

"No. You keep them. Or just throw them out. Whatever suits you."

Monica glanced at my canvas on the easel. She looked out at

the ocean, then back at the painting. "It's good," she said.

"Thank you. I have a small gallery in town. It opens next week if you'd like to stop by and have a coffee."

"I'd love to," she said. I picked up my brush again, expecting she would leave, but she didn't. "Can I show you something?"

"What?"

"I'm not sure," said Monica. "Let me go get it."

I painted while she was gone, but somehow I knew what it was she was bringing back. I did not even look up when I heard her coming. She came up beside me and said, "Here it is."

I looked at the pickle jar she held in her hands, and the caul still perfectly preserved inside it.

"What is it?" she said. "It looks like human skin." She looked at me anxiously, as if some great crime had been committed here.

I laughed, and echoing Etta at my birth said "It's only a caul."

"A what?"

"A caul. It's a membrane babies are sometimes born with over their heads. The woman who lived in your house believed it was good luck to keep it."

"I thought those people were childless," Monica said.

"They were."

"Then who does the caul belong to?" I thought a long while before answering her, but she seemed to understand and only waited. Finally I said, "It belonged to a boy who used to live around here. But he's not here anymore."

"Well, then do you want it?" said Monica.

I took the pickle jar from her and held it carefully in my arms, the way one would hold a baby. I looked down at the caul, and then up at Monica. "Come with me for a second."

She followed me past the front of my house and across the

lawn. We climbed the path that led down the east side of the Cape, scrambling over boulders, until we stood at the edge of the water. She stayed back and watched while I picked my way out to the furthest possible rock.

"That boy's dead," I called back to her. "This is the only part that's left of him. Let's have a burial at sea!"

I raised the pickle jar over my head and hurled it into the ocean. It landed with a splash, went under, then bobbed back to the surface. I carefully made my way back to Monica and we watched as the jar was lifted on the waves and floated off into deeper waters. We stood there a long while, in comfortable silence, and I knew suddenly that this woman was going to become my friend. When a fresh breeze picked up off the ocean, Monica lifted her face into it and said, "God, it's beautiful here." She turned to me. "You know, in the city sometimes it feels like I'm only surviving, but when I'm in Tyler's Cape, it feels like I'm finally living. I'm so glad we come here."

"So am I," I said. We watched the jar float away until it was just a glint of sunlight on the water. For some reason the sight of it had me bordering on a revelation, though what it was wouldn't quite come. Finally the thought broke through like a slant of light piercing storm clouds. Monica had placed her finger on the secret that for all these years I'd been trying to learn. My father knew it. Now I knew it too. There are many reasons for surviving, but there is only one reason for living. To celebrate the awesome glory.

ACKNOWLEDGEMENTS

I would like to thank the following for their support and encouragement during the writing of this novel; Brenda Anderson, Steve Brown, Greg Findlay, Yvonne Greer, Beverly Greer, Jake Linklater, and Monica MacNeil.

I would especially like to thank Sam Mainster and Kim Thomas for critical readings of the manuscript, and Jan Whitford and Richard Wagamese for their professional opinions and early encouragement. This book is also partially dedicated to the memory of the Canadian novelist and historian T.H. Raddall, as thanks for all those great stories of Nova Scotia he told me in his living room not long before he died. It was an honour I won't soon forget.